MW00480366

THE COLOR OF EVIL

By Connie (Corcoran) Wilson, M.S.

Quad Cities' Press
The Color of Evil
© 2012 Connie Corcoran Wilson
All rights reserved.
For information, address:
Quad Cities' Press
2127 3rd St. B
East Moline, Illinois 61244
www.ConnieCWilson.com
Published in the USA by Quad Cities' Press
ISBN 978-0982444856

THE
COLOR
OF
EVIL

Connie Corcoran Wilson

BY

CONNIE CORCORAN WILSON

Dedication:

This book is dedicated to my friends, fellow writers, and readers who helped make the book as accurate and exciting as it is. Thank you from the bottom of my heart.

C. Dean Andersson
David Dorris
Benjamin Kane Ethridge
Donnie Light
Jonathan Maberry
William F. Nolan
Pamela Rhodes
Karen Schootman
Becky Smith
Craig Wilson
Regina Wilson

Introduction

by William F. Nolan, author of *Logan's Run* and *Nightworlds*

Connie (Corcoran) Wilson is a born storyteller! Her new novel *The Color of Evil* is a real page-turner, and a very good one, indeed. I took three working days to read *The Color of Evil*, reading 100 pages a day and I'm very glad I did. I found it very rewarding, very enjoyable. I found myself drawn forward, page by page, held in the expert grip of her narrative.

This is the best writing yet from Wilson, whose previous short story collection *Hellfire & Damnation*, was an early favorite of HWA (Horror Writers' Association) members, (who placed it seventh of 46 entries in the preliminary Stoker voting, while Stephen King's *Full Dark, No Stars* came from behind (10th place) to take the Bram Stoker Award at 2011's Long Island ceremony.)

Wilson deals with a large cast of characters in *The Color of Evil*, yet each character is sharply described, leaving the reader with a clear portrait. She handles the sexual content equally well. Ditto the dialogue. The style is direct, modern, solid and keeps the action moving.

Wilson in this, her second novel, takes time with each character and handles them quite well, jumping back and forth amongst them. She handles the "time jumps" equally well. The reader is kept informed and fascinated. It all works. It moves the story forward, scene by scene, in a controlled way. *The Color of Evil* is total entertainment!

Wilson's got a winner here!

CHAPTER 1

The Birthday Party

It was April 1, 1995 and Tad McGreevy's eighth birthday party. His parents had spared no expense.

"We've got Pogo the Clown coming," Mrs. McGreevy told her friend Sally. "He's the best clown in Waterloo, Iowa. Everybody says he makes great balloon animals. Pogo did the Chandlers' party at their house, but this party is going to make the Chandlers' party look like the Screw-Up at the OK Corral."

Jeannie McGreevy hated Cassie Chandler. She had hated Cassie ever since she realized that Cassie was just using her to obtain summer jobs for her daughter, Belinda.

Sally took another sip of her frozen Applebee's Margarita.

"That sounds really nice, Jeannie. Is Tad excited about the party? I mean...does he want to have a clown and fifty guests?" Sally didn't really care, one way or the other, but she was doing her best to act interested.

Tad McGreevy's frail health and generally weird demeanor were well known amongst the McGreevy's neighbors and friends. Tad was always just a little bit.... different. It wasn't just his androgynous appearance, although he did look "too pretty to be a boy," as many admirers had said of Jeannie McGreevy's son when they saw him in his stroller on the street as an infant.

Since those halcyon stroller days, Tad had grown into a third-grader with a "sensitive" stomach, who often cried for no apparent reason. This made him the butt of other kids' mean-spirited jokes. Many times, he had come home from school with a bloody nose, courtesy of some Waterloo redneck. His mother was always telling him not to be so sensitive, but Tad was Tad.

While Sally's husband, Earl Scranton, worked at Rath Packing Plant slaughtering hogs and cattle with a stun gun on long 12-hour shifts, Jim McGreevy was a lawyer who charged $300 an hour. It was easy to envy the McGreevys. They seemed to have it all: the big house, the cute well-behaved children (Tad and his older sister twelve-year-old Sharon.) Sally was torn between envy, jealousy, and self-preservation. Jeannie McGreevy could do the Scrantons some good in this town, and Stevie Scranton was Tad's best friend. *Lord knows why*, Sally thought as she slurped her glass dry.

Jeannie McGreevy was a size zero. That, alone, made other women hate her. Sally (an average-size twelve), was just being a friend of Jeannie's so that Shannon Scranton could benefit. Sharon's old school uniforms fit Sally's daughter, Shannon, perfectly. Jeannie McGreevy always gifted her good friend Sally Scranton with them, free and gratis, for the Catholic school that both girls attended. Shannon was one year behind Sharon at Our Lady of Victory and the girls were on the same volleyball team. The Scrantons didn't have a lot of extra cash, so every little bit helped. Sally downed the last of her strawberry margarita, even though she knew it was rude to make that sucking sound.

When she got home from the outing, Sally commented to her husband, Earl, who was splattered with pigs' blood from working the late shift at Rath, "I wonder if Tad McGreevy might be autistic. He doesn't say much. He seems so weird. He's got no social skills. Maybe he has that deal where the kid is really smart, but really strange…that Ashburger's Syndrome. Something like what Dustin Hoffman had in that movie."

Earl Scranton was no genius, but he corrected Sally, who was still slurring her words after ten margaritas at Applebee's on Jeannie McGreevy's dime.

"It's Asperger's Syndrome, and Tad McGreevy is just a weird dork." Earl toweled off with the kitchen dishtowel (always a sticking point with Sally) and headed towards the bedroom to change his clothes, thinking to himself that his wife, Sally, was a moron. Marrying her because she had been pregnant with Sharon had not been one of Earl's smarter moves.

* * *

The Saturday of Tad's party dawned cool and drizzly. It was early April. April in Iowa can be unpredictable.

Pogo the Clown had a day job. Pogo, also known as Michael Clay, ran his father-in-law's chicken restaurant, Mike's Chicken Shack, by night, and took paying clown gigs by day, on weekends.

Pogo's costume was classic clown. Big shoes, red hair, striped baggy pants, white pancake make-up, and a large red smile reaching ear to ear. Pogo would be a hit. Jeannie just knew it. She smiled to herself, thinking how much better *her* party would be than the one that Cassie Chandler had thrown for Belinda Chandler last fall. Of course, the Chandlers had even more money than the McGreevys and Sally had rented Black's Tea Room for her daughter's party, but Jeannie McGreevy figured, "It's April and kids want to be outside, running around. Our back yard will do just fine."

Pogo arrived at the McGreevy residence in Cedar Falls, Iowa, at ten o'clock in the morning on April first. Cedar Falls was where all the upwardly mobile people in town lived. Waterloo was strictly blue-collar and largely black. The unincorporated township of Deer Run, Iowa, just across the street from the Rath Packing Plant, was even lower on the socio-economic scale than Waterloo.

Sally Scranton lived in Waterloo—not quite as bad as Deer Run—but she'd met Jeannie McGreevy at the school their sons both attended, Rossdale Elementary. Iowa is a school choice state. The Scrantons had selected Rossdale in order to get the best possible public school education for young Steven, who was bussed twenty miles to and from school every morning and afternoon. They were paying for Stevie's older sister, Shannon, to go to a private Catholic school, because Shannon was smart.

Rossdale was a good public school, good enough for Stevie. Probably better than Stevie deserved, since he wasn't much of a scholar. Getting Stevie to and from Rossdale Elementary really screwed up the family's schedule.

When Tad first saw Pogo, standing there on his front stoop in full clown make-up, Tad turned a strange pale chalky color that rivaled the whiteness of Pogo's pancake make-up. Although Tad always looked pallid, his red curly hair became damp and curled wetly against his pale freckled cheeks, dripping with sudden sweat. Tad began to breathe heavily as he backed away from the approaching clown, retreating to the safety and security of the house, sinking down next to the large aquarium that sat in the middle of the family room.

"What's the matter, honey? You look like you're gonna' be sick," Jeannie said.

No sooner had the words left her mouth than the Fritos Tad had consumed before the party left his stomach, splattering the back of Jeannie McGreevy's pale white couch. Mrs. McGreevy ushered Tad into the bathroom to clean him up.

When he emerged from the family's bathroom, Tad was carrying his asthma inhaler and puffing on it like it was a cigarette and he was experiencing nicotine withdrawal. Jeannie McGreevy, in a peeved voice, was saying to Tad, as she ushered him back into the family room, "Why couldn't you have thrown up in the fish tank instead of on my new couch?"

Pogo was gone. He was outside, socializing with the guests and entertaining the children. He seemed especially fond of the little boys at the party.

"Tad, you look like you've seen a ghost!" said Stevie Scranton, mouth agape, when Tad finally emerged from the house, slowly and hesitantly, to join his own party in progress.

In fact, Tad *had* seen a ghost, of sorts. He had seen an aura surrounding Michael Clay, a pale color, like gray-green decomposing dead flesh, that overshadowed Pogo's white clown make-up. Tad saw "auras," that is colors, around all people. Yellow meant the person was good. Red meant they were prone to be violent. Black meant that they were ill and would die soon or die young. Vivid emerald green was one of the best, health-wise, but Tad preferred the yellows, who were always kind, compassionate, giving souls. Tad's mom was a pink: verging on red, but too timid to be dangerously violent His dad, Jim, was a blue, remote and indifferent to the plight of others. Jim was pretty much a self-contained entity, with little time for emotional output towards others.

But gray-green was the worst. The absolute worst. Tad had only ever seen one person with that dangerous khaki color before, and that was on television. His aura was so strong that the "X" on Charles Manson's forehead barely made an impression on the sensitive young boy watching a documentary on late-night television about the long-ago killing of a movie star and her friends. At the time, the baby-sitter was making out with her boyfriend in the next room.

Tad never told anyone about the colors he saw. People already thought he was weird, and his parents would never believe him, anyway. It was just something he knew about people: whether they were "bad" or "good." The auras told him. The colors told him. And, sometimes, after he went to sleep, he learned other things about these strangers.

"D—d—don't make me go near him," Tad gasped to Stevie. "Tell my mom I'm gonna' puke again."

Stevie knew Tad meant the clown, without asking.

Hearing that Tad might spew again, Stevie Scranton backed up ten paces. Unlike Tad, when Stevie was outside later he was happy to receive a balloon animal shaped like an elephant from Pogo. Stevie even sat on Pogo's lap while Pogo made the brightly colored balloon animal for him. The air filled with strange squeaking sounds as Pogo twisted and tied the plastic pachyderm. The other kids were rioting merrily in the cool spring air. Tad sat apart, looking miserable, seated on the back yard swing set. Tad refused to go anywhere near Pogo the Clown. Jeannie McGreevy was heard muttering to Sally, "Well, there's a hundred bucks down the drain!"

* * *

The bad dreams began two days later.

Tad woke in the night screaming. "The fish! The fish! There's a skull in the aquarium!"

Jim and Jeannie McGreevy ran to Tad's room, comforted him, asked him what he was talking about. Tad was incoherent. His tale of skulls and fish and an aquarium made no sense to them. Even taking Tad downstairs and showing him the aquarium in the family room, resting on the couch table behind Jeannie's now-stained white couch did not comfort Tad. His eyes looked wide and frightened.

The second dream occurred the next night. Tad screamed so loudly that it actually woke the neighbors. He described having a crucifix stuffed down his throat. "I don't know why I had to swallow the crucifix," he said. "It hurt. It hurt a lot." Tad had bitten through his lip. Flecks of blood flew from his mouth as he spoke.

The third night, Tad cried out at three in the morning.

"What is it this time?" said Jeannie McGreevy to her son, wearily.

"It was a man, Mom. A black man. His body was all cut up, all carved up. He was half-in and half-out of a bathtub. His heart was gone. I think he ate it."

"Who ate it?" Jeannie McGreevy was exhausted after three days with little sleep, and Tad's tales were becoming gorier and making even less sense.

"The clown. The clown ate it."

"What clown? You mean Pogo?"

"Yes. He ate it. He cut the boy's chest open and took the heart out and ate it. It was still beating when he ate it." Tad choked back vomit. His shivering was pitiful, but the McGreevys were fast losing patience.

"Tad! You've got to get a grip! There's no clown. There's no killer. You're just having a bad dream. You've got to quit waking all of us up in the middle of the night like this!" That was Jim McGreevy, sounding angry. The family returned to their beds, weary from another night of Tad's imaginative nightmares. Their patience was wearing thin. Tad's sister, Sharon, just put a pillow over her head and stayed locked in her room.

Tad looked peaked, too. Every single day, he looked as though he had been up all night. Some nights, that was true. After his parents and sister returned to their beds and to slumber, Tad was afraid to sleep, afraid of what dreams might bring.

After seven nights of terrifying visions, most of them making little or no sense when the frightened boy related them to his concerned parents, Jeannie and James McGreevy made an April 10th appointment for Tad with the best children's psychiatrist in Cedar Falls, Iowa. Dr. Eisenstadt was expensive, but he would be worth it. It had been ten days since Tad's birthday party, and Tad had had seven nightmares in a row, each one more horrifying than the last. An entire week of screaming and sleeplessness. Nobody was sleeping much at the McGreevy household, and everyone was on edge.

Dr. Eisenstadt tried to take Tad's arm in a friendly fashion and guide him from the waiting room into his inner office, but Tad pulled away from the white-haired man with the black aura in alarm. Jeannie McGreevy rose to accompany Tad into the doctor's office.

Dr. Eisenstadt said, "Please…no…it is best if Tad and I begin the process alone."

For the next hour, Tad poured out gory tale after gory tale. Body parts in vats of acid. Heads in the refrigerator. Skulls boiled and then painted. Beating hearts taken from victims and eaten cannibalistically by a crazed killer.

"Who is killing all these people, Tad?" asked Dr. Eisenstadt. "Do you know this man?"

"Yes, Dr. Eisenstadt," the young boy said, somberly. "It's the clown. He's a killer. He even said, 'If you're a clown, you can get away with murder.'"

Dr. Eisenstadt conferred with Mr. and Mrs. McGreevy after Tad's second week in treatment. It had been twenty-two days (and nights) since Tad's party and there had been twenty nightmares.

No one in the McGreevy house was getting any sleep, but giving Tad sleeping pills just seemed to make matters worse. Not only did Tad still wake up screaming, but, the next day, he was zombie-like in school. One teacher even saw him stagger and sway in the hallway and had to quickly run to catch him before he fell. It was obvious that the various drug therapies that were being tried on the young boy were a case of the cure being as bad or worse than the disease.

"I have one more suggestion," said Dr. Eisenstadt, after thirty days of treatment on May 19th.

"What, Doctor? We'll do anything, pay anything. We are all suffering." Jim McGreevy summed up the family's ordeal, night after night. Jim wanted to say, "Enough already! I need to get some sleep!" All of the McGreevys, to use an old clichéd expression, looked as though they had been "rode hard and put away wet."

"Obviously, young Tad is suffering from some form of delusion that centers on the clown, Pogo, who performed at his eighth birthday party. Now, we all know that Tad is imagining these horrible murders and all the other unspeakable things he describes. But drug therapy isn't working, and Tad keeps maintaining that *we* are the deluded ones and *he* is the only sane one. He told me, at our last session, 'I see his aura. It's gray-green, Dr. Eisenstadt. Only the worst of the worst are gray-green.'." When he shared that particular quote, Dr. Eisenstadt's left eyebrow arched.

"Tad claims that people have 'auras' and he can see these colors around his classmates and teachers and family and friends. In essence, he is saying that he is able to see into the souls of all those around him. Now, I know this is silly, but Tad really believes it." Dr. Eisenstadt released a pent-up sigh. "I think I've done about as much for him as I can."

"Is Tad crazy?" asked Jeannie McGreevy, tears welling up in her eyes.

"We don't like to use the term 'crazy.' Tad has some mental issues. I am unable to determine, here, whether he is obsessive-compulsive, paranoid-schizophrenic, or any of a variety or combination of other more complicated mental conditions. You really should check him into Shady Oaks for evaluation. They can do a more complete diagnosis, a more complete medical work-up. Maybe there is an abnormality of the brain? A tumor, perhaps? An MRI could determine this, but I don't have the necessary equipment here in the office to diagnose Tad's problem. I suggest a one-week stay in Shady Oaks."

CHAPTER 2

May 22, 1995
Shady Oaks Psychiatric Facility, Cedar Falls, Iowa:

Tad entered Shady Oaks the next Monday, May 24th. It had been fifty-two days since his birthday party. There had been at least thirty days of screaming, night terrors and wild tales of cannibalism, murder, skulls, aquariums and violence. In one dream, from which Tad woke shaking uncontrollably, he described the killer trepanning his victim, attempting to keep a nineteen-year-old victim alive for days, making holes in the young man's head and repeatedly raping the young male subject as the hapless victim lay in a near-coma in Pogo's bathroom bathtub. While in Shady Oaks the drugs helped Tad sleep, but the sleep was not restful sleep, and he was groggy and disoriented when awakened. He actually found it difficult to walk the length of the hall the next morning after taking the medications prescribed.

It was this last story from one of Tad's dreams that made Jeannie McGreevy physically gag and run to the bathroom. After that, Jeannie dropped her objections to committing Tad to the clinic on a trial basis for a week. Originally, she had said, "What will the neighbors say?"

Her husband replied, "They'll probably say: good. Now we can get through one entire night without screaming coming from the McGreevys' house." Personally, James McGreevy was looking forward to getting a good night's sleep, his first in over a month and a half.

Jeannie muttered, to her husband, "Another five thousand dollars down the drain," as they walked out of Dr. Eisenstadt's office.

Tad entered the clinic on Monday, May 22nd, fifty-two days after his birthday party.

He quit speaking. He quit eating. He stared blankly into space and would not answer any questions. He seemed to have had a total break with reality. He was now delusional, locked within his own private world. The McGreevys had to take turns spoon-feeding him a soft diet, since Tad wouldn't feed himself and barely chewed his food. He resembled an 80-year-old more than an 8-year-old.

* * *

On the 52nd day after his eighth birthday party, May 23rd ,1995, the local paper in Waterloo, Iowa, the Waterloo *Courier* carried the front-page story of the arrest of Michael Clay, a local businessman who ran Mike's Chicken Shack for his father-in-law. Michael Clay moonlighted on weekends as Pogo the Clown. The papers reported that thirty-three bodies had been found buried beneath Pogo's house. Others had been found in various stages of decomposition in a basement bathroom. The descriptions of what the victims had endured before death were very disturbing.

Early accounts confirmed nearly all the details that young Tad had poured out during his night terrors. Skulls had been boiled. Penises cut off and preserved in jars of formaldehyde. Two policemen threw up when they opened a refrigerator and found two severed heads inside. The picture of the headless nude man, bound to what looked like a dentist's chair, was widely distributed on the Internet. The body in the bathtub was just as Tad had described it to his disbelieving family.

CHAPTER 3

May 24, 1995
Release

The McGreevys conferred with Dr. Eisenstadt. He agreed that young Tad should leave Shady Oaks and return home. Tad had been right about Pogo. This provided little real consolation to the family or to the boy. There was guilt, of course, that none of them had listened more closely or believed Tad's stories.

Who could have known? Who would believe an eight-year-old who said he saw into peoples' souls? None of them really wanted to talk about Tad's strange power or believed in it, then or now. The hope now was that returning Tad to the bosom of his family would help return him to some semblance of normalcy, since his time in Shady Oaks only seemed to have made him worse.

Returned to familiar surroundings, Tad seldom spoke. He didn't answer when spoken to. He rarely smiled or showed any sign of even knowing that others were present in the room. When in his bedroom, he rocked back and forth, holding himself, knees to chest, moaning softly. That was the most emotion Tad displayed. He slept only fitfully, if at all.

The dreams stopped. Although Tad mostly lay in bed staring at the ceiling, the screaming and night terrors seemed to have ceased with the last of the murders.

Sometimes, Tad would be brought downstairs to the family room, in the futile hope that he would, once again, communicate with his family. He spent hours staring at the Puffer Fish in the aquarium. When Tad looked into the eerily human eyes of the Puffer Fish, Tad's own eyes held a look of indescribable terror.

Fifty-three days. Fifty-three nights. Thirty-three victims. The Puffer fish stared back at the mute boy with its large, expressionless vacant eyes, silent, disconnected, aimlessly wandering in an aquarium limbo.

* * *

Some time in July, around Independence Day, Tad began to seem more like the Tad of old. He still was quiet, but he now fed himself and the rocking and moaning had stopped. Since Pogo's arrest, there had been no further horrific dreams. Tad was returning to his former self. Fragile. Sensitive. Intuitive.

CHAPTER 4

EIGHT YEARS LATER
September 2, 2003

School was starting. Labor Day was over. Fall was in the air. First day of Tad McGreevy's and Stevie Scranton's junior year of high school. Sixteen years old. Feeling invulnerable. The two fast friends had hung out together all summer, in keeping with their long history as best friends. They were ready for school to start. Boredom with summer had set in.

Tad had come out of the catatonic state of his third-grade year, but it had taken a long time. He was home-schooled for an entire school year. Because Tad was bright, he was able to rejoin his fifth-grade classmates the next fall when the school year began.

Although Tad still saw auras, he didn't mention them. Since he had not encountered any murderers since Pogo the Clown, if he did dream, it was not a horrible dream filled with unspeakable carnage.

Tad's precognitive intimations of what a certain individual had done or was capable of doing always came in his dreams. The fugue states didn't necessarily happen immediately after meeting "the bad ones," as Tad categorized them. It took a few days before the Pogo dreams commenced. There was no schedule for Tad's dreaming. There was no explanation for Tad's ability to sense that, for example, Cassie Chandler (a mauve), was cheating on her husband with their neighbor, or that Jim McGreevy (a blue) occasionally visited the seamier side of Waterloo to pick up prostitutes after work. These were things that Tad sometimes saw in his dreams. He knew that these things were happening, but he didn't tell anyone. He didn't dare.

Look what had happened the last time he had shared his knowledge of the color of evil? Besides, watching an R-rated sexual dream was far less unpleasant to a 16-year-old than monitoring the vile actions of Pogo the Clown.

School, for Tad McGreevy, always implied a lot of unpleasant things. In the past, it meant bigger kids picking on him in the hallway. Mean comments. Harassment. Dodge ball with the physical education teacher, Mr. Bear, inciting the students to make fun of and verbally abuse the smaller, weaker, less athletic kids in Tad's class. Historically, that group included both Tad and Stevie Scranton.

"Come on, you sissies! Move it! Use it or lose it! You're gonna' get creamed if you don't step lively. Pick up the pace!" Mr. Bear screamed this into his bullhorn. Mr. Bear was so right. All through elementary school, Tad and Stevie did get creamed. Frequently. Tad hated dodgeball, physical education and Mr. Bear, not necessarily in that order.

It did Tad's heart some good that the other kids in the class, even the cool ones, didn't like Mr. Bear, either. They had a variety of names for him. The recitation of those names never failed to elicit a smile from the often silent and taciturn boy. It didn't help Mr. Bear any that his parents had had the bad judgment and insensitivity to give him the first name Theodore. That just opened the floodgates for unkind remarks. The remarks were often from the weaker, more fragile students who had been the butt of Mr. Bear's ridicule during class. It seemed fair to Tad.

Tad wasn't in favor of making fun of anyone else. He knew too well how much it hurt. He'd been the target of many unkind comments throughout his growing-up years. But if anyone deserved to be made fun of, it was Teddy Bear, who was as big a misfit teacher as one could find in the public schools.

Mr. Bear's entire class usually consisted of him sitting on a folding chair at one end of the gym, holding a bullhorn, and yelling at his charges to "move it" or "step lively" or some other abusive order. He always left his grade book on the folding chair. He sat on the folding chair all hour. He never rose unless absolutely necessary. Mr. Bear was at least 100 pounds overweight. His horrible comb-over hairdo made you think of a fatter Donald Trump in gym shorts.

Once, Tad had accidentally knocked Mr. Bear's grade book on the floor when running solitary laps during his lunch hour, all alone, punishment for some minor infraction. Probably Tad's reluctance to shower in a pack, which meant that he was always hanging back. Because he didn't like showering with the pack, Tad was often late to his next class. Mr. Bear, badgered by the other teachers, told Tad, "Ten laps on your lunch hour, Loser. You can't keep being late to your next class. I'm getting heat for it."

Tad had quickly picked the grade book up to replace it before Mr. Bear returned. He glanced at the pages. To his surprise, he discovered that all the pages were blank. The names of the students in class were duly recorded, but absolutely not one grade or remark followed the names of the students in his gym class for a year that was more than half over. This confirmed what the other students had always said about Theodore Bear's unique teaching techniques.

Bear made Miss Sloan, the pretty young girls' physical education teacher, write all the lesson plans. She also had to keep all the records and do all the grading, including painstakingly recording them on report cards. Mr. Bear abdicated all real responsibility in favor of hanging out with his drinking and hunting buddies in a variety of duck blinds and bass boats on weekends. Tad's physical education class was being run by a giant slothful overweight jerk whose main interest in life seemed to be making smaller, weaker human beings unhappy. He did as little real work as possible. T.B. (one of the student nicknames for Mr. Bear) usually just sat there, coffee mug in one hand, bullhorn in the other, shouting insulting comments at his unhappy charges. There were rumors that the "coffee" wasn't really coffee.

"Lead butt! Leary! Get moving! McGreevy! You're running like a girl. Toughen up! Step it up! Stop that sissy stuff, Scranton! Hey, Princess: did you forget your crown? Hike up your pantyhose. Get a move on it!"

Miss Sloan would provide a framework for any real athletic activities, taking charge when the combined classes went outside and played baseball or some other outdoor sport, in the fall and early spring. It was in winter that Mr. Bear hibernated in the gym. His stock-in-trade was mean, unkind comments. He seemed to really enjoy that part of work, even if, rather than working hard, he was hardly working.

CHAPTER 5

September 2, 2003
Stevie Scranton

Stevie Scranton had been born without a fontanelle, the soft spot that allows the brain to expand without damage. Although three subsequent surgeries had fixed the condition before he was two years old, while the doctors were waiting for Stevie to become old enough to undergo the surgery, Stevie's head had taken on an alarming shape. His head looked like a piece of misshapen fruit. It resembled a large twisted grapefruit that had been squished somehow. The fact that Stevie was blonde only added to the impression. Stevie's head was also very large and out of proportion to the rest of his body.

Maybe it was their relatively unique physical traits that caused Stevie Scranton and Tad McGreevy to bond in elementary school. The good news, for Tad, was that he had outgrown his androgynous, wimpy-looking, redheaded freckled little boy phase. Tad was now a healthy-looking, attractive boy with auburn hair, six feet tall. His quiet shyness remained, but intelligence shone from warm brown eyes that watched with good humor and inquisitive interest.

Stevie, however, was not so lucky. His head still looked like squished fruit. He did not do well in school, academically. In fact, because he was resentful of his three-years-older sister, Shannon, Stevie had chosen a role for himself in the family: troublemaker.

Stevie was always in trouble, both at home and at school. This was in marked contrast to Tad, who always tried to behave. Stevie spent a considerable amount of time under the iron hand of Principal Puck, who was meaner than Mr. Bear.

"Old Man Puck is meaner than a horny toad," Stevie said after emerging from one office visit. He always looked shaken after his visits to (hockey)

Puck. Tad worried about Stevie's many trips to Principal Puck's office, but Stevie never listened to his good friend, because he was, after all, the Troublemaker.

Peter Puck had arrived as principal at Sky High three years prior, coming from a Catholic school in Oklahoma, near El Reno. El Reno had a large percentage of American Indian students. The kids called him Pistol-packing Puck when they found out.

Stevie was not a bad kid. (His aura was purple, which Tad had discovered meant that the individual had poor impulse control.) It was surprising to Tad to realize that both Stevie and Peter Puck, the Principal, were purples. Principal Puck, however, also had a rather large streak of red in his aura, which meant he could easily turn violent.

Tad constantly tried to warn his good friend Stevie to stay out of the clutches of Principal Puck, but Stevie was not smart enough to be good at changing the way he normally operated. He blurted things out in class that often got him in trouble. He wasn't a mean kid. He didn't set out to cause trouble. Sometimes the things he came out with were just plain Stevie stupid or the teachers would misinterpret his impulsive remarks as offensive.

Once, in sixth grade English class, Miss Nicholson asked for a word beginning with the prefix "inter" and Stevie blurted out "intercourse." That earned him one of his many trips to the principal's office.

At Christmas-time, Sally Scranton had confided in Jeannie McGreevy that she had taken all of Stevie's Christmas presents back to the store.

"I told that boy, if you go messing around with the presents under the tree before Christmas and start opening them up and peeking, they're all going back to the store! I told him!"

Sally ended that last statement somewhat defiantly. She looked as if she expected an argument or thought someone might contradict her. Nobody argued with Sally. She could be very unpleasant if you didn't go along with her view of things. Nobody needed the hassle.

Of course, leaving Stevie's presents under the artificial Christmas tree, unguarded, was like leaving catnip out for a cat. Stevie couldn't help himself. It didn't seem like much of an infraction. He would just check to see if he had received the Game Boy he wanted. He slyly opened the packaging. Or, at least, Stevie thought he was being "sly." Just a peek.

In reality, the package practically screamed, "I've been opened!"

Back went the toys to the store. When Jeannie McGreevy told her husband, Jim, the story, both of them thought it was mean-spirited of Sally to have followed through on her threat. Kind of odd, too.

It was Christmas, after all. But that was just Sally's way. As Earl put it, "Sally can be as mean as Snow White's evil stepmother, and there ain't nothin' you can do about it when she gets her evil on."

CHAPTER 6

September 3, 2003
Sally Scranton

Sally definitely got out-of-sorts on a regular basis. She had a reputation for receiving messages from her circle of "friends" telling her that they no longer wanted to be her friend, for one reason or another. All Sally's "friends" just dropped her, one-by-one, like a bad habit.

She would sometimes hang up on a good friend, for no apparent reason, even if the discussion were just something topical in the news, which Sally was addicted to watching faithfully at 6 p.m. and 10 p.m. If Sally was at your house as a guest and you didn't have the news on, she'd get up and turn it on, without asking if that was all right with her hosts. Jeannie McGreevy found that off-putting. So did her husband Jim.

Sally was domineering, bossy, always right, and insistent on getting her own way, no matter what. Jim McGreevy called her "the Town Crier" because of her penchant for gossip, which was unsurpassed amongst all of Jeannie McGreevy's acquaintances. Jim constantly told Jeannie McGreevy, "Whatever you do, don't tell Sally Scranton anything you don't want the whole damn town to know!"

Yet, at other times, Sally Scranton could be pleasant, fun and engaging, especially in a social setting. Tad's mom wondered if Sally Scranton might be bi-polar. Jim McGreevy, an attorney, just laughed when Jeannie threw out that theory saying, "Where'd you get your medical degree, Dr. McGreevy?" Both McGreevys laughed. It was true that Sally's mother went on reckless shopping sprees and then had to have some minor shock therapy to bring her back to her senses, but that was Stevie's Grandma and, so far, the ailment had not extended to Sally.

* * *

One of the annoying and mystifying things about Sally that Jeannie had noticed was her "copycat syndrome," as Jeannie used to describe it to Jim McGreevy. If Jeannie McGreevy went out and bought a dress, Sally would immediately rush out to the very same store and purchase the identical item. Once, Jeannie had wallpapered a bathroom, and Sally wanted to know where Jeannie had found the pleasant pink pattern. When Jeannie told her, Sally rushed to the exact same store and tried to buy the exact same wallpaper for her own bathroom. When she couldn't find the identical pattern in their wallpaper books, she actually called Jeannie up and asked her the name of the pattern.

"Jeannie, you got your wallpaper at Carpenter's, didn't you?" asked Sally.

"Well, yes. Why?" Jeannie was surprised that anyone cared that much about where she had purchased the pleasant but ordinary pink floral wallpaper.

"Okay. That's all I wanted to know."

And, with that, Sally hung up and was off to look again at Carpenter's Corners, as the store was called. She never did find the exact same wallpaper. Jeannie was secretly glad.

Plus, as Jeannie told her husband, "I was mortified when we both showed up at the same wedding in the same dress. If I had known that Sally was going to rush to Feminique to buy the exact same dress—especially when she knew we were both going to be at the Henderson wedding—I would have worn something else. From now on, I'll act like I have amnesia if she ever again asks me where I bought something."

"Weird," Jim McGreevy said. "Just friggin' weird. I guess you have to go with the thought that imitation is the sincerest form of flattery, but it's still crazy. And she does that all the time." They both laughed.

Stevie, however, did not laugh about the loss of every single one of his Christmas presents at Christmas in his sixth grade year in school. Life at the Scrantons could be tough, at times, for Stevie. And it was often even more difficult when Stevie was at school.

This trip to Principal Peter Puck's office was one of those times.

CHAPTER 7

September 3, 2003, Just before 1st Period
Sky High High School

"Hey, McGreevy! You on a pass from the loony bin? You on furlough from the Nut Hut?"

That remark from BMOC Jeremy Gustaffson: tall, blonde, a perfect neo-Nazi. Tad thought to himself, *Geez, Gustaffson. Give it a rest. It's been eight years!* But Tad said nothing.

Jeremy had a well-deserved reputation for harassing younger, smaller boys in the class. He was captain of the football team and Alpha male at Cedar Falls' Sky High. He was, in fact, going to be nineteen before he graduated…if he ever did. Tad and Stevie were just two of many that Jeremy enjoyed teasing and bullying.

The correct name of their high school was State College of Iowa University Lab School, but SCI, over the years, had become Sky. The distortion of the true initials of the school, S.C.I., had caught on with the students in the school, who liked it. It had also caught on with the community at large. The school had morphed into Sky High.

Of course, there were always opposing team members who made fairy jokes about the athletic teams of Sky High. But it was a cool name for a relatively normal high school that was a laboratory school for the nearby State College of Iowa, a university which, in its initial years, had mainly prepared teachers. What they used to call a "normal school," which seemed quaint, given the teachers and students at Sky High now. Over the years, SCI had adopted other majors, so teachers were not the primary graduates today. But the State College of Iowa (later to morph again into the University of Northern

Iowa) remained a school that graduated a disproportionate number of teachers, amongst the three state universities in Iowa.

Tad had learned it was best to ignore bullies like Jeremy. While Jeremy stood 6' 2" with a muscular athletic build and had spent his summer pumping iron in the school weight room in preparation for the fall football season, Tad stood just six feet tall. He had spent the summer reading and playing chess and video games. Tad was, however, no longer a shrimp-y, nerd-y kid. He was no longer the weakling who might have sand kicked in his face in the old comic book strips. He was of average height and build, six feet tall, light reddish-brown hair, dark brown eyes, and a friendly face.

In the summertime before school started, Tad and Stevie occasionally went to a movie. The theater had begun to pair one "old" movie with a "new" one at a reduced price, in an attempt to boost attendance on Wednesdays during the summer and again at late-night double features on weekend nights.

In fact, it was at the showing of "Forrest Gump," a 1994 film popular when Tad's parents threw him the ill-fated eighth birthday party that Tad had seen Jenny San Giovanni for the first time. Best friends Tad and Stevie saw the movie at the Cedar Falls Cineplex, paired with the new film "Lord of the Rings: Return of the King." Tad was a big fan of the Lord of the Rings books. He'd only been seven years old when "Forrest Gump" first came out, so both films were new to him. The double feature aspect that the local theater was using (one old; one new) had lured the two boys to the Saturday late night matinee.

It was close to midnight when he saw her for the first time.

Jenny was like a dream, walking. She didn't really walk so much as float, in Tad's mind's eye. She was surrounded by a yellow aura (the best, Tad knew). She was so beautiful that Tad felt as though she must have stepped out of a Disney movie. He caught his breath. He could almost imagine Jenny with butterflies holding the hem of her dress, like Cinderella or Snow White or one of the other Disney heroines he used to love to sketch when daydreaming. Was she a mirage? He actually felt light-headed when he first caught a glimpse of this ethereal creature, this lovely blonde, standing at the popcorn counter across the movie lobby.

Stevie knew Jenny, not only because she was in their class at school, but also because Jenny's older sister, Cynthia, hung out with Stevie's older sister, Shannon.

Jenny had changed significantly with the onset of adolescence. Where she previously had been a slightly chubby blonde child in elementary school with a prominent widow's peak and big blue eyes, when she reached 8th grade and adolescence kicked in, there wasn't a boy in the high school that didn't notice the curvaceous blue-eyed blonde. Jenny was just so nice, always smiling and kind to everyone.

Just as Tad was going to ask his friend Stevie who that beautiful girl was, Stevie casually strolled over to the goddess and said, "Hi, Jenny. What's going on?"

Tad's mouth must have dropped open a foot. He was dumbstruck. The 15-year-old's fresh-faced beauty took his breath away. Her smile was like a caress. She was more beautiful than the character named Jenny in the movie they had just seen. Tad could empathize with Forrest Gump, who loved Jenny purely, but felt unworthy of her affection because he wasn't a smart man.

Tad, however, *was* a smart boy. Although he didn't yet realize it, he was a cute boy, too, although shy. Shy was good with young girls like Jenny SanGiovanni. Tad's shy was sincere. That made it even better.

Stevie Scranton, however, was the short, porky sidekick who was always being picked on by someone. He had the physique of a much older male. His nose hair stuck out unattractively from his nostrils. Jenny was such a nice person, though, that she would never be mean to her friend's little brother, and Shannon was her sister Cynthia's friend.

Jenny turned to greet Stevie. "Who's your friend?"

"This is Tad McGreevy," Stevie replied, barely glancing over his shoulder at the awe-struck Tad. "You remember? Sharon's brother. You know Sharon...right?"

Jenny was already shaking her head. "Oh, yeah. Right. I remember." Jenny could be forgiven for not remembering Tad from earlier years in school, as her family had moved there after her parents' divorce, when her mom remarried.

She turned to Tad. "How are you, Tad? It's nice to meet you?" Her smile would have melted an iceberg. "I'd shake your hand but it's sticky from that oily stuff on the popcorn." She smiled and tried to wipe her hands dry with a napkin from the counter.

Tad felt his throat tighten. He stumbled around in his mind, before saying, "Okay. I'm okay."

Later, he would beat himself up thinking what a stupid response that had been.

Despite the rough start, Tad and Jenny, just like Forrest and Jenny in the movie, "went together like peas and carrots." They were destined to become fast friends...although neither of them knew it at that moment.

CHAPTER 8

October 1, 2003
Tad & Jenny

It had been a month since Tad McGreevy and Jenny San Giovanni had become friends. They talked on the phone almost every night. Their friendship was—so far— platonic. Jenny treated Tad like one of her girlfriends or as though he were gay. Nothing could have been further from the truth. Tad's heart melted every time Jenny smiled at him. He looked forward to their nightly chats about what had happened in school that day more than he could say. He felt very protective of the pretty blonde girl.

There was the inevitable note writing that high school students indulge in, writing them to one another when stuck in a boring study hall or a less-than-riveting class.

Jenny constantly received notes from Tad, but she also received notes from Jeremy Gustaffsson, whom she had dated at the end of last year, her sophomore year. Jeremy was old enough to drive the five miles to her former school, Cedar Falls High School, near Rossdale Elementary, the school which Stevie and Tad had attended.

Jeremy had not passed his senior year. He was back to try to complete his course of study and receive a diploma. A football injury had sidelined him. He had missed a lot of school. Jeremy had been unable to make up the missed classes over the summer because the school had had to cut back on summer classes. Individual tutors were too expensive in this day of budget crunches. Plus, Jeremy's family moved from race track town to race track town, following the ponies. So, Jeremy got a "red shirt" year, a do-over, a fifth year to finish up his high school diploma at Sky High.

For that reason and because his parents did move around a lot with the harness racing trade his father practiced, Jeremy was old for his class. Old, but not mature. Jeremy was eighteen last year, when he had begun dating Jenny, who was only fifteen at that time. Jenny was still fifteen until December. The couple had lied to her parents about Jeremy's true age, but the SanGiovannis had eventually learned the truth.

Every day, during last hour, Tad would start a note to Jenny. It always began the same way: "Hey, Beautiful Girl. What's goin on? Nothin' here. Just writing you from study hall."

After that routine beginning, the notes would go on to discuss happenings in the school that day, various fights, alliances that had formed and reformed. Tad had learned from experience never to tell anyone about his unique ability to read colors, as he had come to call his power to determine good and evil in others. He had learned that lesson well eight years ago. It had led nowhere good.

For now, although his precognitive power remained and Tad still saw auras around each and every human with whom he came in contact, he did not share the information about his ability with anyone. He just used the information he gleaned to protect himself and to protect those he cared about. Tops on the list of those he cared about was his pretty new friend Jenny SanGiovanni.

CHAPTER 9

Oct. 1, 2003
Notes

Today's note from Tad discussed the knifing in the hallway of their school that very morning. Two Hispanic cousins squared off, fighting over the same girl. The boys' parents worked at the Rath Packing Plant where Earl Scranton, Stevie's father, was now a foreman. The police were called. An ambulance took one of the cousins to the nearby hospital with superficial knife wounds.

The school had a full-time Officer Friendly, Lenny McIntrye, in the hallways at all times, but nobody could be everywhere at once. The fight broke out in a hallway not supervised by the policeman at that precise moment.

Homeless Hispanic people had been recruited from the Southwest to come work at the meat-processing plant in Waterloo, Iowa. Many of these workers had originally been found sleeping under bridges in remote Texas Dust Bowl towns. The packing plant offered them money to move north to live and work at the packing plant. Some were mentally ill.

Ever since then, the town had had problems with violence, both at the plant, at the Ramada Inn, and at the high school. The recruits were housed in the old Ramada Inn on the edge of town at first, although some eventually saved enough to move to small houses in a virtual shantytown in Deer Run, near the Rath plant and the railroad tracks. A few even lived in abandoned railroad cars, with no heat, electricity or running water. In time, if they saved their money, they moved to an area of town known as "the Heights." Most of the minority workers did not speak English.

Talking about the knife fight during their lunch hour, Stevie Scranton would describe the excitement in the halls of Sky High when the two Hispanic cousins, children of workers at the meat packing plant, had gone after one another.

"Alex Jimenez pulled a knife on his cousin, Roberto. They both like this same girl, Heather Crompton. But it didn't look like either one of them really wanted to get cut. It was sort of a chicken-shit fight, to be honest. Before they could really get into it, that cop, McIntyre, showed up. Then Principal Puck, Pistol-packing Puck, arrived and broke it up."

"Wow!" That was all Tad could think of to say. "And Mousy McIntyre broke it up?" It had never occurred to Tad that a knife fight would break out in the halls of Sky High. He had seen disturbing auras around both cousins. They weren't gray-green. They were red. But they did carry black shadowy clouds above their heads, like the character Pig Pen in the comic strip *Charlie Brown*.

Tad wasn't surprised that the two would clash, but he was surprised that they would use knives. His idea of a fight was two boys giving each other bloody noses. Knives were a whole other element. He must remember to warn Jenny away from anyone whose aura was black, red or…God forbid…. gray-green.

CHAPTER 10

October 1, 2003
Principal Peter Puck

Principal Puck was one of the people at Sky High with the gray-green zombie-like aura. All students with half a brain tried to avoid the principal, anyway. Any principal.

Jenny San Giovanni was smart. She wouldn't be getting sent to Principal Puck's office. Tad didn't warn her that the Principal was someone she should avoid, because he couldn't conceive of a situation where Jenny SanGiovanni would get sent to the principal's office.

If you were in the presence of the principal, it generally meant you were in trouble and receiving a detention or an after-school or in-school suspension. Jenny was not a troublemaker. Her niceness permeated her being. Tad's mind wandered mentally away from the details of the fight that Stevie was currently sharing, contemplating the girl of his dreams.

Tad did have a student he could legitimately warn Jenny about—as if she and her parents hadn't already figured that out: Jeremy Gustaffson. Jeremy's aura was red and seemed to be growing more crimson each day. Tad had to be careful about directly criticizing Jeremy. Jeremy and Jenny had been boyfriend and girlfriend last year. Despite her parents' ban on Jeremy as a boyfriend, Jenny had sneaked out to see him over the summer twice. Jeremy still thought of Jenny as his girlfriend. If Tad openly attacked Jeremy, it would appear that Tad was trying to win her for himself.

In reality, Tad was trying to protect Jenny from Jeremy. At fifteen, Jenny was too young for him. Jeremy was three—almost four— years older than Jenny. At the end of last school year the SanGiovannis had intervened to put an end to the budding romance.

Or so they thought.

For now, Tad would inquire about Jenny's relationship with Jeremy through his daily notes. He would pretend that he thought Jeremy was an okay guy until he got a chance to warn Jenny about him. Tad did not feel Jeremy was an "okay" guy. At all. But he had to be discreet in how he introduced the topic of Jeremy's character. The time had to be right.

CHAPTER 11

October 1, 2003
More Notes

Tad's notes were not the only ones that Jenny SanGiovanni was receiving. Jeremy, possessive and territorial like a junkyard dog, routinely wrote to Jenny during his classes. He didn't wait till study hall. It would have been logical to kill the boring hour all students were forced to spend in study hall writing notes. Jeremy, however, bored at all times, wrote the notes during his academic classes.

Jenny had reluctantly tried to break it off with Jeremy at the end of last year, telling him of her parents' objections to the age difference. But Jeremy wouldn't take no for an answer. Initially, when Jenny told him her parents objected to them as a couple, he had acted like everything was cool. But that wasn't what he was feeling. He was seething inside.

Jenny was his. Jenny's parents couldn't take her away from him. They had no right.

He isn't even her real Dad, Jeremy thought to himself. *He's just her stepfather. He has no authority over her, really. He can't take her away from me. I'm going to get her back. Just wait and see. Besides, I can tell she still likes me.*

In fact, Jeremy had convinced Jenny to sneak out and meet him at least two more times over the summer. Although Tad and Stevie didn't know it, one of those times was after that showing of "Forrest Gump" and "Lord of the Rings," as Jeremy waited for her outside.

* * *

The note said, "To Jenny, from the worst person in the world. Someone who really loves you."

Hey, Jenny –

What's goin' on? Nothin' here in the library. Just talking to Justin. I haven't given that note to your friend Kelly yet. Things are getting fucked up. Your parents don't want me to be with you, and neither do your two friends. It's gonna be hard to see you now. I dunno 'bout Zack's house cuz Kelly is gonna' be over there, and she don't want me to be there. What the fuck. I still can't think of what I've done to make your parents hate me so much, or your friends. Things are just gonna' keep getting' more fucked up. I don't know what's gonna' happen. Your parents always talk shit about me and tell you to break up with me. Geez. What a great day our five month anniversary is gonna' turn out to be. It's been five months, counting the summer, 'cause we started going out May 1st at the end of last school year. I don't know how you're gonna' deal with all the shit your parents and friends say, but, hey, I gotta go now cuz Math took me most of the period to do.

Jenny, you know I love you more than nething, and I hope you feel the same way.

Happy five months.

I LOVE YOU.

I'm so confused about all this shit.

Jeremy

P.S. I gave that note you wanted me to pass on to your friend Kelly."

CHAPTER 12

October 24, 2003
After School

Jenny walked slowly towards her front door. Her stepfather, Gregory Tuttle, usually got home before her mom did. That was kind of awkward. It wasn't that she didn't like Greg; it was just that sometimes she wondered what was going through his head when they were alone in the house before her mom showed up from work at her real estate office.

Her real dad had moved to Boulder, Colorado after the SanGiovannis' divorce, and Jenny missed him. A lot. She hoped that maybe after she graduated from high school she could go live with her dad, Jeff, and his new wife Tammy, and attend the University of Colorado. Her dad had said she could, when he left. But it was also a decision that his new wife, Tammy, would have to support. So far, Jenny didn't know whether Tammy liked her or not. It almost seemed as though Tammy was jealous of the time that Greg and Jenny spent together. She seemed to want Jeff all to herself, so it might be hard to talk her into letting Jenny come live with them in Colorado.

Maybe I could live in a dorm and just be nearby, so I could see my dad sometimes, she thought. Her father had been the only one Jenny felt she could talk to, when he lived with them. She sighed heavily, thinking about how far away he was now.

When Jenny started going out with Jeremy, she'd talk about her dad to Jeremy. Her dad seemed like he could relate to Jeremy. When she talked about her real father to Jeremy, he volunteered some of his own family history.

"I never knew my father much," Jeremy told Jenny once. "My dad left us when I was about twelve, but then he came back. It's been real hard for my mom to raise three boys without a man in the house. Sometimes, I think that I'm the way I am because of my dad."

"What do you mean: 'I'm the way I am?'" Jenny wasn't sure she understood what Jeremy was trying to tell her.

"You know. All the athletics and stuff. When I fly off the handle like I do some times, I know that, if I'd had a dad like your dad, who paid attention to me and tried to help me control my temper, I'd be different. But when I get mad, I just lose it. I can't think at all."

Jenny had seen this side of Jeremy. He had once administered a beating to another boy who had whistled at her when she was leaving practice and looked cute in her cheerleading uniform. Jenny had to pull Jeremy off the boy.

"Stop! Stop, Jeremy! He didn't mean anything! It was just a whistle."

Jeremy had a sort of glazed look on his face. It took him about five minutes to calm down enough to move away from the bruised and bleeding underclassman.

Then there were Jeremy's constant sexual advances.

"A boy has to get rid of sexual tension somehow!" he once told Jenny.

Teasing, she had responded, "I thought that sexual tension was supposed to be good for athletes. You aren't supposed to have sex before big games or athletic events. Besides, you've got hands, don't you?"

"Who's having sex? You won't let me do anything," Jeremy muttered, frowning.

"Not this discussion again. If anybody found out we were doing it, you could go to jail."

"Nobody'd find out. We could be real careful. You could get the pill. Besides, you'll be sixteen soon." Jeremy looked at Jenny hopefully. She always reminded him of how young she was.

"Not *that* soon. Not until almost next year. My birthday's not until after Christmas. Besides, when can we ever be alone? Your house is always filled with people, including your two brothers, and you know my parents' position on me dating someone who is eighteen—almost nineteen— when I'm only fifteen."

"I know. I know." Jeremy paused. "He's not your *real* dad, though," Jeremy said to Jenny, referring to Gregory Tuttle, Jenny's stepdad. He was thinking, *Maybe I should talk to that Tuttle twit.*

Jeremy continued, "My dad spent time in the joint. That's why he wasn't there when I was twelve. I don't wanna end up in prison like he did." He laughed, "Like father, like son. Both of us locked up 'cause of raging hormones. But he's back now, and doing okay with the ponies. He said I could have his old Pontiac LeMans when we get a new car soon."

"What do you mean?" Jenny asked, puzzled.

She really didn't know much about Jeremy's home life. It was only during their times together talking like this that she learned his family secrets. She had never been to Jeremy's house or met his parents. Her parents would freak out if they thought she had gone to Jeremy Gustaffsson's house alone.

All she knew was that Jeremy's father moved the family from harness racing track to harness racing track on a circuit, with great frequency. Now she had learned that LeRoy Gusstaffsson had been gone for a critical period during Jeremy's adolescence, doing time in prison. Jeremy's schooling had suffered, as a result.

"Rape. My dad did time for rape. He said it was her fault, though." Jeremy shrugged. "Who-the-hell knows, with my old man? My mom was glad when he left, because he used to beat her up when he was drinking. Once, she got a restraining order against him."

Jenny didn't say anything. She was from one side of the tracks; Jeremy from the other. In Jenny's world, husbands didn't come home and beat up their wives, the mother of their children. Gregory Tuttle, her stepfather, was so soft-spoken and meek that Jenny doubted he'd ever had a physical fight with anyone in his life.

Sometimes, in her world, however, fathers fell in love with younger, prettier women and then blamed their first wife, the mother of their children, saying things like, "Your career is your husband. You don't have time for me in your life."

Jenny had overheard that argument one night before her father announced that he was filing for divorce. That was before she learned that her father was seeing Tammy Tolliver, who was now Tammy SanGiovanni.

Last year, when she and Jeremy were a couple, Jenny just felt sorry for the big lummox and said, "I'm sorry, Jeremy. It must have been rough for your mom. It must still be rough for her, now that your dad's back. Jimmy and Jeff seem like a handful."

Jeremy snorted derisively. "I can handle Jimmy and Jeff. They're just a couple of little psychopaths." He laughed. "Last week, I caught them trying to set fire to the neighbor's cat."

Jenny did not laugh. She was shocked. "That's horrible! I hope you stopped them."

Jeremy peered at her from under brooding Nordic eyebrows. "Well, the cat was just an old tabby cat that was sick and threw up all the time, anyway. I heard the lady next door say she wanted to get rid of it."

"So you let your little brothers torture it?"

Jeremy seemed taken aback. "I didn't LET the little pissants do nothin' of the sort. They're hellions. It's a bad age. I'm eighteen, but they're thirteen and twelve and they don't know whether they're coming or going half the time. They're troublemakers. Worse than me," said Jeremy. He laughed when he said it.

"My dad got sent up when I was 12. Jimmy was only 7 and Jeff was 6. I had 12 years of Dad beatin' on Mom and then beatin' on me before he left. But I started to get too big for him to do me like he used to by the time I got to junior high and he got out of the joint. I started doin' sports and working out, and he quit taking after me. Back then he'd spend all his time at the Dew Drop Inn. That's where he met that skank that said he raped her. I don't know if it's true or not. Although it is true that my old man was horny as hell." Jeremy snorted derisively. "IS horny as hell. Another reason not to go to my house, if we try to get together."

That old cliché popped into Jenny's head, *The apple doesn't fall far from the tree.* She was alarmed. Did Jeremy's last remark imply that LeRoy Gustaffsson might make a pass at her...or worse?

They had reached the point near her house where she always jumped out of Jeremy's car so her parents wouldn't know that they were still a couple, that he was giving her rides home. She was still too young for a nearly nineteen-year-old man. After conversations like this one, she could almost agree with her parents and her friends that Jeremy was bad for her.

Her parents would have a cow if they knew she was still sneaking around to see Jeremy Gustaffsson. She had lied to them and told them that she was going to Homecoming with Tad McGreevy. Now, she just needed to let Tad in on that particular secret. It was the only way she could think of to actually go to the dance with Jeremy.

All Tad had to do was agree to the charade of being her date. He'd have to come to her house and pick her up and do the corsage thing.

Jenny thought of Tad as her best friend, most of the time, followed by Janice Kramer when Janice wasn't going boy crazy for anything in pants. After Tad McGreevy picked her up at her house, she'd go off with Jeremy and Tad could go off with whomever he wanted. Although Jenny hoped it wouldn't be Janice.

Tad never talked about who he liked, even though he wrote a note to her every day, faithfully, almost religiously, when he was in study hall. And in some of them, she couldn't help but get the feeling that he disapproved of her romance with Jeremy.

CHAPTER 13

October 24, 2003
Homecoming Plans

To: Jenny-O
From: Your Jeremy

Hey, Babe! I'm in Kellogg's boring chemistry class, and I'm really tired. So, do your parents have to work today? I'm still scared to go to your house after what happened when we got back late and they came driving up and caught us making out in the car. Your dad was hella' crazy.

But we could think about going to your house before either one of them got home from work??? What do you think of that plan? Beats trying to get rid of my crazy-ass little brothers.

But, neway, it's raining like crazy out. I hope we get a lot of rain so we don't have school tomorrow. That would be so freakin' cool! Never happen. Not like snow days. But a guy can dream, can't he? And I dream about you all the time, Jenny Baby. I could tell you my dreams, but you might slap me silly.

Sean Carpenter came up to me in the hall. He said his parents were going to be gone next week from Thursday until Sunday. His dad is gonna' get him some booze. Do you wanna' come over to Sean's house with me and be with me and Sean and his girlfriend, Melody? Your folks don't have to know. Tell them you're going somewhere with one of your girlfriends. Kelly, maybe. She's not as boy-crazy as your friend Janice.

It's kinda weird how we've done basically everything but have sex, but now we have to sneak around to see each other. If we do drink over at Sean's house, I'm gonna' have to watch you so you don't get crazy and break shit like you broke the cup holder in my car off with your knee that time. Ha!

Come by my class after lunch when you are out of that fat bitch Kleeman's English class during your split period. I can see you then, unless you're sick of seein' me. Don't let that old hag Kleeman scare you off. What's the worst she can do?

What color is your dress for Homecoming next weekend, so we can match? You are going to go with me, aren't you? We can find a way.

We have to do somethin' before then. Maybe you'll let me see you naked? That would be cool. (Hahahaha. Just kidding.)

REMEMBER THAT I LOVE YOU.

Your Jeremy

CHAPTER 14

Study Hall
2:30 p.m.
October 27, 2003

"Hey, Beautiful girl! What's happenin'? 'Nothin' goin' on here. Just finished some boring homework for Kellogg's chemistry class.

You said you wanted to talk to me about Homecoming plans. I hope this means that you want to go to Homecoming with me, because I want to go to Homecoming with you.

I really, really like you, Jenny. You're my best friend.

I know how much you like Jeremy. And you know I really don't want to mess up things between you two. But I hope you know how I feel about you. I don't want to be shady and just not tell you. But I think if we are tight, I'm gonna' want to go out with you. I hope you want to go out with me, too. You know that I don't want to cause any problems with you and Jeremy, though. You told me that was all over because of your folks. Is that wrong? Do you still want to be with Jeremy?

I think you should listen to your folks. They want what is best for you. Jeremy is kind of old, even for the senior class. He'll be nineteen soon. I have a bad feeling about him sometimes. You aren't even sixteen yet. (Not until December 27th, right?)

I think that's what your mom is trying to say. He's maybe not a bad person, but he's too old for you. And I worry that there is a side to Jeremy that you have not seen yet.

Sorry that I didn't get on AOL when I got home. My mom was on it doing some of her book club society stuff. I didn't get home till 10:05 p.m. 'cause my sister's car broke down on the way back from the 'Y.'

I haven't written you anything like this ever before, but you said you had something important you wanted to talk to me about, and that it was about Homecoming. Well, I have some important things to talk to you about, too.

P.S. If you can, come to the 'Y' tonight. We can talk about Homecoming, face to face. That will be better.

Your friend forever,

Tad"

Jenny folded the note and put it deep inside her purse. This presented a new dilemma. She had told Tad, through mutual friends, that she wanted to talk to him about Homecoming, but what she wanted to talk to him about was the charade that she had planned, where Tad would act as her date...what they used to call a "beard" ...and she would really be going to the dance with Jeremy.

She and Jeremy had already selected their color-coordinated outfits. Since the Homecoming dance coincided with Halloween weekend, being held the very day of Halloween, they were wearing black and orange.

Jeremy was renting a tux with an orange cummerbund. She had picked out a dress that was more coral than orange, but it would do. She didn't know who Tad was interested in asking, as his date. She had always thought she and Tad were just good friends who could talk to one another about anything and liked the same kind of movies and liked doing fun things together. In the note she had just read, it sounded as though Tad wanted to get with her, to hook up. That was something of which she had been unaware. She hadn't realized Tad had those kinds of feelings towards her.

This can't be good. How do I ask Tad to just pretend to be my date, so that I can go to the dance with Jeremy? I may have to rethink this entire plan.

Jenny decided that it would be best to talk it out face-to-face at the "Y" that evening. One thing was sure: Jeremy would be mad as hell if he thought that Tad liked her as more than just a friend.

She had always told Jeremy that Tad was "just a friend, almost like a girlfriend," and that was truly what she had thought— until this note. The dance was just days away, on Friday, October 31st. Jenny had an appointment to have her nails done and everything. Jeremy wanted her to wear one of those stupid colored bracelets that advertised what you'd do with a boy, but she wasn't going to be suckered into doing that for anybody. Especially not for a fancy occasion. Jeremy didn't know her very well if he thought she was that kind of girl. She had thought about getting her nails painted with black cats or something else that tied in with Halloween. She' d have to talk to Jodi, her nail technician.

For now, Jenny was just thinking about her friend Tad McGreevey. She had never considered the fact that she might be hurting Tad's feelings by going out with Jeremy. Tad was just....well...Tad.

Surely he'd understand?

CHAPTER 15

October 28, 2003, 8:00 P.M.
The Cedar Falls YMCA

When Jenny saw Tad entering the Cedar Falls YMCA, she could see that he looked very happy. He was almost glowing with an inner light. He scanned the room for her. She had a sudden insane impulse to hide from him, but she knew she had to be straight with him and make it clear what it was she really wanted to talk to him about regarding the Homecoming dance. The dance was only four days away. She couldn't afford to let this hang. Arrangements had to be made.

As Tad walked towards her, Stevie Scranton trailing behind, Jenny sucked it up and put on her best smile for her best friend, saying, "Hi, Tad!"

Tad just smiled shyly. He really didn't see what was coming at all. He thought they were going to discuss *their* plans to go to the dance as a couple. Jenny felt more miserable than she had at any time since the night last school year, in the spring, when her parents sat her down and told her they didn't want her going out with Jeremy any more.

"You wanted to talk to me about the dance?" This was Tad's direct way of approaching the logistics of where they should eat beforehand, what color dress Jenny planned to wear, whether he should do something color-coordinated with his tux, what friends they should try to team up with. Usually, a large bunch of couples went to the dance together. *Jenny is very popular. Anyone would want to go to the dance with Jenny SanGiovanni*, Tad thought, and as he held that thought, for a moment he glowed with pride that she would pick him from among all the boys she could have selected. Even Jeremy Gustaffsson.

Then a serious look came over Jenny's previously sunny expression. She took Tad by the elbow and maneuvered him away from Stevie and the others, so she could talk with him privately.

"Tad, I have a big favor to ask of you," she said. Her eyes searched his, looking for a sign that he would grant her wish.

"Anything. Anything for you, Jenny. What do you want?" Tad never saw the bullet that was headed straight for his heart.

"I need you to pretend to be my date for Homecoming this Saturday and come to my house and pick me up and all that. But then you are free to meet up with anyone you want, because Jeremy and I have been planning to go for a long time, and we have our outfits picked out and everything. But you know how unreasonable my parents are about me going out with Jeremy, so I need you to come to the house and pretend to be my date."

Tad felt as though a one hundred pound boulder had crushed him. As one little girl on the playground he had overheard had once said, "That hurt all the way to God!"

"Do you think that's a good idea, Jenny? To trick your folks, I mean? If they find out, they'll be really mad, and they'll be mad at me, too." Tad's eyes were cocker spaniel eyes. It was all he could do to keep his voice from breaking. He wanted to tell her so much more. He wanted to level with her about Jeremy and the danger Jeremy posed. He wanted to tell her he loved her.

Jenny looked at him, and she sensed that something strange was going on, but she didn't know exactly what it was.

"You know I was dating Jeremy at the end of last year...that we were going steady...right, Tad?" Jenny asked with hesitation.

"Of course," Tad replied. "It's about all we talked about when the year started. Whether you should do what your folks said and break it off with him. But you said he had a terrible temper. You said that you thought you could help him control his impulses. You said that he needed you."

"He does need me, Tad. He doesn't have a good family behind him, like you and I do. His dad drinks too much and is gone a lot. He basically has to be the man in that house for his little brothers. Plus, his dad gets violent with his mom sometimes. Jeremy has to step in to stop it. You know this. I've told you all this. I'm the only one he can count on. He tells me that all the time. I can't let him down." Jenny's eyes were pleading with Tad to understand.

Tad tried very hard to keep his voice even and not say anything he would regret, but he just had to warn Jenny about the evil inside Jeremy, the evil he could see that Jenny could not.

"Jenny, I think you should listen to your folks. There's something wrong with Jeremy. I don't know exactly what it is, but he's not like he pretends to be. He's broken inside somehow. Sure, he says he needs you, but why does he say that? Does he have some ulterior motive?"

Tad had seen a few of the notes that Jeremy had written to Jenny. They all implied Jeremy's desire to move forward sexually, and none too subtly. They asked about seeing her naked and "how much would you be comfortable doing." The notes suggested she wear the colored bracelet that indicated the girl would give a blowjob to a willing male recipient (there were plenty who would, but Jenny was not among them). The multi-colored lightweight rubber bracelets were all the rage. Girls wore them in multiples…unless their teachers made them take them off or did not allow them to wear them to class. Sometimes there was active trading of the bracelets that occurred during class.

The notes Tad had seen referred to Jeremy's being banned from more than one person's house in a 24-hour period of time. In one note Jeremy wrote, "Huh! I've gotten banned from two houses in one day. Your dad kicked me out of your house last night, and Sean Carpenter's mom said she didn't want me hanging around with Sean so much, so I got banned from two houses in one day.

Plus, I hear they are going to start doing random drug tests at school. I am so fucked if that happens. I'm trying not to smoke pot, 'cause I know you don't like it, but sometimes I have to have just one doobie before school starts, to get through boring classes like Kleeman's English class and Kellogg's chemistry class. I want to quit. I really do. I want to do it for you, because I know you want me to."

An ongoing theme in the notes was Jeremy's constant marijuana use and Jenny's disapproval of it. Another ongoing theme: constant references to how "sexy" Jenny was and how much Jeremy desired her. They always ended with Jeremy professing his love for Jenny.

Tad had seen these notes. He was concerned that Jeremy, who was big for his age and old for his class, was the kind of overgrown bully, who, some day, would not take no for an answer. Tad had seen Jeremy's aura. It was red…redder than Mars. He had a violent nature, deep down, which he had, so far, hidden from Jenny except for that one incident involving the underclassman who had whistled at her. Quite frankly, Tad was surprised that Jeremy had not beaten the shit out of *him* yet. But now he understood. Jenny didn't like him in that way and she had made this perfectly clear to her boyfriend, Jeremy Gustaffsson.

Tad was crushed. But he was still going to watch over Jenny SanGiovanni, no matter what.

After his line about the ulterior motives Jeremy might have, Tad turned and walked quickly into the men's rest room, unable to hold it together any longer. He didn't want Jenny to guess how upset he was. Nothing had been solved.

CHAPTER 16

October 28, 2003, 8:45 P.M.
Cedar Falls YMCA

The announcement rang out. "Attention: the Y will be closing in fifteen minutes. Please return all ping pong paddles and billiards equipment to the main desk. Thank you."

Tad looked in the mirror while in the boys' dressing room, and he looked into his soul. He could not, in good conscience, help Jenny fool her parents and go to the dance with Jeremy by pretending that he was her date for the night. For one thing, he wanted to actually *BE* her escort for the night. For another, he was afraid of Jeremy Gustaffsson's temper. He was afraid for himself, but he was more afraid for Jenny. *I have to go out there and tell Jenny I can't do it*, Tad thought, summoning his courage.

Tad's sidekick Stevie Scranton had followed him into the locker room.

"What's up, dude?" Stevie asked his friend.

"Jenny wants me to pretend to be her date for Homecoming on Saturday, so she can go with Jeremy."

Stevie looked at his friend, and he could see that Tad was suffering.

"That's messed up, man," Stevie said. "That Jeremy guy seems like he's half psycho all the time. Have you ever seen him on the football field? He acts like he wants to kill the other players!"

Tad looked at Stevie with irritation. Stevie wasn't the brightest guy, Tad knew, but this was dim even for him.

"That's considered a plus in football, Stevie. That's not the problem. He can be as violent as he wants on the football field, but I'm worried about him *off* the football field. What is he like around Jenny? What will he do if she continues to say no when he wants her to say yes? I can't come out and oppose

Jenny's relationship with Jeremy. If I do, it will look like I'm just saying it because I like her and want her for myself. But, honestly, that's not the only reason."

Stevie, who stood just slightly over 5' 4", looked up at Tad. "Well, what other reason do you got?" he said.

Tad almost opened up about the red aura that surrounded Jeremy Gustaffsson. Then he remembered what had happened to him eight years ago when he had been honest about Pogo the clown. He said nothing. Tad just looked miserable, eyes troubled and brooding.

"I have to go out there and tell Jenny that I can't do it. I can't make her like me and want to go to the dance with me, but I'm not going to be used so that she can sneak around with Jeremy Gustaffsson." Tad seemed to be pulling himself upright, gathering his courage to do the right thing.

"Good for you, guy," said Stevie, cracking his gum. "But aren't you worried that Jeremy might beat *YOU* up, if you don't play along?"

"If he does, he does," said Tad with finality.

He pushed open the door to the locker room to return to the lobby area of the YMCA.

CHAPTER 17

October 28, 2003, 9:00 P.M.
Cedar Falls YMCA

Tad walked from the men's locker room to the lobby, fully expecting to find Jenny and her friend Janice Kramer waiting for him and for Stevie, but they were gone. Either they had been shooed from the emptying facility by the help or Jenny had sensed that Tad was upset and wanted to avoid a confrontation.

"What are you gonna' do now?" Stevie asked.

"If she's not online tonight to talk in instant messages, I guess I'll have to write her a note at school. I just can't do what she asked. I'd be happy to be her date, but not her fake date."

"Who are you gonna' ask to Homecoming?" Stevie asked.

Tad just ignored the question.

As if there were any other girls he would ever want to be with, except Jenny SanGiovanni. Sometimes Stevie was so dense that he wanted to slug him, just to wake him up. The boys sometimes joked around, using the phrase, "Hit me upside the head with a shovel, hard," to confess they had not been paying attention. *Stevie needs a good shoveling*, thought Tad.

* * *

In study hall on October 29, Wednesday, Tad wrote his usual note:

"Hi, Beautiful Girl. What's goin' on? Not much here in study hall.

About that favor you asked me for, I can't do it. I can't pretend that I'm your date and let Jeremy be your real date.

There are some reasons why, and I think you know what a couple of them are: (1) I don't want to be put in the position of playing your folks. If they ever found out, they'd never let us be friends again. They'd never trust me again. I'd hate for that to happen.

(2) I really really like you, Jenny. I don't know what I'll do if you don't like me back, but I do know one other thing.

(3) Jeremy Gustaffsson is bad for you. You should not get with him. He is too old for you and he wants more than you are willing to give, from what you've told me and from what he's said in notes.

Please think about it.

Your friend forever,

Tad."

When Jenny got the note from Tad, she kept it, as she always did, and, later that night, she tucked it in the small brown chest where she kept all her notes from her friends, including those from Jeremy and from her other girlfriends.

Lately, Jeremy's notes had been more and more sexually demanding and sexually suggestive. If her parents ever saw those notes, she didn't know what they'd do. They might even call up Mr. or Mrs. Gustaffsson and demand that Jeremy quit bothering her…(not that he was.)

I can handle him, Jenny thought.

But deep down she wondered if she really could. She'd seen Jeremy lose his temper, and it wasn't pretty.

CHAPTER 18

October 29, 2003, Wednesday
Study Hall

"Hey, Sexy, what's goin' on? Not shit here in study hall. Just about to fall asleep. Jen, I just saw the sickest thing ever. Chris T. and Angie were kissing in the hallway. Ewwww. So, who was your first kiss? Was it me? Or am I just the best kisser you know? (lol)

This weekend we should actually do something with Angie and Chris. That kid is hilarious. Who ever heard of playing the clarinet in band? Duh. I'm tired, so I'm gonna' sleep now. Write me back. Don't forget that you owe me a back massage still. And let me know if Tad is gonna' step up and help us out about Homecoming. We could even ask Angie and that clarinet kid Chris to eat dinner with us, if you want them to.

I LOVE YOU,

Jeremy"

Jenny put that last note from Jeremy carefully inside her purse, for filing later. Lately, every note ended with protestations of "love." It made her nervous. She had told Jeremy that they were too young to be talking shit like that, but he just kept it up. She had told him that she couldn't tell him that she loved him back. She had promised her mom and dad (and stepdad) that she would get a college education before she got serious about any boy. What could be more serious than telling someone that you loved them? She didn't know what her feelings for Jeremy were. She decided they were more lust and a feeling that he needed someone. Those two things did not add up to "love."

She was also afraid of what Jeremy's reaction would be when

he found out that Tad wasn't going to help them with their Homecoming plans.

However, Jenny had another good idea, which might spare Tad. She would tell her parents that she and her girlfriends were going stag. Then, she and Jeremy would meet up at the dance. She hoped that would satisfy Jeremy. She didn't want him mad at Tad and taking his anger out on him. It would be horrible if Jeremy beat Tad up like he had beaten that poor freshman kid who whistled at her that time at the game.

She turned the lights out and tried to go to sleep.

CHAPTER 19

October 30, 2003, Thursday
Sky High parking lot, 8:00 A.M.

Tad was just pulling his backpack from the front passenger's seat of his Honda Civic to the driver's side door when he saw Jeremy Gustaffsson making a beeline for him. Jeremy, who usually was the largest and most heavily muscled boy in any group of boys on campus, had a scowl on his face. He was wearing his letter jacket.

Jeremy's feet crunched on the gravel as he approached Tad's car, the other boys hanging back slightly, to let him have a word with "the weird McGreevy kid."

"Hey, Tad...Jenny says you won't cover for us for Homecoming. Why not?" Tad thought, *Well, at least he hasn't hit me yet. He does get right to the point.*

Tad straightened up from dragging his heavy book bag across the driver's seat and looked Jeremy right in the eye. "It's nothing personal, Jeremy. It's not that I'm trying to make trouble for you or for Jenny. In fact, I'm trying to keep Jenny from getting *in* to trouble. You and I both know that her parents don't want her going out with you because you're eighteen...almost nineteen. She's only fifteen. You can blame me for that, if you want, but it's the truth. It's just the way it is."

Tad took a deep breath to calm himself. He saw that this was not what Jeremy hoped to hear.

"Yeah, I know her folks don't like me. So what? She does, and that's what counts. Age is just a number."

Ruefully, Tad almost agreed with Jeremy out loud. Instead, he said, "Yes, I do know that Jenny really cares for you. She's a very caring person and she's told me so. And I hope you care for her as much as she cares for you. I'd hate to see her get hurt."

Jeremy's voice sounded coarse and rough when he responded. "You don't need to worry about Jenny's and my relationship. We're doin' just fine. The only problem we have is her folks, and that's what she asked you to help us out with. Why don't you be a good kid and a good friend to Jenny and do as she asks?"

"If I were to pretend to be Jenny's date, I'd be deceiving her parents. A relationship should be built on trust, don't you think? If I did that to Mr. and Mrs. SanGiovanni, they'd never trust me again. And I care about that, even if you don't." Tad started to hoist the backpack to his shoulders from the car seat.

Tad could hear Jeremy snort.

"I don't give a rat's ass what that wimpy stepfather or her dikey mother think of me. It's what Jenny thinks of me that counts, and we're in love."

"Has Jenny told you that, herself?" Tad couldn't believe that Jenny had been spouting off about "loving" Jeremy, even if Jeremy constantly threw the word around casually to her in his notes.

Jeremy looked embarrassed...like a kid caught in a lie. "She doesn't have to," he quickly responded. "I can tell. And I can tell that you want her for yourself."

This conversation was getting painfully close to the truth. Tad had wrestled with his conscience over his reasons for refusing Jenny's request, both when Jenny asked him and when he was alone later. He still felt that he was doing the right thing. He was prepared to take a beating, if he had to, to stand up to Jeremy Gustaffsson.

"Jeremy, you're not wrong about my feelings for Jenny. But she obviously doesn't return them. And that's okay. I've been her good friend for quite a while, and I hope to remain her good friend, no matter who she goes out with. I just don't think that the person she is going out with should be you."

There. Now he'd gone and said it.

Tad didn't see the right cross coming. It hit him so hard that he would have fallen to the ground if he hadn't been backed up against his dad's old secondhand Honda Civic. The first punch hit him on the right cheekbone. The second punch caught him in the nose, which immediately began to bleed. Jeremy's entourage rushed forward. Some of them grabbed his upraised right arm, which was ready to strike another blow. Tad was still standing; he hadn't fallen.

"Jeremy...leave him be. Old man Puck'll have our balls if we get caught fighting out here. We're just lucky that that lame cop isn't on duty yet." The friend talking was Zack Porfino, an Italian kid from his neighborhood whose dad was one of Leroy Gustaffsson's drinking buddies.

Jeremy stopped and seemed to mentally assess the situation...as much as he was capable of mentally assessing anything when he was this pissed off.

"Right. You're right," he said to Zack Porfino and Stewie Truitt, his toady friends. "He's not worth it, anyway."

If Tad had been lying prone on the ground, Jeremy would have spit on him with those words, stepped over his body, and walked into the school. Since Tad was still upright and trying to staunch the flow of blood from his nose with the sleeve of his long-sleeved blue shirt, Jeremy just turned on his heel, the ranks of toadies closed around him, and he walked off towards the entrance to Sky High.

CHAPTER 20

October 27, 2003, Monday
History class

Stevie Scranton was at it again. He was on a roll. The other kids were laughing at his attempts to be witty, and Miss Anderson, the history teacher, was writing out a referral slip.

Oh, well, Stevie thought. *At least my referral can't be as serious as the one that Jeremy Gustaffson and Sean Carpenter got for smoking reefer on the bus this morning.* Everybody had heard about it. Mr. Limkeman turned beet-red with anger when Sean and Jeremy showed up for detention.

Mr. Limkeman told everyone, "When I retire, I'm going to write a book about being a detention supervisor. Kids today have no respect. We never used to talk back to our teachers. Now kids talk back ten times a day. And here you two are, smoking dope on the school bus. Dope is the right term for it and the right description for you two. I'm going to use this referral to start off my book. How stupid do you have to be to light up a joint on a school bus?"

Usually, Jeremy would not have been on the bus. He would have been driving the car his old man told him he could use, an old maroon Pontiac LeMans, but his father Leroy was pissed off at him. Jeremy had been helping his dad at the barn with the horses. As usual, he didn't do things well enough or fast enough for dear old Dad.

In addition to smacking him up alongside the head with a pitchfork they were using to break apart a bale of hay for the horses, LeRoy Gustaffsson had seen fit to tell Jeremy that he couldn't drive the Pontiac for the rest of the week. And, of course, this was Homecoming weekend.

That's just great, thought Jeremy. *I'm gonna' take it, anyway! Otherwise, I won't have a car to make out in, and I sure can't take Jenny back to my house. Jenny's Mom Andrea and her stepdad don't approve of* me. *But by this weekend, my dad will forget he said I couldn't use the Pontiac, especially after he gets a snootful. That won't be too long after he gets home. If he does remember, I'll be gone by then.*

It was always dicey, though. You had to hope and pray that your father's memory was as bad as usual and his follow-through typically nonexistent. When LeRoy Gustaffsson was pissed off, he didn't remember half the shit he said. Jeremy was counting on that. If his father did remember, well....Jeremy wasn't that frightened of his father any more. *If I need the car, I need the car,* he thought, his jaw set with determination.

Jeremy wasn't sure he liked Mr. Limkeman's tone at the moment. Mr. Limkeman might just find he had a flat tire or sugar in his gas tank if he kept up with this insulting shit.

But, right now, Jeremy was feeling pretty mellow from the doobie he had shared with Sean Carpenter on the bus. Besides, he was too tired to worry about it. He'd been up late hanging out at the track with his old man until after midnight, helping him with the horses. He was as tired as a quarterback at the end of a game where he'd played every quarter, as Jeremy usually did.

Maybe I'll stop at Jenny's house before her mom or stepdad get home. We can talk about how we are going to hook up at the dance. If that Twinkletoes stepdad shows up, maybe I can convince him to let me date Jenny. He let Limkeman's annoying voice roll from his subconscious, like spilled milk on a flat surface, dripping to the floor below. *No worries.* Jeremy smiled.

But in Principal Puck's office, Stevie Scranton, red-faced with humiliation, was clutching the waistband of his pants and backing away from Peter Puck. This was not the first time the principal had threatened to expel Stevie from school entirely for all his many classroom escapades. Unless Stevie did as he was told and kept his mouth shut, that is.

Peter Puck was a short fat balding man, who had once dressed up as Abraham Lincoln for a school patriotic day. That was funny enough, but the really funny thing was that another teacher, Mr. Ross, had also come dressed as Lincoln that day.

Mr. Ross was tall and thin and he really did resemble Lincoln because he had a long, scraggly, really unattractive natural beard. On this day, Mr. Ross had trimmed it to emulate the real Abe Lincoln. Mr. Ross' beard looked the best it had ever looked.

Somehow, the two of them, Ross and Puck, had ended up on the flat roof of the school, yelling at each other and pushing each other like twelve-year-olds. The students down below were hoping one or the other would fall off.

"How dare you steal my idea!" shouted Puck. Stevie remembered it like it was yesterday. The kids down below were flabbergasted. The two teachers had almost fallen off the roof as they tussled on the rooftop, but finally stomped back inside. Stevie remembered thinking, *Somewhere, the REAL Abe Lincoln must be spinning in his grave like a chicken on a spit!*

The next year, Mr. Ross was nowhere to be found amongst the faculty.

But the unfunny thing about Peter Puck was his fondness for boys. He always found a way to get the smallest and nerdiest boys in school alone. After that, it was all about how much he could demand from the weakest of the pack.

"Unzip that fly, Stevie. You've been a bad, bad boy."

Stevie Scranton felt as small as he had ever felt in his life. If he didn't do as he was told, he'd probably be expelled and never graduate. And so the familiar pattern that had begun in Rossdale Elementary with a different pervert evidenced itself again. Stevie didn't dare speak up. All he could do was try to disassociate. He'd pretend this wasn't really happening to him.

He slowly unzipped the fly of his Chinos as Principal Peter Puck approached, leering with a lop-sided grin.

CHAPTER 21

October 27, 2003, Monday
10:00 A.M.

When Stevie returned to Study Hall from Principal Peter Puck's office, after being sent to the office from Miss Anderson's American History class, Tad could tell something was very, very wrong. He was hoping to be able to talk to Stevie after school, to find out what was bothering him. Tad had known Stevie a long time. He had seen that look before. It wasn't good. Often, Stevie would withdraw for days at a time after that look appeared on his face.

Stevie was nowhere to be found when the final bell rang. He had gone to the nurse and gotten a pass to go home early.

That Stevie Scranton is always coming in here with his nervous stomach complaints, Nurse Ramirez thought. *His parents really ought to have him examined by a doctor.*

But, as was her custom, she obligingly wrote him a note allowing him to go home one-half hour early. *I've got kids knifing one another, for Pete's sake. Who's going to miss one kid who feels like he's going to be sick?*

Those would turn out to be prophetic words in the weeks to come.

* * *

Sharon McGreevy's cell phone rang. She glanced at the number, but didn't answer. *That creep Kellogg. How old is he, anyway? He's got to be pushing 40. Why doesn't he give it a rest?*

Sharon didn't answer, instead letting the call roll over to her messaging system.

Sharon was, at that exact moment, replacing the electrical outlet plates on the wall of her new apartment near the University with prettier brass plates.

Sharon had graduated from Sky High two years before. She was starting her junior year of college, her first year in an apartment by herself with no roommates.

She was soooooooo glad to be out of high school, her parents' house, and the dormitory her parents had made her live in for her first two years of junior college. She had painted her new bedroom yesterday; she was replacing the furniture and faceplates today.

Sharon didn't want a roommate. She'd had enough of interrupted sleep cycles and people screaming in the night. She still remembered the period of time eight years ago when every single night for over a month all of them at her house were up waiting hand-and-foot on her little brother. *It was always all about Tad*, Sharon thought. Even after Tad came home, his care and feeding were paramount in her parents' minds.

She loved her little brother, but talk about a dysfunctional little shit! He sure had been back in 1995, anyway. She hoped he was getting more normal in his junior year of high school, but, frankly, she didn't see that much of him these days. She blew the stray strand of hair out of her eyes and went back to work with the Phillips head screwdriver.

The phone rang again. Sharon checked the number and, this time, she answered.

"Wassup?" It was Belinda Chandler, her friend from high school and the volleyball team. Belinda was cute in a dark Italian way, with slutty eyes and a Kathleen Turner voice.

"Not much. How's it going with the apartment?"

"Really well," Sharon responded.

Belinda was a friend that Sharon never could have over to her house in high school. Now that her mother wasn't her keeper, she could do as she pleased.

Sharon's mom had always hated Belinda's mom, Cassie. Therefore, Jeannie McGreevy discouraged Sharon from fraternizing with Belinda. Sharon thought that Belinda was cool, if a bit promiscuous. Besides, Belinda had worked at Sharon's dad's office, helping with filing and typing, just as Sharon had done all through her high school summers, and the shared work experiences had helped the two girls to bond.

Both girls had been on the volleyball team at Sky High, coached by Kenneth Kellogg, the chemistry teacher, and both girls had received phone calls from him since graduating.

"I just got a call from that Kellogg creep," Sharon told Belinda. "Why doesn't he give it up and go after someone his own age?"

Belinda said nothing. She had always had a soft spot for Coach Kellogg. She'd been having sex with him for the past six months. She didn't want to tell Sharon, because she knew that Sharon felt that a 37-year-old teacher—their former teacher and coach—shouldn't be calling up his former students, even if they *had* graduated. Belinda was secretly glad that Sharon had no interest in Kenny Kellogg, as she had enough interest in their ex-teacher for the both of them.

Belinda had a sneaking suspicion that Kellogg, or Cereal Man, as she called him when they were in bed together, was diddling someone who was his *current* student. That bothered her.

But what was wrong, really, with dating a *former* student like her ? That would not be the case if Cereal Man really was putting it to any of his underage charges. Belinda hoped he wasn't, because she'd probably get dragged into it somehow. She wouldn't suffer in silence if he was two-timing her with some 16-year-old chippie from Sky High!

Both Sharon and Belinda were entering their third year at the State College of Iowa, (now known as the University of Northern Iowa). Belinda was actually there on a volleyball scholarship. Her relationship with Kenny Kellogg, Cereal Man had begun when he offered to recommend her for that volleyball scholarship at SCI/UNI.

When she had been granted the scholarship, she felt indebted to him. Kenny had helped that along when he said to her, at a local bar, "Wouldn't you like to show your old coach a little gratitude?" The gratitude she showed him that night took place in the alley. Since then, they had moved on to better venues and more creative foreplay.

Kenny Kellogg had offered to help her with some pointers for her game. Belinda had an inkling that the game wasn't volleyball, but she played along. After all, sometimes older men made the best lovers, if they knew what they were doing. Lord knows that her high school honeys didn't have a clue. *Alex, may I buy a clue?* Belinda thought. She smiled.

Belinda wanted to become a physical education teacher, like Miss Sloan. Everyone at Sky High knew that Miss Sloan did all the real work and planning while Mr. Bear just coasted. If she found herself in a school situation where she was the brains of the outfit and some lame-ass male phys ed teacher was coasting on her coat-tails, like Bear did on Sloan's, she at least wanted to know what she was doing, so she could do well for the both of them.

If Kenny Kellogg could help her become a better teacher, or even help her get a job when she graduated, where was the harm in that? Justification? Maybe. But it made sense to Belinda Chandler. So she was happy to hear that Sharon McGreevy was indifferent to good old Coach Kellogg's charms. She just hoped she was wrong about her suspicions regarding Coach Kellogg and his preference for young stuff. He wasn't much to look at, it's true, with his double chin, nose and ear hair and sparse military style crew cut, but she'd had worse.

Sharon McGreevey had a less positive attitude towards the entire experience of receiving phone calls from an unattractive former teacher. She thought he was a pervert. She reminded Belinda of it every time Cereal Man called either of them.

Sharon was not a phys ed major and did not plan to become a teacher. She had no idea what she wanted to become, at this point in her young life. She just knew that she had to go to college, because her parents said so. Besides, it was a good way to get out of her parents' house.

"Why are you so hot to move out and have to pay rent, when you could live at home rent-free?" Belinda had asked Sharon.

Sharon responded, "Too much drama."

Sharon didn't explain what she meant by that, but Belinda thought she knew. There was Tad, her weird-ass little brother with the emotional issues. There was Jeannie McGreevy, the size zero Bitch of the Year.

I wonder if Sharon would appreciate knowing the drama going on in my life? thought Belinda.

But she remained silent on that subject. For now.

CHAPTER 22

October 27, 2003, Monday
7:00 P.M.

It was getting dark. Shannon Scranton was getting worried. Shannon and Stevie had made plans to go bowling together after school was over for Stevie and Shannon finished up at work. Three years older than her little brother, she didn't make plans to do things with him that often.

Shannon was working for Layne Insurance Agency now. She didn't have that many free nights. She had better things to do in her spare time than go bowling with pimply-faced, strange-looking short little high school nerds, like her brother Stevie. But he was a good kid in a weird way, and she had less-than-enthusiastically adopted his plan that she give him some pointers for the bowling unit he had to take in Phys Ed next semester. Shannon was a natural athlete, good at almost every sport she tried. Stevie: not so much.

Her dad was working the late shift at the Rath plant, so he wasn't around to get worried. Shannon was worried enough for both of them. Sally Scranton usually didn't get home from her on-again, off-again job cleaning houses for some of the wealthier folks in Cedar Falls until 7 p.m. or later—especially if she knew that Earl was going to be working, anyway—but Shannon had cut short her work day to be here at 4 p.m. In fifteen minutes it was going to be 7 p.m.

Shannon heard the sound of the garage door going up.

Must be Mom, she thought. *Maybe she can tell me where the little dweeb has gotten himself to.*

Shannon had helped herself to some cookies while she waited around for Stevie. She brushed the crumbs from her 38D chest as she waited for the door to the kitchen to slam, indicating that Sally had made it through the mudroom.

"Hi, Mom! Any idea where Stevie is?"

Sally emerged from the hallway. "No. Isn't he here?"

"No, and we had a date to go bowling when I got off work. I even got here early, but no Stevie."

Sally said, "He probably got himself into some kind of trouble at school again and got an after-school suspension."

"Yeah. I thought of that," said Shannon, "but usually they give you a day's warning if you have to stay after. Do you think Tad would know?"

"It's worth a try, Honey. Why don't you call him?"

Shannon pulled out her cell phone and dialed Tad McGreevy's home phone number. *Tad should be home by now*, she thought. Shannon had the McGreevys' home phone number in her directory because of Sharon, one year younger, who had also been on her volleyball team. Tad wouldn't be serving any after-school suspensions. He ought to be able to shed some light on Stevie's whereabouts.

Tad answered on the first ring. He was hoping it was Stevie. Instead, it was Shannon.

"Hi, Tad! Do you know where my little brother is?"

"No, Shannon, isn't he home yet? I'm worried about him."

A slight chill caused Shannon to shiver. It was as though an ice cube had inadvertently slipped from her lips and fallen into her ample bosom.

"Why? What do you mean?"

"Well, he got sent to the office from Miss Anderson's class. Then, I saw him on his way to his last-period study hall after that, and he just looked......funny." Tad didn't know how to accurately describe the red-faced look of shame, hurt and embarrassment that he had seen on Stevie's face as he entered the rest room after his session with Principal Puck. If Tad hadn't already been late to his own class, he would have followed Stevie to ask him what was wrong.

"Funny how?" Shannon was becoming more and more disturbed by Tad's observations. Tad knew Stevie better than anyone. If Tad was worried, there was good cause for Shannon...and, for that matter, Mr. and Mrs. Scranton...to be worried.

"Well, I saw him come out of Principal Puck's office and duck into the rest room immediately. He almost looked like he was going to cry or something. Of course, Principal Puck probably lit into him for acting up in Anderson's class."

"Yes, I can understand that Puck would give him trouble, but it wouldn't exactly be the first time Stevie has gotten in trouble and been sent to the principal's office. He should be a pro at handling that, by now," Shannon said, somewhat sarcastically. She doodled with the pen and pad on the kitchen counter, where she now sat in a hard-backed white wooden chair. She was sketching what looked like a slinky on the white notepad.

"I don't know, Shannon. I looked for him everywhere after school, but he was not any of the places I thought he'd be. I've been worried about him ever since." Shannon detected genuine concern in Tad's voice.

Shannon hung up the phone and turned to give her mother the news.

CHAPTER 23

October 28, 2003, Tuesday
8:00 A.M.

It was not official for 24 hours…or so the cops said…but Stevie Scranton was missing.

When he wasn't home by 10 p.m., his worried parents had called the authorities. The police had not been very helpful, stating that they really needed to wait till morning to make sure that Stevie wasn't on his way home. Also, they needed to retrace the final hours of his school day. He really wouldn't be an "official" missing person until close to 3:30 p.m. today. The new laws about abducted children and the Amber Alert changes had coaxed the police into looking for the missing boy earlier than twenty-four hours out, although they generally figured the missing kid was probably just playing hooky. Or the kid might have actually run away from home.

Bright and early, the Scrantons, Shannon in tow, trekked over to Principal Peter Puck's office. It was the beginning of a new school day. The Tuesday crowd filling the office had the usual concerns. The office was able to verify that Nurse Hernandez had seen Stevie shortly before Tad saw Stevie enter the restroom. Nurse Hernandez had authorized Stevie's one-half hour early release from school. Stevie had told her that he felt sick to his stomach.

"Stevie often comes to me and says he feels sick to his stomach. You should consider having him looked at by an internal medicine specialist."

Earl Scranton thought, *I should consider doing a wood shed number on him like my old man used to do on me!*

Earl was a plainspoken man of the people. He didn't pussyfoot around with his son when Stevie came home red-faced and crying like a baby.

Earl would ask, "What's the matter?"

"I got sent to Principal Puck's office," Stevie would say.

"That weird pudgy prick?" Earl asked.

"Yeah. He's weird, but he's large and in charge."

"Stay the hell away from Principal Puck. Quit being mouthy and getting in trouble, and we wouldn't be having this conversation. Let's not, and say we did."

Stevie would slink away to his room. It wasn't as though Stevie and Earl had much in common. They didn't really talk. Earl wasn't much of a talker with Sally or with Shannon, either. Earl just criticized Stevie for whatever mischief or fuck-up he had gotten himself into this time.

The only person that Stevie really confided in was Tad McGreevy. Tad had said he didn't know what was bothering Stevie when Stevie went home early from school. He didn't even know that Stevie had been to the nurse right before his last hour of class. It didn't surprise Tad when he heard that bit of news.

So far, nobody seemed to know anything, really, and Principal Peter Puck was not shedding much light on the situation.'

"Yes, Miss Anderson sent Stevie to me to be disciplined for some foolishness he engaged in during her 5th hour American History class. He was only here for a few moments before he said he felt sick and wanted to go to the nurse. Naturally, I sent him to Nurse Hernandez immediately."

Not quite immediately, Peter Puck thought. *There was time for a little interpersonal R&R first.*

"Now, if you'll excuse me, I have some pressing business to attend to. I'm sure that Stevie is just hiding somewhere. Perhaps he feared your reaction when he got home?"

"Why would Stevie fear our reaction?" This was Sally Scranton speaking.

"You know how Stevie is. He's a bit of a rapscallion at times. Perhaps he feared you two would be upset with him?" Principal Puck raised his eyebrow in a familiar way when he said the word "rapscallion."

"Look, Mr. Puck…"

"Dr. Puck," Peter interrupted him archly, his porky features betraying his pride in his advanced education degree. He'd gotten it from the online college, Sphinx, so his pride was misplaced.

This time it was Earl's chance to speak. "Stevie has been getting into trouble for as long as I can remember. That's why he went to Rossdale, instead of that hoity-toity school that Shannon attended. But, despite the crap he pulls, he's a good kid. He's never done anything that would cause us to over-react or become this worried. I hope you aren't implying that we said or did anything to Stevie to cause him to run away, because that seems to be the chief theory the police have. I seriously doubt that those clowns could find their ass with a flashlight."

Earl Scranton looked as though a dark storm cloud were gathering. His kid was missing and he was stuck listening to this wimpy Pillsbury DoughBoy guy use terms like "rapscallion" to describe the little shit.

"Oh, heavens no, Mr. Scranton. Please excuse me if my comments were misconstrued." Puck cleared his throat, " I simply meant that Stevie, himself, might have felt that he was going to be grounded or incur some other disciplinary measures. Therefore, he might have temporarily chosen to absent himself from the family home."

"If my bullshit detector and translator is working, you mean you're with the cops in thinking he might have run away from home. But, where would he go?"

"Yes, where would he go?" This was Stevie's mother, echoing her husband Earl. She was truly worried.

It had now been seventeen hours since Nurse Hernandez had seen Stevie at approximately 3:30 p.m. the day before. Even though Stevie wouldn't truly be an official missing person until after twenty-four hours, seventeen hours since Stevie dropped from sight was looming. Earl, Sally and Shannon Scranton were frantic to find Stevie.

CHAPTER 24

October 28, 2003, Tuesday
10:00 A.M.
Study Hall

"Hi, Beautiful girl,

Did you by any chance see Stevie any time after school or just before school let out yesterday? He didn't go home and his folks and his sister are worried sick. If you know anything about where he might have gone, write me back right away.

Your friend,

Tad"

Tad didn't feel it necessary to bother Jenny with the gory details of his confrontation with Jeremy and his minor bloody nose in the parking lot yesterday. It would just make Tad look like a big wimp and a colossal loser. Besides, nothing was really hurt but Tad's pride. His nose made a "snapping" sound when he straightened it out. It was no big deal.

His sister Sharon said, "It will give you some character. It's kind of cool that you were defending the lady fair." Tad wasn't exactly sure why she described the minor dust-up that way, but he wasn't going to argue.

Sharon had stopped by the house to pick up a lamp. She had no light in her bedroom, right now, and her parents wouldn't mind if she borrowed one of their standing lamps till she got one of her own. She had noticed Tad's bloody shirt, and he told her the story behind it.

"It was just one quick shot. He cold-cocked me. I didn't see it coming. Next time, I'll be ready." Tad did the jock adjust thing. He noticed the more macho boys always did that, to make themselves look and sound like they were alpha males.

Tad knew he wasn't an alpha male. He was perfectly happy being a beta male. Alpha males didn't worry about sensitive stuff, like Tad did. Alpha males didn't have dreams that predicted the future, as Tad sometimes did. Alpha males didn't give a rat's ass about auras.

He was worried about Jenny and Jeremy. He was thinking about the SanGiovannis and how they would react to Jeremy, Jenny and him, if they thought he was mixed up in Jeremy's continuing to date their daughter. He had a terrible sense of forboding regarding Jeremy. What was his dad's old expression? "An accident waiting to happen."

He had had a dream last night where Jeremy was pounding and pounding on some helpless person. He held something silver in his hand, but it didn't look like a knife. It had a more substantial handle. Jeremy loomed over the person in the dream. Tad didn't know who was getting beaten up. *Is that me? Is that Jenny? Who is it?* He woke up before he could discover the answer to that question, but whoever it was had taken a terrific physical beating from Jeremy Gustaffsson. Just as Tad awakened, he noticed that the leg he could see in his dream was female. He didn't know whose leg it was, but it was most definitely a girl's—or a woman's—leg.

Besides the dream, there was one thing on his mind that bothered him more: *Where is Stevie?*

As for Jenny and Jeremy, she'd said she had worked it out with her folks so that her parents thought she was going to Homecoming with a bunch of girlfriends. Janice Kramer. Kelly Carter. Heather Crompton. Besides, Tad was too worried about his oldest friend in the world to think about a stupid dance that he wasn't even going to attend.

Sharon left, taking the family's standing lamp from the McGreevy's family room. Tad went back to phoning their mutual friends and surfing the net looking for someone that Stevie might have told where he was going after school yesterday. He tried a couple of chat rooms on AOL that Stevie sometimes hung out in. No luck.

Stevie had vanished.

CHAPTER 25

October 28, 2003, Tuesday
Midnight

It was well past the time that Tad McGreevy normally went to bed on a weeknight. Tomorrow was Wednesday…or, really, today was Wednesday, since, as he watched, the clock ticked past midnight, the dawning of a new day.

Tad had exhausted every avenue he could think of. He had been on the phone non-stop since Sharon had left with the standing lamp, just before Jeannie and Jim McGreevy got home.

Jeannie McGreevy seemed disappointed that Sharon hadn't stayed for dinner. "Oh, I wish she would have stayed and eaten with us. What did you say she came for, again?"

"She came and took the lamp from the family room, Mom. I've told you this twice now."

Tad was tapping away at his laptop computer, checking to see if there had been any communication back to him from Stevie or anyone else he had contacted.

Tad must have sounded irritated. He was intent on getting in touch with every one of his and Stevie's mutual friends, either online or on the phone. A typical conversation would last five to ten minutes before Tad was told the same thing, time after time: "No. I never saw Stevie at all yesterday after he got sent to the office."

Everyone seemed to remember Stevie horsing around in Miss Anderson's class. After that, no one seemed to know what path Stevie had taken. Many of the people Tad contacted mentioned Rodney Black and the tattoo comment that Stevie made to Rodney. Tad knew Rodney, whose father shot film on a free-lance basis for their local television station and covered the athletic events at the high school. Rodney was too lazy to go to the bother of trying to catch Stevie to beat the crap out of him. Rodney was laid-back—and stoned, most of the time.

Tad was in a different section of American History, a section for the brighter kids. Stevie and he actually had very few classes together. It wasn't that way in their days at Rossdale Elementary, when there had only been one section, through sixth grade, but once they went to the middle school (7th, 8th, 9th) level, and other feeder districts fed students from other suburban communities into Sky High, their paths crossed much less frequently. They still had lunch at the same time, and the study hall placement depended on whose homeroom the student drew. That was purely luck. Tad suspected that the more unruly students were given to the teachers who could handle them the best, but the administration would argue that students were randomly assigned to homerooms.

Whatever the reason(s), Tad and Stevie had been in the same study hall last year, but they were not in the same study hall this year. Tad was assigned to Kenneth Kellogg, the chemistry teacher, for his homeroom assignment. Stevie drew Miss Anderson, who was what used to be termed an Old Maid schoolteacher. The phrase had passed from the language, but the plain teacher with no husband, no children, and no life other than her teaching career still existed in education.

Study halls were usually held for the final 45-minute portion of the day, although some were held in morning hours. Outside detention supervisors were brought in to monitor those morning detention students and were paid minimum wage. Tad had never been sent to an outside supervisor's study hall or to detention study hall. He had always toed the line and stayed out of trouble.

This year, Kenny Kellogg and Tad sat within five feet of one another (Tad sat in the front row to be able to pay better attention to lectures). Last year, Tad had been assigned to Kleeman's study hall. The pudgy Ms. Anderson had little tolerance for troublemakers. She wanted the students seated in the orderly rows of her classroom to behave themselves and work on tomorrow's homework. She did not want to have to deal with the Stevie Scrantons of life.

According to the reports that Tad had been able to piece together from various students who were also present when Stevie rattled Miss Anderson's cage, he had been kidding around with another student, Rodney Black. Rodney was a dirt bag. He had a tattoo of a heart, crudely drawn, on his left bicep. An arrow pierced the heart, but there was no girl's name attached to the arrow. Not that it showed in class, but Rodney also had a tattoo covering his entire back that depicted a human brain being put through a washing machine ringer. In gym class, when asked, he said, "Brainwashing. Get it?"

Rodney thought it was brilliant.

Everyone else in his phys ed class, when it was revealed in the shower, thought it was just lame.

Stevie had been trying to engage Rodney in light banter regarding the smaller, more visible tattoo.

"Hey....Rod....when did you get that tattoo?"

Rodney Black just looked at Stevie as though he were a bug under a microscope. His long hair fell in greasy strands across his forehead. The only description that Tad could give, to compare Rod's greasy hair to anyone famous, was fat Elvis. Emulating Elvis, who had been dead for decades, made Rod an anachronism. Most of the punks had spiky hair or piercings or other Goth touches. Rod looked like he had walked out of an old Elvis movie, a movie where Elvis was ugly and fat.

Rod didn't respond to Stevie's jibes, so Stevie kept it up.

"Maybe you didn't hear me, Rod. I asked you who gave you that handsome heart tattoo? When did you get it?"

When Stevie asked the question with the adjective "handsome" added, Rod took offense. He was a big fat kid. The desks were close together. He took the toe of his motorcycle boot and pushed Stevie's chair over. It was the kind of desk where the chair is separate from the desk. It was a good thing, with kids the size of Terry Wilkinson in there. If the desks had been the one-piece kind, half of the students in this particular study hall would not have been able to fit in their desks. They would have had to stand all hour or sit on the floor, which Mrs. Anderson would not have liked at all. Many of them, like Jeremy Gustaffsson, were repeating, spending a second year in the same class. They were physically too big for the puny desks, which had needed replacing five years ago.

With the push from Rod's boot, unaccompanied by any further repartee, Stevie's desk chair crashed to the floor. Stevie rode the chair to the ground like a rodeo cowboy. His misshapen head hit the tiled floor with a clunking sound, the sound of someone thumping a watermelon especially hard, hitting it with a wooden implement, like a canoe oar.

Miss Anderson looked up from the papers she had been grading. Seeing that it was Stevie Scranton—again—she automatically handed him a pink referral slip. Stevie was embarrassed to be laying flat on his back in the middle of the aisle. On the other hand, he recognized the opportunity to be a star. Negative attention was better than no attention at all.

He scrambled to his feet, unhurt, and said to Rodney, before exiting, "Well, whoever did that tattoo, you oughta' ask for a refund."

As he left the classroom and swaggered toward the office, he had a defiant grin on his chubby face.

CHAPTER 26

October 29, 2003, Wednesday
Start of School Day

Tad felt really tired. And weird. He couldn't believe that there was a hiding place or a favorite spot of Stevie Scranton's that he didn't know about. He and Stevie had built forts when they were little kids and fished when they were slightly older. Basically, he and Stevie had spent all their free time together. Until recently, that is, when the high school class schedule had split them up, except for lunch and after-school hours.

Stevie wasn't at the cabin, the one that belonged to old man Isham. Ike Isham was in a nursing home now. The boys had discovered that the key to his unused cabin was in a very obvious spot: inside a flowerpot beside the front door. There were some plastic flowers in the pot, true, but if you picked up the fake geraniums, there was the key to the cabin. This had allowed Stevie and Tad to enjoy their own secret hide-away since 8th grade.

They were always fearful that Old Man Isham would die in the nursing home, or that one of his relatives in town would suddenly decide to check on Ike's abandoned fishing cabin deep in the woods near town, but that had not yet happened. It was a cool place. Tad had a wild idea that maybe Stevie had needed a place to hide from his old man. Maybe whatever was upsetting Stevie that last day at school—which no one seemed to be able to clear up to Tad's satisfaction—had driven him to want to be alone in the woods for a while, sequestered even from his best friend Tad.

However, when Tad had visited the cabin early this morning, long before he was to be at Sky High, there was no sign of anyone having been there since the last time the two of them had gone there.

After that, Tad had wandered down to the old Yundt Theater. The theater was a favorite hangout, but it had recently closed, the victim of a new Multiplex at the Crossroads Mall on the edge of town. It looked as abandoned as it had the day the owner, Able Yundt, locked the door and closed the place for the final time. It was like "The Last Picture Show," signaling the end of an era. Now, it was all about the mega-mall and the movies that were the big hits of the day, with a room off to the side for games that were increasingly wild and crazy.

The Yundt Theater had always featured old-fashioned movies with good guys in white hats and bad guys in black hats. There was also a spate of odd films: Laurel & Hardy shorts, the Three Stooges. Throwbacks to a long-gone era. Once 80-year-old Able Yundt gave up trying to make any money from the run-down former Opera House that had been converted to a movie theater, it was only a matter of time till the theater chains moved in, showing the homogenized crap of the day.

Mr. Yundt's theater had been a true gem. He even showed his own home movies, with a recliner in the middle of the aisle that his German Shepherd Solomon would jump up in to watch the show. But quirky businessmen like Able Yundt were not in keeping with the films or the theatergoers of 2003. The place today remained shuttered and dark. A forlorn "For Rent or For Sale" sign hung crookedly on the closed and locked door.

After traipsing all over town to their favorite haunts...at least five of them.... and contacting everyone in their class who had ever been Stevie's friend (as well as a few who had not), Tad had no idea where to look next. The Scrantons and the police and the principal had already asked him this question.

He noticed that Principal Peter Puck...Dr. Peter Puck, as he preferred to be called...acted strangely when being questioned. His sickening gray-green khaki hue was deeper than usual. The color of evil, Tad mentally dubbed it.

"Did Stevie ever confide in you that anything in particular was bothering him?" the principal had asked Tad. Tad thought, later, that Dr. Puck was looking at him particularly keenly, the look of a bird of prey regarding its next victim.

"No, Sir." Tad answered honestly. Although he could tell that something *was* bothering Stevie, all of Tad's hints that he could be a good listener if

Stevie was bothered by something at home or at school had not led to any disclosures of trouble. Stevie just shrugged and changed the subject.

Tad had done everything he could think of to try to help locate Stevie. His efforts had been futile.. The gray-green aura of Principal Puck made Tad want to keep his answers short. He wanted to get out of Puck's office as quickly as possible.

Tad was still worried about Friday night, two days away, when Homecoming would coincide with Halloween and Jenny and Jeremy would dance to the strains of the hired dee-jay, while he would be at home worrying about his missing best friend.

CHAPTER 27

October 30, 2003, Thursday, 5:00 P.M.
Day Before Homecoming/Halloween

Jeremy had been thinking about Jenny SanGiovanni all day. He wanted to see her naked. He wanted to take her to bed. He wanted to make her his for all time.

She belongs to me. Nobody else can have her

As the Homecoming dance approached, Jenny had been acting very cool towards Jeremy. She was "busy" with this activity or that whenever he suggested giving her a ride home.

"I can't tonight, Jeremy. We have cheerleading practice." Then she would hurry off down the hall.

Just as Stevie and Tad had few classes together, Jenny and Jeremy had literally none together, not even lunch, since Jeremy was a senior (albeit a 5th year senior) and Jenny was "one of the smart kids," as Jeremy proudly called her.

Jeremy wasn't dumb. He had a certain cunning that his father called "street smarts." Jeremy wasn't considered academically bright, but he knew a lot. He knew enough to know that Jenny SanGiovanni's attitude towards him was changing. It seemed as though she had grown ten degrees cooler ever since that Scranton kid had turned up missing the first of the week.

I don't know why that little dweeb going MIA makes her mad at me. I didn't have nothin' to do with that scrawny little geek disappearing.

That part was true. Jeremy Gustaffsson had no interest in weird little guys who didn't even come up to his shoulder, kids with strange-looking heads and dopey friends like Tad McGreevy.

Thinking of Tad McGreevy made Jeremy's skin flush red. He was going to have to have a talk with that kid, and this time the boys wouldn't pull him off of that runty smart ass.

This time, I'm gonna' drive home the point that Jenny and me—we're a couple—now and forever. There ain't nothin' her folks can do about it, and there ain't nothin' Tad McGreevy can do about it, either. Maybe I should make it clear to Jenny, first, Jeremy thought. *It wouldn't hurt to clue in her dip-shit stepfather that we're gonna' see each other, and there's not one damned thing he can do about it.*

* * *

Belinda Chandler rode Kenny Kellogg like he was a prize pony and she was a champion rodeo-style cowgirl. She almost felt like letting out a war whoop as she came. Kenny just put his tongue in the side of his mouth, an affectation she swore he had swiped from Michael Jordan. He did a lot of grunting when he came, but he didn't say much. He was, however, quite considerate of her. Kenny would make sure that she had as good a time as possible, which was more than she could expect from the boys her own age.

Kenny wasn't much to look at. He had a ridiculous old-style flattop buzz-cut Marine style haircut. He did stay in fairly good shape, as far as his body. His body had gone about as far as it could, with her. Belinda didn't mind the fact that he was getting that old-man hair sprouting from his ears look. *At least he has hair some place*, she thought. She still had some pubes in her mouth from going down on Cereal Man. *An occupational hazard.* She smiled, remembering the old saying, "There's no such thing as a bad blow job."

Belinda had once won an after-school informal contest for giving the best B.J. in the school, and she was very proud of her skills. She also didn't mind the fact that Kenny had a curved penis; it was a sizeable tool. She enjoyed fondling it. She called it "my little pony." This pony was fun to ride. Of course, at thirty-seven, Kenny Kellogg couldn't keep up the pace that she would have liked, but he knew a few tricks that her younger suitors did not.

Once, Kenny showed up with a cock ring. Janice had never "done it" with someone wearing a cock ring.

"What's the idea behind this thing?" she asked her older lover as they lay in bed. Janice had to borrow one of her girlfriend's apartments to meet Kenny for sexual trysts, because she was still living at home. Her girlfriend Billy's apartment was way-the-hell-and-gone out towards the woods where some people had summer cabins. In this case, the deal with Billy was that she and Lover Boy would be gone by dinnertime. That was when Billy got home from her day job as a waitress at the Maid Rite.

Kenny explained. "This will keep me hard longer. Want to try it?"

Did she! Janice loved anything that would keep her sexual partners from becoming Minutemen. The only time she wanted to hear that phrase was in reference to orange juice or history. Not in reference to her sexual partners.

They were really going at it when something happened. She was never sure exactly what, but apparently Cereal Man blew a gasket. The pressure on his dick caused a huge blood vessel to erupt. It was purple and looked like it hurt. It looked a lot like a tire with a heat bubble about to explode. Their fucking came to an abrupt halt. Belinda laughed uncontrollably. She couldn't help herself. The sight of her former teacher hopping around clutching his purple penis made her nearly hysterical with laughter.

"Shit!" Kenny seemed much more upset than he should have been.

"Does it hurt that much?" Belinda was gradually calming down. It occurred to her that maybe Kenny had really hurt himself. The little purple pony looked like a tire with a blow-out. Belinda was feeling remorseful that she had laughed…if Kenny was really in that much pain.

Without thinking, Kenny blurted out, "It's not that it hurts. It's how it looks."

This caused Belinda to stop and say, "Well, you're not married. Who else is going to be looking at your dick?"

At that, Kenny Kellogg, "Cereal Man", clammed up.

That was when Janice suspected that her old volleyball coach was definitely screwing somebody else. Somebody younger than her, perhaps. Certainly not her good friend Shannon Scranton, who despised him. Belinda Chandler was going to find out who Kenny was seeing, besides her. If it was some underage chippie from school, and her former teacher was doing a high school girl, Belinda was going to make sure that he paid for two-timing her and paid dearly.

CHAPTER 28

October 30, 2003, Thursday
After School

Jeremy had been brooding about Jenny.

Jenny needs to know who's the boss in this relationship, he thought. *It's no good her cutting off my balls this way. I'm not some housecat that can be neutered to make a calmer pet. That stepfather of hers should step off, too. He's not even her real dad.*

Brooding was not a good thing for Jeremy. He tended to act out when he focused on how he had been wronged. It seemed, sometimes, like the entire world was out to get him. *It's not my fault that my dad's a drunk and I have a shitty life. People should consider how much I've had to overcome to get as far as I have.*

After all, Jeremy was the starting quarterback, for the Sky High Eagles. During basketball season, as the tallest boy in his class, he was the center and leading scorer. This year, his fifth year in high school, he ought to really be able to rack up the points, since the conference was going to give him another year of eligibility because of the timing of his blown knee last year.

Before I talk to Jenny about things, I ought to try to have a talk with that sissy stepfather of hers. Maybe I can con him into thinking that I don't have any sexy plans for his stepdaughter. After all, Jenny's not even his kid!

Jeremy knew that Greg Tuttle was usually home long before anyone else in the household. Tuttle was a financial advisor. As far as Jeremy could see, that meant that he did very little real work anywhere. He did have an office, but he seemed to have no set time that he visited his office in Union Square downtown. He was always just drifting around, doing whatever. Greg often was at the house, especially whenever Jeremy hoped that the house would be empty. Mom Andrea would be at her real estate job at SanGiovanni Realty and step-daddy Greg was supposedly out investing other people's money...or whatever it was he did.

Tuttle looked and acted like a real candy-ass. Jeremy had no fear of the slight-of-build almost feminine-looking Gregory Tuttle. He knew that Jenny deeply loved and missed her real father, but she gave off mixed signals about her feelings for Greg Tuttle.

Even Andrea SanGiovanni had not cared enough about old Greg to take his last name when they got married. She kept SanGiovanni. Who could blame her? However, whatever Gregory Tuttle did or didn't do, it appeared that Greg Tuttle brought in some do-re-mi, and that was something that Jeremy Gustaffsson did have respect for: the Almighty Dollar. Jeremy had precious few dollars of his own. His parents had very little money, either. And it didn't look like Jeremy was going to win the lottery any time soon.

What Jeremy did have was a fearlessness towards other males, a physicality that was imposing and at its peak, and a passionate obsession with Gregory Tuttle's stepdaughter, Jenny SanGiovanni.

Just because I think about Jenny all the time doesn't mean I'm nuts, thought Jeremy. He remembered one dictionary definition he had seen, which described an obsession as "domination of one's thoughts or feelings by a persistent idea, image, or desire."

That's all it is. I am preoccupied by thoughts of Jenny and our being together. If her parents would just let nature take its course, we'd be together and everything would be fine.

Interest does what it can; obsession does what it must.

Jeremy Gustaffsson thought it was about time that he and Mr. Tuttle had a little talk.

* * *

Immediately after school, the day before the Homecoming dance, Jeremy set off early, ditching his last-hour class (Kellogg's chemistry class: BO-RING) to make it to Jenny's side of the tracks when Greg would come marching home. Jeremy knew that Jenny had cheerleading practice after school tonight. She wouldn't make it home before 6:00 p.m. at the earliest. Andrea SanGiovanni never got home before 8:00 p.m., even on a good night. It was work, work, work for the Slum Queen, which was what Jeremy's mom and half the town called Andrea SanGiovanni.

Andrea's own obsession, a preoccupation with her business career, was why she had already lost one husband. From what Jeremy had heard, she was in danger of losing Tuttle, husband number two, as well. In a town this small, when you checked in to the *Westward Ho* motel with someone other than your wife, word traveled fast. Andrea's late arrivals on the home front were caused by her need to attend to her properties, many of which were in the area known as The Heights, where the Mexican-American families primarily resided. That was why Jenny so often had to start dinner for the family on her own.

The family meant Andrea, Greg, Jenny's college-aged brother Frank, who lived at home and went to Cedar Falls Junior College, her older sister Cynthia (who had an apartment near her office job at Layne's Insurance, but sometimes dropped by at dinnertime) and Jenny.

Jenny told Jeremy, "I'm a good cook!"

Jeremy believed her. "There's nothing you can't do, if you put your mind to it." *I have a few things I could teach her, if she'd let me*, Jeremy thought, leering as he considered his plans for Jenny on Homecoming night. *She could be World Class if she'd only let old Jeremy tutor her.* He smiled in anticipation of the day—or night— when he could instruct Jenny SanGiovanni in some areas he was very interested in. Cooking was not one of them.

Jeremy, driving the battered maroon Pontiac LeMans, cut across the fields that separated the housing development from the older part of town on a rough gravel road. His father had told him not to use the car, but when did Jeremy ever listen to dear old Dad? Usually, the locals using the road were driving four-wheel drive vehicles, but Jeremy drove like he was being pursued by the FBI and the old Pontiac LeMans wasn't in mint condition.

Jenny and her family lived in a new subdivision on the south side of town called Harvest Homes. The area had once been a farm field. Only in the last ten years had the town grown large enough that this area was incorporated and Harvest Homes became a new housing development.

Jeremy lived way out on the north side of town where an abandoned railroad depot stood. He was, literally and also figuratively, from the other side of the tracks. People just called Jeremy's stomping ground Old Town. The area had been there since the 1850's. It looked like it, with crumbling, crummy buildings in need of painting.

Jeremy sat in the Pontiac LeMans and waited, radio cranked, his new Bose speakers filling the air with heavy metal chaos.

Soon, he saw the brand-new BMW sedan that Gregory Tuttle had recently purchased. The garage door of the house began to ascend, triggered from within Gregory Tuttle's car. *Business must be good in financial advising,* Jeremy thought. Jeremy got out of the car and waited for Mr. Tuttle to emerge from the garage, so that he could talk to him on the driveway.

But Gregory Tuttle either hadn't seen Jeremy or didn't want to see Jeremy. As Jeremy stood there, fully expecting to have a civilized conversation with Mr. Tuttle about escorting Jenny to Homecoming tomorrow night, the garage door began its descent.

Wh-a-a-a-t? Jeremy thought,

Jeremy reacted quickly, as only an athlete could. He ducked and rolled under the descending garage door, to confront a very surprised and possibly very frightened Gregory Tuttle.

"What did you do that for?" Jeremy asked. "I only want to talk to you." His blue eyes took on the blue of a Nazi storm trooper. Jeremy was becoming angry. Obviously, Gregory Tuttle was attempting to avoid speaking to him.

Gregory Tuttle had seen the Pontiac LeMans, maroon and dirty, sitting outside his house. He knew that this was Jeremy Gustaffsson's car. His stepson, Frank, referred to it as "the pimpmobile." Greg did not want to know why Frank called it that. Gregory Tuttle was afraid that if he asked Frank for an explanation, Frank would give him one and Greg wasn't at all sure he would like it. Better to chalk this term up to teen-aged slang and not inquire too deeply. If he found out something he didn't like, he would be put in a difficult position, as Jenny's step-father. He found it was a balancing act all the time, much like a circus trapeze artist. He couldn't go too far in disciplining his wife's children, and he didn't really want to, anyway. He'd rather remain blissfully ignorant of anything problematic, and he hoped that his wife and children would remain blissfully ignorant of his own activities.

"I just want to know why you won't let Jenny go to Homecoming with me," Jeremy began.

Gregory Tuttle was in no mood.

He had had a horrible day in the stock market. It was the kind of day that made strong men jump from windows. This was not any of his concern, anyway. Jenny was not his kid.

Second, Greg was well aware that his slight frame and light build would be no match in a physical fight with the likes of a Jeremy Gustaffsson. Just in case Jeremy had come to cause trouble, he didn't want to get badly beaten up. He'd taken enough of a beating at work today.

Third, Gregory Tuttle had just had a little afternoon delight with Cassie Chandler at a small seedy motel out near the west edge of town. The Westward Ho was aptly named, Greg thought. Gregory Tuttle really didn't want to harsh the tiny bit of mellow that he had managed to achieve today.

"I'm sorry, Jeremy. It's not my decision," Greg said. "Andrea is Jenny's mother. I'm just her stepfather. I have no control over Andrea's decisions." With that, Greg Tuttle turned his back to Jeremy, standing there inside the garage, heading for the door from the garage to the house.

Rather than placating Jeremy, this particular bit of issue-dodging simply enraged Jeremy. Jeremy lost it.

"Well, hell, man! She's your woman! You had *BETTER* have some control over her decisions. Otherwise, what good are you as a man? You should step up and make yourself heard."

With that closing statement, Jeremy hit Gregory Tuttle as hard as he could, a real haymaker, coming from out of nowhere.

Greg Tuttle fell backwards, bleeding, stumbled once, and sank to the concrete floor of the garage, unconscious.

Jeremy thought, *Shit! Now I've done it!!* This always happened when the red impulsive rages overpowered his ability to think.

A minute or two later, the cunning side of Jeremy emerged. He realized that no one would have seen him hit Gregory Tuttle. The garage door was down and they were inside the garage. He just hoped no one had seen his maroon car parked outside the house. Even that would be okay, if no one had seen the BMW enter the garage.

Furtively, Jeremy exited the side door of the garage. Fortunately, the door opened onto the fields he had driven through to arrive at the house. There weren't many houses out here yet. The few houses in the subdivision were new and expensive. The only neighbors the SanGiovannis had were the Chandlers, half a mile away. Jeremy almost tiptoed to the concrete apron of the driveway, heading towards his maroon Pontiac, still parked at the curb in front of the house.

Then he thought a moment about Jenny and the conversation he had just had with Gregory Tuttle before he knocked him out. Jenny would be along soon. He ought to stay and have a talk with Jenny and make her see that they belonged together.

Returning to the garage, Jeremy grabbed some electrical cord from the workshop area on the garage workbench, bound Gregory Tuttle's ankles and wrists together with it, and sat down to wait for Jenny. Just for good measure, he placed a piece of silver duct tape over Mr. Tuttle's mouth. Wouldn't do to have him screaming his head off. A short while later, Jeremy would change his mind once again and decide that the "waiting for Jenny" idea was a bad plan. He needed to stash Greg Tuttle somewhere for a while, until Greg came to, then release him with warnings about what would happen to him if he pointed any fingers of blame. Jeremy wasn't much of a planner, but he settled on taking Greg to Ike Isham's abandoned cabin and letting him regain consciousness there, away from prying eyes.

He ain't hurt that bad. He'll be fine, once he understands the way things are and the way things are gonna' be. I'll let him loose a little bit later. And if Gregory Tuttle felt like pressing charges, Jeremy would blow the whistle on his after-work gymnastics sessions with Cassie Chandler at the Westward Ho motel.

Now that Jeremy had calmed down, he realized that he could easily transport Greg to the cabin, let him cool off for a bit, untie him when he woke up, give him a stern talking to, and then release him. Since Greg was getting it on with Cassie Chandler with great regularity and often came home late as a result, nobody would be looking for him for a while, anyway. Greg could always think up some excuse if he had any permanent marks from the blow Jeremy had unintentionally inflicted. And Jeremy could use his knowledge of the romantic ramblings of Greg Tuttle to blackmail him into keeping quiet about this little encounter in the garage.

What Jeremy didn't realize was that Cassie Chandler, one-half mile away in her kitchen, peering at the SanGiovannis' house through her binoculars, had seen Jeremy exit and then re-enter the SanGiovannis' garage. She, too, had just arrived home from the *Westward Ho! Motel* She was looking through her omnipresent binoculars to catch one last glimpse of Greg Tuttle before he returned to his role as husband and stepfather and left his role as her sometime lover.

CHAPTER 29

October 30, 2003, Thursday
Tad McGreevy's House

It was not yet dinnertime at the McGreevy house, because Jeannie and Jim McGreevy were not yet home. Tad didn't care. In fact, he was glad for the chance to lie on his bed and try to think about where Stevie might be.

The strain of thinking about his missing buddy had thoroughly drained Tad's soul. It was a psychological strain, like the fatigue you experience when someone close to you is sick and in the hospital. He kept going over in his mind the possible places Stevie could have gone, the possible causes for his departure. Nothing made sense. Tad was worried. He was tired. His stomach churned.

Why does my mind always get so upset? It's normal that I should be upset now, with Stevie missing, but I get upset over really stupid stuff. Stuff that shouldn't make me anxious at all. It's crazy how my mind becomes this database. I worry about things that are so arbitrary, things I can't do anything about. I always put a lot of thought into my actions. But then, you know, my stomach will be just like a cement mixer, just churning and upset over the smallest thing. I'll be totally anxious about something ridiculous. My mind just won't shut down. At night I can't sleep for thinking. I turn situations over and over in my head, looking at each aspect of a situation as though it were one facet of a diamond. I have to stop myself during the day and say, 'It's just not worth it. Stop it!' But, at night, I can't stop my mind from thinking. And when it is something that's worth agonizing over....

Tad drifted into fitful slumber. Despite his chronic insomnia, he was exhausted. It was not like him to take afternoon naps, but the strain was getting to him. He felt as though someone had placed a needle in his bones. Something had drained out all his energy. An energy vampire had sucked him dry.

It was during sleep and the REM dream state that Tad would sometimes have precognitive episodes. He only saw violent actions. Sometimes the actions were occurring right then, sometimes they had already occurred, and sometimes his visions predicted future violent acts.

While he knew the auras of all those around him, seeing the future didn't predict for any but the violent offenders, like Pogo the clown. If one of the gray-green or red auras were to attack someone, Tad might dream about it. Fortunately, he had not had any such episodes since the age of eight when Pogo had been caught, tried, found guilty and sent to prison in Fort Madison Penitentiary. Michael Clay (aka Pogo) was now serving a life sentence.

Things were different this evening, though.

For one thing, Tad was under tremendous pressure and feeling the strain. He had tried to help the police find Stevie, using his extensive knowledge of his old playmate's favorite haunts. He had even visited a few places that he forgot to mention to the police, usually before the school day started. All Tad's searches proved fruitless.

As Tad drifted into slumber, he experienced sudden, fleeting flashes of color. He saw an arm rising and falling, rising and falling. The arm belonged to a tall, blonde individual, an athlete. He saw the figure only from the back. He could not tell exactly what was happening at first. Watching the implacable rise and fall of the figure's arm was scary.

Tad became aware that the object the figure held in his left hand was metal. The metal thing was dripping wetly with a red liquid that looked like blood. The hand, frenzied, rose sixty-three times. *Was the object a knife?* Tad began hyperventilating. He started to moan slightly.

He had not yet seen the knife-wielding figure's face. His build, his coloring, his athleticism:.. all signs pointed to Jeremy Gustaffsson. Tad began to whimper like a small puppy, still deep within his dream.

Who is the figure on the floor? What is Jeremy doing?

When these visions took over Tad's subconscious, he was helpless against them. He couldn't turn the visions on and off at will. He became like a possessed person, a possessed animal. The noises he made, the emotions he experienced were similar to those a helpless kitten might experience if a cruel owner were abusing it. He had no ability to awaken himself. When someone else woke him up, he would remember the dream, but often he would be too upset to share the dream's contents.

After the events of eight years ago, who could blame Tad for not admitting to any precognitive dreams? Upon awakening, he would attempt to shrug off any such experience as "just a nightmare." Jeannie McGreevy referred to these episodes as "night terrors." She pretended as though she and the entire McGreevy family had completely forgotten Tad's visions of eight years ago.

No one had ever acknowledged how accurate Tad's predictions had been in the sordid Pogo the Clown case. Dr. Eisenstadt was bound by patient/client privilege, and the McGreevys, including Tad, just wanted to move on from the embarrassing episode. Everyone wanted to move on and forget. The family just wanted Tad to forget. To behave normally. To go along to get along. *God forbid Tad should ever mention one of those horrible visions again.*

What Tad had spilled out in vivid detail at age eight had condemned him to a mental institution for days. It had taken him a year to recover and become a reasonable facsimile of your average kid next door. Nobody in the McGreevy household wanted a repeat performance of Tad McGreevy's experiences after his eighth birthday party.

* * *

In his mid-day dream, Tad still could not tell who the victim of the attack was, but just before his mother came upstairs to summon him for supper (since he had not answered when she called his name), he saw a woman's leg and shoe just to the right of Jeremy's body. The male figure, seen from the back, was still blocking his view of the violent, vile acts.

Jenny? Was that Jenny?

Just then, Jeannie McGreevy shook Tad into consciousness.

CHAPTER 30

October 30, 2003, Thursday, Evening
The SanGiovannis' Home

Cassie Chandler put the binoculars down on the kitchen table. She was puzzled. Greg hadn't said anything about meeting with Jeremy Gustaffsson. She knew that neither Andrea nor Greg wanted Jenny to continue dating Jeremy. When Cassie and Greg met, usually at the Westward Ho! Motel, the two talked frankly about their respective spouses and children. It was one of the things they had bonded over.

"Charles doesn't understand that Belinda is an independent young woman now," Cassie told Greg on one occasion." I mean, she's a high school graduate. She supports herself on the salary she makes at Layne's Insurance. We can't be telling her how to run her personal life when she's paying her own way. But whenever she stays overnight with us, Charlie seems to think that he can give her a curfew like he did when she was twelve." Belinda took another drag on her cigarette. "You know how bossy cops are." Another drag. Charlie Chandler had been on the Cedar Falls Police Force for almost 40 years, ever since Cassie and Charlie had gotten married, right out of high school.

Cassie and Greg had been meeting at the Westward Ho! Motel for a little "R&R" as she liked to call it, for six months now. It had done wonders for her marriage to Charlie Chandler.

Cassie found Charlie about as exciting as a pick-up truck. Charlie had never sent her a love note, never written her anything mushy, sometimes he didn't even remember her birthday. He drank too much, always came home late from his shifts at the department—if he even made it home— and, for a cop, he never had much to say. If anything exciting ever happened on his job, she never heard about it. They never had sex any more…hadn't since Belinda graduated from high school and left home, which was going on two years ago now.

Greg Tuttle, while not particularly athletic-looking, was hung. His equipment was superb. He made her husband Charlie look like an earthworm, by comparison. And, more importantly, since Charles was older than she was and was fast approaching his late fifties, Greg, who was only in his forties, could go all night long, which was exactly what Cassie Chandler wanted at this stage of her life. While she was only a couple of years younger than her middle-aged husband, she had aged well. She was light years younger than him, sexually-speaking.

Greg and Cassie had struck up a conversation at the gym they both belonged to. The gym also had a hot tub where one could relax tired muscles after a workout. Cassie believed in working out, sex, and not getting caught…not necessarily in that order. She didn't want any trouble, and she knew that Greg didn't, either.

Greg's chief complaint about Andrea SanGiovanni was that she didn't have time for him. If Cassie remembered correctly, that had been the complaint when Andrea's ex hooked up with Tammy Tolliver, dumped Andrea, and headed for a new life in Boulder. Old patterns die hard. Here was Andrea, now driving the same wedge between herself and her second husband, Greg Tuttle.

A man as endowed as Greg Tuttle should be enjoyed,… savored even. He should never have to whack off alone in the bathroom, tired and lonely, thought Cassie. Their meeting was pre-ordained by the gods of hedonism. So far, it was working out beautifully.

Because the Chandlers and the SanGiovannis were next-door neighbors in Harvest Homes…although that usually meant at least the length of a football field between houses…she often got her binoculars out and checked to see that Greg had gone home to his wife and kiddies…or step-kiddies. She secretly hoped he would strip naked in front of the bedroom window and head for the showers. He was a slight man, but he had the largest penis she had ever seen. And Cassie had seen a few.

This time, when she gazed through her binoculars (Charlie thought she was bird-watching) she saw something slightly peculiar. Jeremy Gustaffsson, Jenny SanGiovanni's boyfriend from last year, tip-toed out the side entrance from the garage and then went back in.

I wonder what that's all about? thought Cassie.

Something about what she had just seen didn't feel right. It wasn't that she had seen Jeremy do anything. It was the mere fact that he was there at all. He was a nineteen-year-old Neanderthal.

I'll bet Jeremy is hung like a horse, too, Cassie mused idly.

Then she had an idea. Apparently Greg and Jeremy were there alone. Jenny did not look as though she was home yet, and certainly Andrea would not be there for another couple hours. Maybe Cassie should pop over and say "hi" and pretend she needed to borrow a cup of sugar or something. She'd like to see Jeremy Gustaffsson up close and personal. She'd only seen him on the football field or the basketball court prior to this. He did look to be a healthy hunk.

What can it hurt to just stop and say 'Hi!' After all, we're next-door neighbors.

Cassie Chandler had no idea what awaited her.

CHAPTER 31

October 30, 2003, Thursday, 7:00 P.M.
The SanGiovannis

Charlie wasn't home from his golf league yet. Some of his old high school buddies played on a regular basis and they usually went out for beers after golf. They were all the class of '63: Earl Scranton, Mike Murphy, Lloyd Carpenter and Charlie. This was their last chance to play golf this season. Cassie knew Charlie would be late, and she knew Charlie would be drunk. He'd be as useless to her tonight as always— which was pretty useless.

Cassie walked to the garage, grabbing her Toyota keys as she went. Cassie liked the fact that her environmentally friendly Prius was virtually soundless when driven. It would be easy to sneak up on the SanGiovannis' house and do a little reconnoitering. If the truth were told, she had already done that a few times, just to see if it looked like Greg was home alone. Greg had warned her about being too inquisitive. He had told her that they must confine all their activities to the west side of town, but still Cassie liked to poke around, just to see what was happening.

This was a time when Cassie should not have investigated.

* * *

As Tad emerged from his late-afternoon nap, shaken by his mother who wanted him to come downstairs to a late supper, he had the urgent intuitive feeling that he must try to get to Jenny. He had to make sure that Jenny was all right.

At first, Jeannie McGreevy could not make sense of the gibberish that Tad was spouting. Then, she realized that he had had one of his "spells." She shuddered. *Not this, again.*

She quickly left the room with just one phrase, "Come down and eat your supper."

* * *

True, it had been over eight years since Tad had his episode of violent visions, but for several months…really all of his fourth grade year…Jeannie had thought he was lost to them. He didn't communicate at all for a very long time. When he did, he was not himself.

The short-term commitment to Shady Oaks had been a nightmare for all of them. Jeannie wasn't so sure that Shady Oaks, itself, might not have been the culprit in turning Tad from the sunny, if fragile, fun-loving boy he had been as an eight-year-old into the morose, depressed, withdrawn creature that he was until the age of nine. She still remembered how Jim had complained about all the expenses they incurred: private psychiatric sessions with Dr. Eisenstadt; the stay in Shady Oaks; an at-home tutor for one full year. Tad's night terrors had cost them a pretty penny!

After nearly one year of home tutoring and private sessions with Dr. Eisenstadt in his office (no more Shady Oaks), Tad had eventually come out of his almost catatonic state. He resumed life as a normal kid. True, he sometimes had a sad, lost look in his eyes, but he was able to rejoin his classmates at Rossdale Elementary School in fifth grade. The McGreevys always listed the ailment that had kept him out of school for a full year as "mononucleosis" on school admission forms.

In a town as small as theirs, the real reason did sometimes surface. It was usually in the form of a kid who threw a taunt at Tad about his flirtation with mental illness. But no one ever spoke of Tad's night terrors or his precognitive dreams about Pogo, the Clown, again. Dr. Eisenstadt had expressed an interest in testing Tad further, but Jim McGreevy said, "Over my dead body. That'd be another $5,000!"

Jeannie McGreevy, for one, was very glad when they sentenced Pogo to life in prison. She would have liked it if they had put the needle in Pogo's arm, but they lived in a no capital punishment state. Michael Clay, aka Pogo, paid for his crimes with the rest of his life behind bars, Charles Manson style. No more Pogo. No more clown dreams. No more troubled Tad.

Or so it had seemed.

Now, after eight years, Tad had experienced a "future-telling" episode again. All Jeannie McGreevy could get out of him were the words "knife," "Jeremy Gustaffsson" and "Jenny." It surprised her that his troubled moment of terror in his dream hadn't involved his missing friend Stevie. Jeannie thought that that might have been helpful. Stevie Scranton had been missing now for two days. It was all over the news.

Why can't Tad use his power...if it is a power...to help his best friend? Jeannie McGreevy just didn't understand the situation. That old cliché applied, "If you can remain calm while all those about you are losing their heads, you just don't understand the situation."

Jeannie McGreevy didn't understand the nature of Tad's precognitive episodes, and she was not inclined to do further research on them, or to let anyone else do it, either. Tad was fine. He was just a typical sixteen-year-old kid who occasionally had a bad dream. Nothing to worry about.

Alone in Tad's bedroom, hugging the sweaty, gasping, sixteen-year-old while he composed himself, his mother had even articulated this sentiment. "Tad. If you really can see the future, see Stevie's future and help the Scrantons find him. It's been two days! They're frantic."

"Mom! Don't you think I'd like to help Mr. and Mrs. Scranton find Stevie? He's my best friend. But it doesn't work like that. I see the colors, yes, but I only see what is happening ahead of time if it's a bad thing that's happening. I see murders. I see violence. I'm glad I haven't seen Stevie in my dreams, because it means that he must be okay. He must still be alive. But I saw something bad happening in this dream. Some woman...I... I have to go to Jenny's house to make sure it's not her."

"Wait a minute, Little Mister. What, exactly, was happening in the dream?" Jeannie acted annoyed.

"I told you. I don't know, for sure." Tad was upset and still somewhat incoherent.

"Are you sure it was Jenny you saw? Are you certain that the location you saw in your dream was the SanGiovannis' house?"

Jeannie was asking logical questions, but she was asking them of a troubled youth who had just been awakened from what Jeannie liked to call a night terror. (even though it had occurred in the late afternoon, before 6:00 p.m.)

"I want to go over and make sure that Jenny is all right." Tad was composing himself, but just barely.

"Honey, I know you like Jenny, but you said you didn't even recognize who was doing what in this dream of yours. You don't even know if it was Jenny. You need to come downstairs and eat first. No running off on a wild goose chase until you get some food into that skinny frame of yours. It's probably just hypo-glycemia or something."

Jeannie McGreevy always liked to read about the latest ailments in a variety of women's magazines. She always hoped she could find a logical explanation for whatever was wrong with her family members. It was ironic that she was a size zero, because she always acted as though food would cure everything. Unlike Andrea SanGiovanni, who rarely cooked anything, Jeannie made wonderful home-cooked meals for her husband and children. She didn't eat very much of the meals herself, but she made the food for others as a token of her love.

Sometimes Jeannie would pose as the latest expert on attention deficit disorder or bulimia or anorexia or whatever ailment the magazines were trumpeting that week.

To Tad she now said, "You aren't going anywhere until after you've eaten dinner. There's a lovely crock pot roast, with potatoes and carrots and gravy. It's ready to go right now. Eat first, and then we'll see which direction you should be going off in... if any." She turned and gave Tad a wan smile, "And I don't want any left-overs."

Jeannie took Tad's hand in her own and pulled him to his feet, guiding the troubled boy downstairs to the family dining room.

CHAPTER 32

October 30, 2003, Thursday
The SanGiovannis

Cassie rolled soundlessly up to the edge of the SanGiovannis driveway in her salsa red Prius. She didn't park directly in front of the house. She parked to the immediate left of the driveway. She got out of the car and approached the house. Cassie felt like a thief in the night.

This is nonsense, she thought. *I've got to get my shit together and have a legitimate reason for coming over here, in case anybody besides Greg is home. I'll ask to borrow sugar...say I'm in the middle of baking cookies and ran out. Something domestic like that. That is, if it's just Greg and Jeremy and one of the kids here. I know Andrea can't be home yet. She never gets home this early.*

Cassie approached the side door that led into the garage. It was ajar. She stepped though the open door, which led directly to the interior of the unlit garage. Cassie thought, *Good, I can check to make sure that Andrea's car is not here.*

If Andrea's car was there, parked next to the brand-new BMW sedan she had helped Greg select at Hunter's Car lot where she worked part-time, she'd skedaddle back to her house without ringing any bells or knocking on any doors.

No reason to use that lame cup of sugar excuse unless I have to, she thought.

When she stepped inside the garage, she pulled the door shut behind her. She saw that there was only one car in the garage, Greg's. That meant that he might actually be here alone. Or, if not alone, Greg might be talking with that Gustaffsson kid inside the house. She thought she could make out something in the extremely dim light of the garage. It looked like a pair of men's shoes protruding from an area close to the rear bumper of Greg's new car.

Cassie's eyesight wasn't the best. She refused to wear her prescription glasses. She felt they made her look ten years older. She couldn't tolerate contact lenses. She was saving up from her part-time job at Hunter's Car Lot to have her eyes lasered, saving for the newest lasik procedure. Until then, in the interest of vanity, Cassie just squinted and tried to bring things into focus as best she could. It was not a particularly great way to tell what you were looking at.

Many times, Cassie had misidentified common objects. She mistook her gray cat for a rock at twenty paces, once, and almost ran over Lucy on their John Deere riding mower. She didn't mind using the riding mower to do their two-acre lot. It gave her a sense of power that was often missing in her personal life. Besides, Charlie never seemed to be around when the lawn needed tending.

But lawn mowing was the furthest thing from Cassie Chandler's mind as she slowly approached the pair of men's shoes she could see just behind the back left tire of Greg's spiffy new BMW sedan.

As she neared the bumper and saw that the feet were tied together with electrical cord, she realized that the shoes and feet were attached to Greg Tuttle, and that Greg Tuttle, himself, was bound and trussed like a Thanksgiving turkey on the floor of his own garage. There was one almost surreal moment when she thought this was some kind of joke.

Just then, she felt a sharp pain in her back. She fell, landing atop the body of Gregory Tuttle, who let out an "oomph" sound from behind the silver electrical tape covering his mouth. She was now atop her paramour Greg Tuttle's stomach, just as she had been earlier in the evening at the Westward Ho! Motel, but not nearly as happily.

* * *

Jeremy Gustaffsson had crouched behind the back left rear tire until Cassie was within striking distance. He grabbed a tool from the tool bench in the garage— a screwdriver with a black handle.

"You silly whore! Why didn't you mind your own business?" He plunged the screwdriver into Cassie's back, puncturing a kidney on his first blow. After that, he lost control and he lost count. The coroner would later testify that there were sixty-three separate stab wounds.

"You deserve this," Jeremy shouted, in a rage. He was completely absorbed in his moment of madness. "You're a low person. You sicken me. I know you've been sleeping with Jenny's step-dad! See how you like this!" With that, Jeremy stabbed Cassie Chandler in the back again and again, driving the silver metal part of the screwdriver into her body up to the black-handled hilt.

Cassie screamed loudly after the first blow. Blood from the attack flew from the silver shaft. In his dream, Tad was seeing Jeremy Gustaffsson driving a screwdriver into the body of Cassie Chandler sixty-three times, frenzied, shouting, out-of-control.

As for Cassie, she never saw it coming.

Gregory Tuttle, who had almost roused from his unconscious stupor, shit his pants and passed out again.

"Shit!" Jeremy grunted in disgust. It was the right comment.

Jeremy saw a blue tarp that the SanGiovannis used to cover their hot tub in cold weather near the tool bench in the garage. He was not about to spend the night before Homecoming cleaning up Gregory Tuttle's shit or blood from that stupid cow Cassie Chandler. In a town as small as this, everyone knew everything about everybody else. Even Jeremy knew about the trysts between Greg SanGiovanni and Cassie Chandler, but what did he care? It would just make Jenny feel bad if he told her, and there was nothing in it for him. Until now. It was the perfect blackmail leverage to keep Greg from having Jeremy Gustaffsson charged with assault and battery.

I'll make them both disappear for a bit, thought Jeremy. *When anybody comes around, they'll be looking for Greg Tuttle, not me. I've got to get these two out of here. I've got to get my car away from out front. And I'll have to move the Chandler woman's car, too. I'll let Tuttle go—after a while, but first I've got to get rid of this Chandler cunt.*

Jeremy decided that moving the two bodies, one dead, one unconscious, would be best accomplished if he wrapped them both up in the blue tarp from the hot tub and put them in the trunk of his car. Or, better yet, he could use Cassie Chandler's red Prius. He knew a place to take them: an abandoned cabin in the woods near the maximum security prison that had been built there two years ago, to take care of the overflow from Fort Madison. Some old fart now in a nursing home used to use it as a fishing cabin. That old fart, Mr. Isham, was now in the same nursing home as Jeremy Gustaffsson's grandmother. Ike Isham used to tell Grandma Gustaffsson about his days on the Cedar River in his cabin. Jeremy knew where the cabin was. He knew that it sat empty. He had been considering it as the location for a romantic tryst with Jenny following tomorrow night's dance.

It took only a few minutes to drag the two bodies to the trunk of the car. Jeremy was able to lift them into the cargo area of the newer car and shut them inside, after he lowered the seats in the back of the Prius. *These cars really are roomy*, he thought. Jeremy slid behind the wheel and drove to the wooded area known as Burnham Woods.

Jeremy didn't know why it was called Burnham Woods. Jenny once said it had something to do with Shakespeare. Jeremy Gustaffsson didn't know anything about Shakespeare.

He dumped the dead woman and her still-unconscious boyfriend, wrapped together like a human enchilada, in the cargo bay of the Prius and, when he reached the deserted cabin (only ten minutes from the SanGiovannis' house), he dumped the two of them inside the cabin.

As he thought a bit more rationally, Jeremy decided to throw Cassie Chandler into the low ditch behind the cabin. *I'll cover her with leaves until I can bury her better.*

Jeremy was panting now, but he was in good shape. He knew he could jog back to the SanGiovannis and remove his own car long before either Jenny or Andrea returned home. All that cross-country running was paying off.

If Gregory Twit Tuttle wakes up, he won't know about Cassie Chandler's murder. He was out like a light. If he wakes up and there's no Cassie in the cabin with him, he won't be able to blow the whistle on me when I let him go. Plus, he won't want anyone to know he's been putting it to the Chandler woman, so I'll just sneak back after dark, cut him loose, explain the rules and get my car. Jeremy Gustaffsson's Guide to Life. Jeremy smiled.

Jeremy didn't want to be accused of killing Jenny's stepfather. The Chandler woman deserved what she got, but that was an accident. Jeremy hadn't meant to hit Gregory Tuttle in the first place, but Greg and Andrea Tuttle—and Jenny, too, for that matter—needed to realize that he and Jenny were in love. They belonged together. Nothing anybody else said or did would change that. Jenny might not be sixteen yet, but when she was, she and Jeremy could even run away together. Jeremy was thinking all these thoughts as he jogged back to the SanGiovanni house to retrieve his car.

Jenny is mine. No one else can have her, Jeremy thought as he ran back to the SanGiovannis, Gregory Tuttle's car keys and his own jangling together in his jacket pocket.

Jeremy Gustaffsson was able to run back, get the shovel and some other tools from the garage, and throw them in the Pontiac's trunk in less than twenty minutes. He shut and locked the side door to the garage.

Upon reaching the San Giovanni's house, Jeremy let himself back into the garage through the unlocked side door and entered Gregory Tuttle's car, just for fun.

Nice car, he thought. *Great leather seats. What a great make-out mobile this would make.* Of course, that was Jeremy simply wishing for what he couldn't have.

Jeremy realized that tomorrow night might not happen exactly as he and Jenny had planned it, if her stepfather went missing and the SanGiovanni family was in an uproar. It was important that he cut Gregory Tuttle loose before a hue and cry was raised. Midnight sounded about right.

Even if the Homecoming dance goes down the tubes, it's still Halloween, he thought. *Jenny and me ought to be able to find some way to be together on Halloween, if Jenny loves me as much as I love her.*

It never crossed Jeremy's mind that never, not once, had Jenny ever said the "L" word to him, verbally or in writing. He just assumed that she loved him because, after all, he loved her. She was his girl.

For the moment, Jeremy had no better plan than to bury that cunt Cassie Chandler in the woods and see if Gregory Tuttle's absence might make him a prime suspect. Half the town knew Greg Tuttle was porking Cassie Chandler, even if Jenny didn't. That, alone, would make Greg a prime suspect in Cassie Chandler's disappearance.

And what about Charlie Chandler? It was usually the husband who did it when there was a death of a spouse. Jeremy had seen enough "CSI" and "Law and Order" episodes to know that much.

Of course, if Jeremy had his way, nobody would find Cassie Chandler's body for a very long time. He'd bury her deeper in the loam-like earth behind the cabins when he returned to cut Greg Tuttle free. As long as animals didn't dig her up, it might be a very long time before Cassie Chandler was found.

Charlie Chandler, would, of course, be "a person of interest" in the disappearance of his wife. Jeremy Gustaffsson wasn't too bright, but he liked the way this was playing out. Greg had been unconscious throughout the slaying of his girlfriend, so he wouldn't know Jack or Squat. When he awakened in Old Man Isham's cabin, he'd be bound hand-and-foot. It would probably take him some time to free himself, if he even could manage to do so on his own. Jeremy didn't expect that to happen. Greg Tuttle was a wuss, and a worthless wuss at that. He'd never get out of his bindings on his own, but Jeremy would take pity on him after midnight and untie him, explain the deal (Greg's silence for his freedom). And he'd bury Cassie before he cut Greg loose, and get his car back.

Greg Tuttle might tromp into police headquarters to lodge a complaint against Jeremy, but not if he wanted Jeremy to keep the knowledge of his sexual trysts with Cassie Chandler a secret. The cops would probably be looking for Greg Tuttle in the disappearance of his girlfriend, next-door neighbor Cassie, so that might work out more to Jeremy's advantage than to Greg's.

After all, assault and battery is a far less serious charge than murder or kidnapping. Maybe old Charlie suspected his wife was stepping out on him and followed her or something? The spouse is almost always guilty.

Jeremy's imagination was working overtime. It just wasn't a particularly highly developed intelligence. He had street smarts and he was cunning, but most of Jeremy's talents were confined to a football field or a basketball court.

Just then, Jeremy heard a sound. He was finally back inside the SanGiovannis' garage. He had entered the sedan to luxuriate in the Corinthian leather of its seats for a moment and dream a little dream of using this car as a mobile pleasure palace. He had climbed back out to get the shovel he needed to bury Cassie Chandler. The garage stank of blood and shit. When he heard a sound, Jeremy also saw the door handle to the garage side door, which he had just unlocked, turning. Jeremy crouched down beside the BMW.

God, I hope this isn't Jenny coming home.

Then Jeremy thought, *Why would Jenny come in through the side door of the garage? She has a key to the house.*

When that thought crystallized, Jeremy realized that he must be ready to take care of yet another unwanted visitor to the SanGiovannis' house tonight.

Geez! They oughta' install a revolving door in this garage, he thought.

Jeremy watched a pair of size ten Nike tennis shoes approach the back of the sedan, heading towards the door to the house. The shoes paused at the sight of blood and the accompanying foul odor. Whoever was inside the shoes stepped around the mess on the garage floor, heading towards the door to the house. It was at this point, as the intruder cleared the puddle of Cassie Chandler's blood, that Jeremy, clutching the shovel he had retrieved from the tool bench,, slammed it down on Tad McGreevy's head, knocking him out instantly.

Jeremy grabbed the shovel to take to his car outside, pressed the button to automatically open the garage door, and began to put the rest of his plan into play, transferring the tools from the SanGiovannis' garage to his Pontiac, closing the garage door with the outside alarm pad button, and preparing to drive back to the remote Isham cabin.

CHAPTER 33

October 30, 2003, Thursday Near Dusk
Christmas in October

The cabins in Burnham Woods were primitive, especially those, like Old Man Isham's that were among the original structures. Ever since Alzheimer's had taken his mind, Old Man Isham had been a resident of Fernwood Home. Mr. Isham's abandoned cabin in the woods near the prison grounds was one of the first places Tad had looked for Stevie Scranton, after Stevie's disappearance.

Others, like Jeremy Gustaffsson, eventually had learned of the availability of the place, but the cabin was pretty rudimentary. It would be roughing it to use the cabin for date night. Even the running water was unpredictable.

Nevertheless, the cabin had a fireplace and a couch and a bed and a kitchen table and some chairs and running water and electricity. The kitchen would do if you merely wanted to cook a fish you had caught or fry up a squirrel you had trapped in the woods.

The thought of just such a place ran through Michael Clay's mind as he fled the guard tower of the Iowa State Penitentiary on the horizon. This prison was a modern structure, built to augment Fort Madison's ancient prison. Michael Clay, aka Pogo the Clown, had been transferred here from Fort Madison because of overcrowding.

The new Cedar Falls Prison was supposed to be a state-of-the-art facility. After the state built it, they ran out of money. The new facility sat idle and empty for almost a year. But there had been a push to open it in the last year, since the undermanned, overcrowded Fort Madison facility was so ancient and two men had successfully escaped from it in the recent past. The escapees had not invited Michael to accompany them as they used furniture upholstery fabric to rappel down the walls, but, then, Pogo was on the list of the most dangerous inmates of the place. The authorities kept him very securely locked up. He would have been on Death Row, if Iowa hadn't abolished the death penalty in 1963.

Jesus! thought Michael. *The place opened up in 1839...just one year after Iowa became a state. It's an antique! I'm damn glad to be getting out of that hellhole. With any luck, I can escape entirely. Maybe make it down to sunny Mexico.*

When Pogo pronounced Mexico, he usually did a bad Spanish imitation, pronouncing it, phonetically, as "May-hee-co."

Clay did know the roads around here, since this had been his home town. He knew of a large dip in the road that the driver of the van was blithely unaware of as the young escort sped towards the prison gates with just one prisoner to convey, racing along at least twenty miles over the speed limit. This would be the new prison guard's first and last time conveying a death penalty prisoner from one facility to another.

Michael had been working on the grating between the back area and the front seat with a piece of metal from the metal shop. They made license plates at Fort Madison. Michael had been on that detail many times over the past eight years since his conviction and life sentence. When he heard he was going to be transferred to the new prison near Cedar Falls, he decided to help himself to some metal pieces "just in case."

When he was placed in the back of the vehicle, a grated grill separated him from the driver's area. He could see that the driver was just a kid. In fact, it was Jim Kinkade's first week on the job. Kinkade was supposed to have been accompanied by a grizzled veteran, but the grizzled veteran only had two months to go until retirement. The veteran guard was using up his sick days, one by one. He had called in sick at the last minute.

Understaffed as they were, the warden and prison authorities had decided that Jim Kinkade, even if he was new, could handle one lifer prisoner transfer riding solo. After all, Michael Clay had been a model prisoner since his conviction in those grisly slayings of young men and boys eight years ago. He worked making license plates. He painted pictures of clowns. He was quiet and weird and queer.

As soon as Jim Kinkade cranked the radio on the van, Michael began working on the bolts that held the grill in place, twisting the purloined pieces of license plate metal into a makeshift screwdriver. He didn't need the opening to be big enough for him to crawl through. Hell! He was a big man. He weighed over 300 pounds. To get the grill open enough to let him crawl through he'd probably need much more time and an opening the size of a rhino.

No, what Michael Clay had in mind was simply to loosen the protective grill enough that, when the formidable bump in the road that he was aware of (but Jim Kinkade was not) presented itself, Michael could ram the grill into the unsuspecting driver and, hopefully, cause a crash. Even if the van only went into the ditch, that would mean that Jim Kinkade then would have to come to the back of the van and open the door to check on his prisoner's well-being.

Michael Clay knew many methods to silence a boy the size of Jim Kinkade, shackles or no shackles. With his metal tool, he would be able to free himself from the handcuffs and restraints. It would be mano a mano from that moment on. Jim Kinkade was no match for Michael Clay, who outweighed him two pounds for every pound on the guard's boyish frame.

One of his favorite techniques, when Pogo had kidnapped teen-agers, was to tell them to try on his handcuffs and see if they could get out of them. He made it sound like a game.

"Don't you want to see if you can escape? See if you're meant to be the next Houdini!" he'd say with a smile. The boys were always eager to try the game.

They weren't so eager to play the game after Michael refused to release them and subjected them to hours of torture. Michael always represented the handcuffs as being "trick" handcuffs. The only trick was the one Michael Clay was going to play on his next victim.

Most of Clay's victims had been men and boys of slight build, many of them teen-agers. Michael was an equal opportunity killer. If he had to, he wouldn't think twice about offing a woman. But he liked boys, especially, and small men, if no boys were available. The feeling of being in control of another human being, another man's destiny at the moment their life ended, was heady stuff. It was sexually satisfying to him. Michael found, after the first few victims, that he no longer could get off without the added thrill of the chase and the kill.

Pogo did occasionally try to keep a few of his victims alive, so that they could stay with him and become his friend. He was sure that if they just understood the rules, they would learn to like him. But, inevitably, the victims struggled and tried to flee and screamed and would not take the time to find out that Michael Clay was someone they could trust, someone they could bond with. He sighed as he thought of all the lost opportunities amongst his thirty-three dead victims.

At the right moment, Clay threw his entire 300-plus pounds at the loosened grate. The grate smashed into Deputy Jim Kinkade just as he hit the large pothole going well over 70 miles per hour. The effect of the grate (and body) ramming him from behind, just as the prison van hit the bad spot in the road, sent the vehicle out of control, just as Pogo hoped it would.

Everything is going according to plan, Pogo thought. *I'll be outside in Burnham Woods in no time. After that, Mexico. Sunny Mexico.*

When the van careened into the ditch, the officer behind the wheel was temporarily knocked unconscious, body slumped against the steering wheel. The van had gone nose-deep into the shallow ditch. Michael now worked feverishly to further loosen the grating. He needed to get a space large enough so that he could reach into Jim Kinkade's pocket and find the key ring that unlocked his shackles. That feat accomplished, Michael needed to get out of the van. He was able to do that using the metal implement he had fashioned from tools in the prison metal shop.

Out of the van now, back door ajar, Michael walked around to the driver's side and tried to open the door. Jim Kinkade was still slumped unconscious behind the wheel. Michael intended to make sure that Kinkade remained unconscious forever. The door was locked. Clay used the keys he had picked from Kinkade's pockets and from the truck's ignition, found the van key on the car key ring, and opened the van's door. He climbed into the van. With a quick twisting motion, Pogo snapped the young man's neck as easily as you might snap the dried wishbone of a Thanksgiving turkey. Then, he pushed Jim's body onto the driver's side seat— the seat that should have been occupied by the second guard.

Michael Clay backed the van out of the shallow ditch and drove it into the woods. There was a rudimentary gravel road that existed just past the dip.

When he was sure that no one could see the van from the highway, he turned off the motor and climbed out.

The air was chilly with fall, but it was fresh air. It smelled of fall and burning fires and freedom. Heady stuff for a man who had just spent eight years living in the armpit of a decaying prison system.

Pogo set off into Burnham Woods towards the area where the older cabins had been located when he had lived in Waterloo, nine years earlier. The newer cabins had all been built closer to town, but the older ones, like Old Man Isham's, were often run-down and deteriorating. Sometimes abandoned. They were from the old glory days of Route 66 and the fifties. Michael Clay wanted to find one that had no residents.

Ahead, he saw a beat-up maroon Pontiac LeMans parked outside a dilapidated-looking cabin, with a red Toyota parked behind it. He sneaked up to the window of the cabin to look inside. As the last of daylight was fading, he thought, *It must be Christmas and this is my early Christmas present! Christmas in October!*

What Michael Clay saw, through the filthy window of the Isham cabin, was a slightly built man who appeared to be bound, hand and foot, with electrical cord, and also had pieces of silver electrician's tape over his mouth. He saw no other people in the cabin. The bound man appeared to be unconscious.

Next, Michael, emboldened by the lack of any sort of normal human activity in the cabin, walked to the Pontiac while scanning the surrounding area for any signs of life. The car was a beater. Old. Maroon. Dented. The keys were in the ignition.

The red Toyota looked newer and in better shape from the outside. It looked like a Ford Focus. Upon closer inspection, Michael saw that it was a brand he had not heard much about in the slammer. It was a Toyota Prius. He opened the unlocked door of the much-newer looking vehicle. No keys. He also noticed a large flat screen in the middle of the dashboard. *They have TV sets when they drive now?* he thought.

The gear shift stuck out at a funny angle, jutting into the cabin of the car. Michael knew how to jump-start a car, but he had never seen a car like this one before. It was a newer vehicle. But did he really want to take the time to hot-wire it, when the older Pontiac had the keys already in the ignition? The answer was no. Besides, there was something very odd about this vehicle.

Michael's time in the slammer had caused him to lose a step or two, technologically-speaking. This hybrid vehicle would have proven a challenge, had Michael Clay attempted to hot wire it. Wiser to take the older Pontiac.

Dog-gees! Michael thought. *I must be living right. As long as that old Pontiac can get me to Mexico, it might as well be a limo!*

Inside the cabin, a helpless unconscious man. Outside, a vehicle with the keys in the ignition. It was almost as though his daddy had known he was going to break out of prison and had left him a tasty man morsel for dessert and a car to use for his getaway. Michael smiled. His chubby cheeks made him resemble an evil pig.

He walked slowly towards the cabin door, scanning the area for any signs of life or any signs of the law with darting looks to the left and right. *Sometimes, people just walk away from their lives*, he thought. *And sometimes, life just walks up and grabs you when you're least expecting it.* He smiled a self-satisfied smile.

At that moment, Michael Clay was a very happy serial killer. All his senses were on edge. He was hyper-vigilant. He had some ideas about what he might do with the helpless man inside. It had been a long time, but he had some very interesting ideas. *It's just like riding a bicycle. You never forget*, Michael thought.

He became sexually excited just thinking about how he would spend the next few hours.

CHAPTER 34

October 30, 2003, Thursday, Dusk
The San Giovannis' House

When Jenny SanGiovanni let herself into the house after cheerleading practice, it was almost dark outside.

Practice had taken from 4:00 p.m. to 6:00 p.m. She needed to get dinner started. Her mom never made it home much before 8:00 p.m., but Greg should be there. Her brother Frank was over at Buddy Attenza's house, playing video games. She knew he'd probably be there until dinnertime, which meant at least two more hours.

She opened the door to the garage to see if Greg's car was inside. The BMW was parked inside. There was a bad smell in the garage. She noticed a puddle of liquid on the floor. And then she saw Tad McGreevy.

Tad had been dragged to the far side of the garage and thrown onto some old gunnysacks that once held wood chips, near the corner by the tool bench.

Jenny was completely unprepared for the sight of the unconscious boy lying on the floor of her garage. She wondered where her stepfather was.

Where is Greg?

She rushed to the far corner of the garage where Tad lay unconscious. Even in her haste, she tried to avoid stepping in the liquid on the floor. When she flipped on the light switch to the garage, bathing the area in harsh fluorescent light, she saw that the puddle appeared to be blood. And that smell! It was definitely shit.

Is it human or has some animal been in here? Maybe Tad encountered a wild animal in the garage. He had to kill it. But where is the body of the animal? And why is Tad McGreevy in my garage at all? And why is Tad unconscious? Thoughts tumbled through Jenny's mind like numbers in a lottery pool drawing basket, dropping randomly one after another.

Tad was not tied up. He was also not conscious. There was blood dripping down the right side of his face. Jenny noticed that the tool bench area of their garage, near where Tad lay, looked as though it had been ransacked. Things were in disarray. She didn't know what to do. Tad needed medical attention.

Calm down, Jenny, she told herself. *Be calm. Do the right thing. You have to get help for Tad!*

First, she would go inside the house and ask her stepfather Greg. He was almost always in the house before she got home. She'd let Greg decide if they should call 911 or just put Tad in the car and drive him to the hospital themselves.

Then she thought, to herself, *But why isn't Greg out here? Surely he'd hear a ruckus in the attached garage if Tad were fighting with some animal?*

Jenny was totally confused.

Jenny ran back into the house shouting, "Greg! Greg!" She wished her older brother Frank was here to help her decide what to do. For that matter, she wished that her older sister, Cynthia, still lived at home, but Cynthia had moved out and gotten her own place, a small one-bedroom apartment near the office where she worked. She could call Cynthia, though. She'd rather have Cynthia involved than bother her mom at work. Frank almost never picked up his cell when he was in video game mode, so calling him would only waste precious time.

Jenny dialed Cynthia SanGiovanni's number and waited. There was no answer. Just an answering machine saying, "I cannot come to the phone right now. If you leave your name at the tone, I'll get back to you as soon as possible."

Shit! That doesn't help at all.

She dialed 911 and briefly answered the operator's questions.

Then she took a deep breath and dialed her mother.

When her mother picked up, Jenny said, "Mom, I think you should come home right away. Something's happened to Tad McGreevy. He's in our garage. He needs help. He was unconscious when I found him. I can't find Greg to help take him to the hospital, so I dialed 911."

"Why is Tad McGreevy in our garage?" asked Andrea SanGiovanni. At her desk, she put down her ballpoint pen. Her brow furrowed.

"I don't know, Mom. I don't know what's wrong with him, either. He looks like he was hit on the head or something. Maybe he had a fight with some animal that got inside our garage?" The young girl's voice sounded calm, but the sound resembled the light breeze that is the calm before a storm. She sounded as though she really wanted to be hysterical and cry and let her emotions out, but Jenny was struggling to hold it together.

Jenny was reaching. She knew it. So did her mother.

"What are you talking about? What animal got inside our garage? Why was Tad there in the first place?" Andrea SanGiovanni did not understand anything that Jenny was saying.

Jenny didn't know what she was describing, either, and she was beginning to become hysterical.

"I've already called 911, Mom."

" Why? Why did you do that?" Andrea's question was logical, but it also sounded critical.

"Tad's hurt. He looks like he might be hurt bad. He's unconscious and he's breathing funny, and there's a lot of blood and shit." Now Jenny's words were rushing, coming faster and faster.

"Blood? Where do you see blood?" Andrea asked this and then added, "And where is Greg? Can't he help you?" From her office in the city, she was far removed from the reality that Jenny was dealing with. She was much less worried about Tad McGreevy than Jenny, her daughter.

"Greg's not here, but his car's here. I called Cynthia and she didn't answer. Frank is over at Buddy Attenza's house playing video games. He never answers when he's playing video games. I'm going to call the McGreevys next." Jenny tried to get a grip. She tried to explain logically what was happening. It was particularly hard when Jenny really didn't know what was happening.

"Yes, well, I wish you had called me *first* and then called for help, but nevertheless, lock all the doors until I get home or the cops arrive. Do you understand me?" Andrea's tone was chilly. She was using her "in charge" voice.

Andrea was not happy that the local papers would print a report for a 911 call at her house. She was a realtor, after all. Bad press was not good for business. On the other hand, if someone was hurt and needed medical attention, Jenny had done the right thing. But Andrea seldom told her daughter she had done anything well. Andrea was the Critical Queen.

"I'll be right there, Jenny. Sit tight and don't let anybody in but the police or Greg or me." That was the protective mother coming through and winning out over the hypercritical businesswoman. After all, her daughter was home alone and doing the best she could, under the circumstances, reasoned Andrea.

Andrea SanGiovanni grabbed her keys and raced for her car.

CHAPTER 35

October 30, 2003; Thursday, 8:00 P.M.
The Paramedics

The paramedics were loading Tad McGreevy into the back of an ambulance, his body immobilized on a board. They placed the teen-ager's body on a gurney. Tad had a large collar, a neck brace, around his neck. He was moaning slightly. He was not totally conscious.

Andrea SanGiovanni arrived right after the paramedics. She hugged Jenny and took in the scene, which now included the wailing of police sirens approaching the remote housing subdivision.

"Are you all right?" She hugged her daughter tightly. Andrea loved her daughter, but she didn't often show it. On the way over, she had begun to realize that Jenny might be in danger. She was feeling less critical and more concerned.

"Yeah. I'm fine, but I don't know where Greg is." Jenny looked like she was struggling not to cry. Jenny knew this was bad. She was understandably upset. In the midst of all those emotions, she was worried that her mother would be critical of how she had reacted, the split-second decisions she had made. She just knew that whatever she had done would be wrong. It was never possible to totally please her mother.

"Maybe Tad knows what happened here and he can tell us when he regains consciousness. What's this about blood?" Andrea's hazel eyes reflected her concern. She looked deeply into Jenny's cornflower blue eyes as she asked the question.

"Some of the blood was on Tad's head. It looked like something hit him. Pretty hard, I think. He's probably got a concussion. It might have been something from Dad's tool bench, because it looks like some stuff is missing.

Some other blood is right here, right before you step into the house. See that puddle? " Jenny opened the door to the garage and pointed to the messy patch of blood and human excrement that Cassie Chandler and Gregory Tuttle had created.

Andrea put her hand to her nose. "Christ! That stinks! What do you think happened? Did you know that Tad was coming over here this afternoon?"

"I just got back from cheerleading practice. No— I didn't know Tad was coming over. I have no idea why Tad was here. I didn't invite him over or anything like that. He never said a thing about coming by. I don't know where Greg is, either. Do you?"

Andrea responded, "I haven't talked to Greg all day." She thought to herself, *We've been talking less and less every day.* Andrea honestly didn't know how Greg occupied his time or where he was half of the time, since the rift between them over helping her with her realty business. She felt as though it was best if she didn't inquire or act overly interested. It was the old saying, "What you don't know can't hurt you." Or can it?

Andrea and Jenny sank into hard-backed kitchen chairs just before the police arrived.

"Did you try to call Frank?" Andrea asked her daughter. Jenny had already told her mother about her initial calls for help, but she repeated her answer now.

"No. I called Cynthia first. You know how Frank is…he usually doesn't even answer his phone. He just lets it roll over to the answering machine."

Their conversation was interrupted by the entrance of the first policeman on the scene, a fifty-ish gentleman with a pale complexion.

"I'm Officer Nels Peterson," he said, entering through the front door to the kitchen. "What happened here?"

"I wish I knew, Officer Peterson," said Andrea.

"Who found the McGreevy boy?" Officer Peterson addressed both of the women.

"I did," said Jenny. "I had just gotten home from school, from cheerleading practice. I started to look for my stepfather, because he's usually home by the time I arrive home. I came out here to see if his car was in the garage. When I came out here, I saw Tad." Jenny was repeating this for at least the third or fourth time. She would repeat it many more times before the night was over.

Peterson opened the door to the garage, but first he used a handkerchief to prevent his fingerprints from adding to those already accumulated on the doorknob.

The stench hit his nostrils immediately. It was a mixture of the acrid copper-y smell of blood and the shit smell inside a public porta-potty. In the hot, stuffy air of the garage, the odor was almost tangible.

"Was there some kind of disagreement between you and young McGreevy, Jenny?" Nels asked Jenny, quickly shutting the door to the garage.

"No, Sir," said Jenny. "Tad and I are good friends. He could come over any time he wanted. But I didn't know he was coming over tonight. I don't know why he was unconscious in our garage. And I don't know where my stepfather is. I tried to find him to help me with Tad."

"What's your stepfather's name? " Peterson addressed this to Jenny, but Andrea answered.

"My daughter is talking about my husband Gregory Tuttle, Jenny's stepfather. He's a financial advisor and works in the Union Building downtown. He's usually home by now. Neither of us has seen him since this morning, but his car is in the garage." Andrea's brow wrinkled in a worried manner as she answered the routine questions.

"When did you arrive, Ma'am? Were you here when your daughter discovered the boy in the garage?"

"No. No. I just got here. Jenny called me at my office. I own SanGiovanni's Real Estate. I was at the office, finishing up some work. Jenny called and said she had dialed 911. She couldn't get her older sister or brother on the phone. She couldn't find my husband."

"Was there some kind of disagreement between you and your husband earlier in the day?" Peterson was going for the jugular.

"Absolutely not," said Andrea SanGiovanni in an annoyed tone of voice. "Whatever happened in that garage is something that Tad McGreevy is going to have to shed light on, when he wakes up. Neither my daughter nor I were here when whatever happened went down. We're as confused as you are, right now, Officer."

Andrea rose and moved towards the refrigerator to get a bottle of water.

The influx of crime scene investigators, photographers and other personnel filled the night with the crackling of walkie-talkies and the sound of trouble.

CHAPTER 36

October 30, 2003, Thursday
The Hospital

Colors. Light. A jangle of noise. Tad heard all this, yet didn't hear it. He was half-awake, half-unconscious.

In his mind, he was seeing images of his old nemesis, Pogo the Clown. But Pogo was in a forest. He was entering a cabin. Pogo bent down to inspect something on the floor. Then, he went to the kitchen and came back with a knife. *Why is Pogo in my dreams again?* Tad thought he had seen the last of Michael Clay and Michael Clay's victims. He moaned at the thought of having to see more of Pogo's gruesome handiwork.

Then, in his dream, his eyes panned to the figure on the floor. The room was dimly lit. Night was falling. The male figure on the floor looked familiar. He was slight of build. His arms were tied behind his back with electrical cords. His legs, too, were bound. Silver duct tape muted the man's desperate moans.

I know this man, Tad thought. *It's Jenny's stepdad. Where is he? Why is he in a dream with Pogo?*

The larger man approached the figure on the floor with a knife. Michael Clay looked menacing, even though he had done nothing to the bound figure— yet. And then he did something to the figure who lay there, helpless. He drove the knife into the helpless man's right shoulder. Gregory Tuttle, who had been semi-conscious, wriggled and squirmed and showed every sign of experiencing intense pain. To Tad, it looked like what it might resemble if a human were being put on a fishing hook as bait, rather than an earthworm. There were noises coming from Gregory Tuttle's taped mouth. The noises didn't sound human. They were the sounds an animal makes when it is being slaughtered. That was what Tad began to see in his dream: an animal being slaughtered.

All the while he cut and abused the bound man, Pogo spoke to him, saying things that made no sense: "You could be my friend if you'd only try. I'm not such a bad guy. You'd like me if you only tried." Pogo asked the bound man questions about his home, who was there. He'd briefly lift the tape to let the man answer. He removed his captive's wallet, keys, cell phone, watch.

More moans and guttural noises from the bound figure. The failure of the bound prisoner to respond intelligibly seemed to send the man with the knife into a frenzy.

"Why won't you try to learn to know me? Why are you like all the others? Can't you at least try?"

The knife flashed. Blood flew.

Tad moaned as he watched the systematic, inhuman torture of another human being in his dream state. He knew this victim. It was Gregory Tuttle. Tad was still only half-awake, deep in a sort of fugue state. He was not able to cry out or articulate what he was seeing. His head throbbed.

When the violence in the cabin was over, Tad became almost comatose. He didn't want to emerge into awareness. Awareness would mean trying to tell others what he had just seen. No one ever believed him. He should just lie here. He should just remain still. Maybe if he just lay still, everything would go away. Things would return to normal. None of this would have happened. Nurses were trying to rouse him, but he didn't want to be awakened, he didn't want to be conscious. He just wanted to slip into a limbo-like dream state until all of this horror faded from memory—if it ever did.

How long would it take, this time, to try to forget? It took over a year when I was eight years old. Will it be any easier now? These were Tad's unconscious thoughts and the answer he gave himself was not positive. Although he had recovered from the horror of his eighth year of life, he had done so by partitioning off his mind. He told himself that that time in his life was "only a movie." He was able to retain his sanity by convincing himself that none of it was real.

This time, when he actually recognized the victim, it was all too real.

The constant drumming refrain that he heard in his mind, the refrain that had driven him from his family's dinner table mid-meal was, "I've got to find Jenny. I've got to get to Jenny. I've got to save Jenny."

CHAPTER 37

October 30, 2003, Thursday
Jenny

Jenny SanGiovanni sat in the waiting room with her mother. She wondered if her mother was angry with her for contacting the authorities before calling the real estate office.

It doesn't matter what I do. It's always wrong. Nothing I ever do or ever will do is ever 'right.' I had to call for help for Tad. He was hurt. Mom will just have to deal with it.

Jenny tried to re-position her head against the back of the orange plastic hospital chair to be more comfortable. Her mother was sleeping in a similar chair in the family waiting room.

Jenny hated hospitals. It wasn't just the smell of medicines and the feeling of impending doom, it was everything about them.

One thing I know, for sure. I don't ever want to work in a hospital.

Andrea SanGiovanni had frequently hinted that Jenny, who was a straight "A" student, might want to consider volunteering as a candy striper to boost her chances of being inducted into National Honor Society and give her something extra-curricular to list on her college admissions forms. Or she might wish to consider a career as a nurse or a doctor. Jenny never spoke up and told her mother how much she loathed hospitals. It would just cause a fight, and Jenny didn't like unpleasantness and tried never to be disagreeable. She was a pleaser.

I don't ever, ever, ever want to be mucking about in other people's bodily fluids, she thought.

Jenny had no real career ambitions, at this point. Whenever she was asked, she said she wanted to go to "a large out-of-state school." What Jenny wanted hardly ever mattered, anyway. It was more about what her mother wanted for her. She always did whatever she thought everyone else wanted her to do. However, if her mother started to push her towards a career in medicine, that's where she'd draw the line. She couldn't bear the thought of spending every waking moment in a place like this. Maybe she'd go work at Layne's Insurance like her sister Cynthia. Maybe she'd work in real estate, like her mom. But no medicine for this girl.

A tall orderly approached them. His nametag said George Bates.

"Are you the family of the young boy who was brought in with the concussion?" he asked.

"No," Andrea answered, rousing herself from half-slumber. "We just brought him to the hospital. That's Tad McGreevy. The McGreevys are on their way. Is Tad conscious?"

"No, he isn't. We've been trying to get him to wake up and speak to us. He isn't responding to smelling salts. He seems to be sinking deeper into unconsciousness." George flipped a page on the chart he held in his hand. "Will you let me know when his mother and father arrive?"

"Certainly," said Andrea SanGiovanni, readjusting the light jacket she had grabbed as they left the house. It wasn't that it was that cold outside. It was that it was that cold inside. Andrea wondered how the patients managed to stay warm. It was frigid in the hospital corridors and the waiting room was like a deep freeze.

Just then, Jeanne, Jim and Sharon McGreevy entered the emergency room area of the hospital, looking concerned and confused.

Jeanne saw Andrea and Jenny SanGiovanni and made a beeline for them. Jenny had called them to tell them to come to the hospital.

"What's wrong with Tad? Where is he?" she asked.

"We don't know, Jeannie. Jenny came home from school and found him in our garage, unconscious. It looked like there might have been a struggle. He'd been struck on the head. Jenny called 911, and then she called me."

As she relayed this information, Andrea thought, ruefully, I *wish that she had called me first and then dialed 911.*

"Can we see him?" Jeannie addressed this question to George, the orderly. He led them down the corridor to Tad's bed in the ICU.

As they entered the ICU room, Jim McGreevy said, "I wonder how much this room goes for, a night."

The orderly answered, "$1,200."

"Figures," said Jim McGreevy, in a not-that-happy tone of voice, under his breath.

The orderly withdrew to leave the family unit alone with the pale teenager, but, before he did, he said, "Usually, we only allow two family members in here at a time. They can only stay for ten minutes. But, since you just got here and everyone is going to be asked to leave for the night in fifteen minutes, just make yourselves comfortable. No cell phone calls. No outside food or beverages. Try to be reassuring. See if you can get him to wake up. The police would like to talk with him."

"We'd like to talk with him, too, Mr. Bates," said Jeannie McGreevy in a peeved tone as George Bates left the room.

"I'd feel a lot more reassured if this room didn't cost over a grand a night," Jim McGreevy muttered under his breath. Jeannie shot him a dirty look.

Business had not been good recently. The election of George W. Bush as president had not provided the boost in business that McGreevy, Sanders and Slade had hoped for. Since Jeannie didn't work but was an expert at spending money, Jim McGreevy was trying to watch unnecessary expenditures. Last time Tad had these episodes, it cost more than $20,000.

Sharon moved to the side of Tad's bed and said, "Tad! Tad! Wake up! It's Sharon. It's Sharon, your sister. Can you answer me? Can you hear me?"

Tad did not respond. The family finally looked around the sparse room for chairs. There was only one chair in the room. Inside a wardrobe, there were two folding chairs. Jim McGreevy set them up so that the family members could sit by Tad's bedside until closing time in fifteen minutes, when it would be nine o'clock.

"What do you think happened, Jim?" This was Jeannie, asking her hassled husband the question on all of their minds.

"How the hell should I know?" Jim McGreevy responded, in a gruff voice. "What did he say to you when he left our house?"

Jeanne responded, "He suddenly said he had to find Jenny, that he had to save Jenny. He wouldn't eat dinner. He sat down, but he just pushed the food around on his plate. Then he got up and bolted for the door."

"It looks like he did a piss-poor job of saving himself, let alone saving Jenny," said Jim McGreevy, the worried father and payer of all family bills.

"I can't imagine what happened. Why isn't Greg Tuttle out there with Andrea and Jenny and the kids?" Frank and Cynthia had straggled in and were talking with Jenny about her discovery of Tad in the garage, but Gregory Tuttle was still missing.

"I don't know, Jim. I only know that Tad wouldn't eat dinner because he had it in his mind that he had to get over to Jenny's house to 'save' her. He wasn't specific. He didn't say what it was he was 'saving' her from. You know how Tad is when he gets like this." Jeannie looked at Jim McGreevy with a pleading look.

"Yes, I know how he is, and the whole town knows, too. I sure hope this isn't some sort of repeat performance of all that trouble when he was eight." Jim cleared his throat and reached into his pocket for his handkerchief. Outside, thunder rumbled in the darkness.

"Well, whatever it is, we have to help him. It's important that he regain consciousness. We have to do our best to let him know that he is safe and that we are here."

Jeannie smoothed the coverlet of Tad's hospital blanket. She smoothed the brow of her only son. Tad didn't move a muscle. He had been given pain medication and he was breathing deeply. He looked like a marble statue, pale and cold to the touch. Jeannie and Sharon were close to tears as they looked down at Tad's form, lying there helpless in the hospital ICU unit. Although he was now sixteen, they both remembered the thin, frail, eight-year-old boy lying unconscious in a similar hospital bed eight years ago.

"Right," said Jim, and turned his gaze towards the light rain that was beginning to fall outside the window.

CHAPTER 38

October 30, 2003, Thursday night
The Hospital

Lights. Headlights. Tad knew this girl's face. Usually, the victims he had seen Pogo attack were anonymous young men and boys. This was that friend of his sister's.... Belinda Chandler. Her cheek looked as though it had been scraped somehow. Gravel? She was on a gravel road. Maybe she fell? There were long rivulets of blood running down her right cheek. Her face seemed to be pressed against the leather of a car, an old car. The leather of the car's seats had rips in it. She was bound, but not yet gagged. She was whimpering. "Please don't hurt me. I'll do anything you want. Just don't hurt me."

Tad's mind's eye view moved to the front seat of the car. He saw that the driver of the vehicle was Michael Clay, the same man he had just seen doing unspeakable things to Gregory Tuttle.

Belinda was not in that dream. Where did Belinda Chandler come from?

Tad was almost in a fugue state. His eyes, beneath closed eyelids, were darting from side to side. Unfocused fugitive eyes. His head hurt. It was throbbing. It truly felt as though the top of his head might explode. He thought his head could burst at any moment. Tad had seen that happen once in an old movie called "Scanners." He wasn't so sure that it wasn't possible for it to happen in real life, the way his head felt right now. Tad watched the visions and the auras. He was powerless to help the girl in his dream, the girl who was a friend of his sister Sharon's. Pogo's aura, gray-green and red. Smile forming at the corner of his fat little face. Eyes narrowed to ugly slits. Michael Clay was not going to just let Belinda Chandler go. Something awful was going to happen to her.

Tad thought, *Please don't make me see it in my dream. Please, no. Not again!*

* * *

As for Michael Clay, he was feeling very mellow. *Mellow yellow*, he thought as he smiled.

Pogo flipped on the radio of Jeremy Gustaffsson's Pontiac LeMans and turned up the volume to drown out the pleas of the young girl he had picked up walking along the road near the cabin. Pogo had no interest in the young girl, but he couldn't leave any witnesses. Sooner or later, someone would find the corpse of his victim inside the cabin, his early Christmas present, that wimp with the truly huge penis. Then this one would be telling how she was just walking along near the cabin when this fat little man in an orange jumpsuit walked out of the cabin, got inside Jeremy Gustaffsson's car, and drove away.

That wouldn't be good. That wouldn't be good at all, thought Michael Clay.

Michael liked the feel of the car's steering wheel. He liked the souped-up sound system. Dire Straits was playing "Money for nothin' and the kicks for free" on an oldies station. *Or was it chicks for free?* Michael could never tell what the lyrics were. He always thought the lyric to "Bad Moon Rising" was "There's a bathroom on the right." Lyrics were weird. *What about that one where they ride to the desert on a horse with no name*? thought Michael Clay. *How can you tell what any of these mouth-breathers are singing? Dude looks like a lady...what-the-fuck?*

Michael wanted to drive this car as far as possible. None of those new-fangled cars like that weird red one parked back at the cabin. Michael would have liked to drive the Pontiac straight south to the Mexican border, to sunny "May-hee-co."

But it was starting to rain and he was hungry, thirsty and tired.

* * *

Belinda Chandler had a fight with her boyfriend. She got out of his car. Her last words to Kenny Kellogg were, "You're going to be very sorry that you started diddling underage girls. I'm going to make sure that everyone knows what you've been doing. You'll lose your job, and you'll go to jail."

Kenny looked stricken. Who knew that Belinda would give him the third degree and force him to confess his other flings? It wasn't like they were engaged or anything. And after he had helped her get that volleyball scholarship, too. The teen-aged girls on his volleyball team were just innocent fun. They weren't any different, to Kenny, than playing a round of golf or working out with weights in the weight room. They helped him to forget the fact that he was still living at home with his mother, still deeply in debt from his student loans. They liked it; he liked it. Where was the harm? It's not as though some sixteen-year-old chippie was expecting him to make a life-long commitment.

For that matter, Belinda Chandler had enough of a reputation that he didn't think she was serious. Why was she so pissed off? Belinda was not the girl of his dreams. She was a good lay. That was all. He certainly couldn't believe that he was her Knight in Shining Armor. They had good sex and some fun and games. That was all.

This had all started because of that ridiculous sex toy he had brought to one of their sessions, that cock ring. When he commented on how noticeable the bruised bulging vein, (the "blow-out," as she called it), was, she had begun poking around in his cell phone. She had found the other numbers. Well, so what? One thing led to another, as it always does. Ultimately, Kenny had confessed, somewhat irritably and in a defiant manner that he might have "one or two" other interests, socially, and they "might be underage."

That didn't set well with Belinda Chandler. In fact, she flew into a jealous, possessive rage. This fit of hers took Kenny Kellogg, chemistry teacher and volleyball coach at Sky High, completely by surprise. He didn't view Belinda as anything more than an enjoyable diversion. He couldn't see how he was anything more to her. It wasn't as though they were going to have mutual friends in common. They couldn't meet and do things with other couples he knew, even if she were of legal age.

Belinda had stormed from her girlfriend Billy's remote apartment near Burnham Woods, the pad the pair borrowed for their trysts. She began walking home. She took the gravel path through the woods. It was taken less often than the more-traveled dirt road ("the road less traveled" she remembered from Anderson's English class). She didn't want Kenny driving along beside her, trying to coax her back into the car.

She was angry and offended and hurt.

Then Jeremy Gustaffsson's Pontiac LeMans had pulled up alongside, crunching to a halt, offering her a ride. Tears streaming down her face, she had barely glanced at the driver behind the wheel.

CHAPTER 39

October 30, 2003, Thursday
Gregory Tuttle and Jeremy Gustaffsson

Andrea SanGiovanni had an uneasy feeling. *Where is Greg?*

In all the hubbub involving the discovery of Tad McGreevy in their garage and the subsequent summoning of the ambulance and the police and the trip to the hospital, Andrea had felt a nagging bit of concern lodge itself in the nether regions of her mind.

Initially, she had found it odd that Greg was not yet home. She had called his cell phone. The message rolled over to voice mail. This did not alarm her when it was dusk. Now that it was close to midnight, she was beginning to turn her attention to the very realistic possibility that, whatever had happened, perhaps Greg was in danger. Andrea didn't want to "borrow trouble," as her mother used to call it, but she also knew that sometimes, people walk away from their lives. Just look at how thoroughly Stevie Scranton seemed to have disappeared a few days ago. She and Greg had not been getting along that well lately. Had he run off with someone else? Perhaps he just left his car behind in the garage to throw people off his trail?

Lately, Andrea had been neglecting Greg in much the same way that her ex-husband, Jeff, used to complain that she had neglected him. She was always busy at work. She was always late getting home. If it weren't for Jenny's efforts, there would not have been a home-cooked meal for any of them over the past several months. Jenny, who had numerous after-school commitments, couldn't cook for them all every night. The SanGiovanni house had become "take out city." It was Colonel Sanders or tacos or pizza or Chinese four nights out of every seven.

Andrea knew that she should devote more time and attention to her spouse and her children. But this was SanGiovanni Realty, a business she started from scratch, seeing an opportunity in the influx of Mexican immigrants hired to work at the packing plant. Andrea had tapped into her divorce settlement money to expand. She bought up many of the empty homes in The Heights. She and Greg managed them together. Greg knew the law. He certainly knew enough to draw up a lease and collect rent. Andrea had been grateful for his help. They had grown closer as she became busier.

But, after her divorce, when she and Greg were married, Andrea had frozen Greg out of the major decisions in her business affairs. She suggested that he become more active in his own financial advising business. Greg had done so, but not without resentment. Greg didn't hide resentment well. Andrea could feel his disapproval of the new business tack she had taken. It didn't include him. She still used him to help collect rent and show properties, but he was not the key player he had once been.

Now, Andrea was the resentful one. She could use some help figuring out what had happened in her garage. She wanted Greg found. She was getting worried. Greg sometimes didn't surface till midnight, so she'd give him that much time before she melted down. Finally, Andrea decided that she would have to instruct the local police to find her missing husband. If Nels Peterson hadn't already put out an APB bulletin, she'd get her next-door neighbor Charlie Chandler to do it. He'd see that the men in blue found her missing husband.

* * *

Jeremy Gustaffsson had thrown his bloody Nikes into the Cedar River on his way home, after burying Cassie Chandler in a shallow grave near Ike Isham's cabin. As he got closer to his house, he also took off his blood-spattered pants. He put his bloody sweat pants in a trash can a few blocks down the street.

So it was that Jeremy Gustaffsson, star quarterback of the Sky High Eagles and starting center for the Eagles basketball team, entered his own house wearing nothing but a gray tee shirt, jockey shorts and socks.

Jeremy didn't really expect to see anyone as he entered the house through the back door that led to the kitchen. There sat his brothers, Jimmy, an eighth grader, and Jeff, a seventh grader. They were doing homework. Very out of character for the duo.

When they looked up, the younger of the two asked the obvious question, "What happened to your pants, Jeremy?" Jeff snickered a bit after he asked the question.

Jimmy chimed in, "Yeah, Jeremy, what happened to your pants? And what happened to your shoes?"

Jeremy gave his brothers a look of disgusted dismissal as he walked through the kitchen on his way to his room. Then he said, "It was hot outside."

The two younger boys looked at one another. Their eyes grew as big as saucers. The pair erupted in peals of laughter.

"Hot? You always just take your pants off when you get hot?"

Jeremy was now out of sight in the bedroom. He shouted back, "Yeah. Sometimes I do. When you two losers get old enough, maybe you'll be interesting enough to make somebody hot."

The two boys looked at each other, arching their youthful eyebrows. They tried hard to conceal their amusement at the sight of their pants-less brother entering the house, shoeless, through the back door, but the pair just kept giggling. It was contagious. One would stop, but the other would start in again. That continued for a long time.

Jeremy yelled back, from the bathroom near his bedroom, "Are you two actually doing homework? Or is this some kind of stunt you set up to convince Mom and Dad that you are hard-working students...NOT?"

The two younger Gustaffsson boys were not good students. It was not entirely their fault. The family moved around so much following the ponies that it made it hard to keep up academically with their classes. They started at the beginning of the year in one school. Then, they moved to some other school, mid-year. Who knew where the new school's curriculum might be at the moment Jimmy and Jeff Gustaffsson arrived? Jimmy and Jeff were studying together at that precise moment because biology had just reached the unit on the human reproductive system. They weren't so much studying as looking at dirty pictures.

Jeremy strolled out to the kitchen, now wearing a pair of gray sweat pants that matched the gray tee shirt. He'd had the tee shirt on underneath the sweatshirt he threw away. He saw what the two younger boys had been looking at in the biology book.

"Oh, I get it now. You're boning up." He doubted if his brothers would get the joke.

Jimmy, the older of the two, quickly shut the biology book. Jimmy repeated the question he had asked earlier.

"What happened to your Air Jordans? I hope you didn't lose them or something, because those are really expensive. I want them after you're done with them."

Jeremy had a well-known penchant for having to have the latest and most expensive footwear. He always justified it by citing his athletic prowess. "I can't do good if I don't have the right kind of shoes, Ma," he'd tell his long-suffering mother. She would just sigh. Dad Leroy usually had a smart-ass comeback, but, secretly, he was proud that Jeremy was such a hot-shot football, basketball and track star. If all it took was the right pair of shoes for Jeremy to continue that winning tradition, Dad didn't object to his oldest son indulging his affection for popular brands touted by billionaire athletes.

Jeremy, still toweling his damp hair from the dunking under the sink faucet, said, "My shoes? Somebody stole 'em."

Jimmy and Jeff thought that was funny, too. They giggled uncontrollably, like a couple of ninnies.

"Stole them from where?"

"I was lifting some weights in the weight room after school. I took off my shoes and put them in my locker, but I forgot to lock it." Jeremy finished with the towel and tossed it towards the hamper visible in the corner of the laundry room. He missed.

"So, in one day you lost a pair of pants AND your newest pair of Air Jordans," Jimmy said, summarizing the half-baked story that Jeremy was peddling.

"That's right. Wanna' make something of it?" Jeremy approached his younger siblings. He had a menacing look in his eyes.

The younger brothers knew that look. They knew that that look often preceded a pummeling from their older brother. Jeff became silent immediately, but Jimmy fired one last salvo across the bow. "So, when the thief got in your unlocked locker, did he take your money and your wallet, too?"

Jeremy wasn't thinking that quickly. He finally responded, "What money? What wallet?"

Jeff said, "Your brown wallet that you always have. Didn't you have any money in it? Did the guy who stole your shoes rip off the money in your wallet? Or maybe take the whole wallet, with your driver's license and stuff? If he did, you'll have to cancel your bank debit card and get a new driver's license."

Jeremy was amazed that his youngest brother would have such a practical thought. He also realized that he was going to have to account for not having lost his wallet to the locker thief.

Jeremy responded, "No. I still have my wallet. I took that with me when I lifted weights. I had my wallet in the weight room."

Both of his little brothers just looked at him as though he were saying something outrageous like, "I just kissed a Martian."

"So, you were just walking around in your underwear and socks holding your wallet while you were getting ready to lift weights in the school's weight room? I'll bet Coach Bear liked that!"

Jimmy and Jeff resumed the giggling, sniggling sound that they had been making previously.

"Look. When you two retards make it out of middle school...if you ever do...and make it onto any teams.... if you ever do...then you can start making fun of my workout practices. Until then, zip it." Jeremy's face was flushed red.

It was true that neither Jimmy nor Jeff had inherited the athletic prowess that Jeremy possessed. Jeremy was unique in the family. He actually had some outstanding ability in an area, even if it wasn't academic.

Jeremy walked back to his room and cranked his headphones. Death Cab for Cutie. "The Sound of Settling." He sang along to the line "Twisting my stomach into knots." He smiled at the line, "If you've got an impulse, let it out."

Oh, he had definitely let his impulses out. Now, he just had to try to pin his handiwork on somebody else. Maybe that wimpy Greg Tuttle. Maybe Charlie Chandler. Didn't matter so long as he was never connected to that cunt Cassie Chandler. When or if they ever found her body. He hoped it would be a very long time before the shallow grave where he had left Cassie's battered body yielded its secrets. He planned to dig her a deeper one slightly before midnight, when he got his car back and cut Greg Tuttle loose. He'd have to give some thought to how long to wait before going back to untie poor old Timid Gregory Tuttle. He thought maybe a few threats about what could happen to Greg Tuttle if he started making trouble for Jeremy Gustaffsson would shut him up. Jeremy knew he had it all over Gimpy Greg in the physicality department. He wasn't afraid of the man, simply because he was older and had more money. And there was the Cassie Chandler leverage.

When I untie him to let him go, I'll put the fear of God in him so that he doesn't say a word to anybody. Maybe midnight. He probably hasn't been neutered so bad that he can't stay out alone until midnight without reporting to Mommy. After all, everybody but Jenny and her mom know he's been putting it to Cassie Chandler for months. He must have some pretty creative excuses he can float with that dikey wife of his. I'll wait until midnight, go back, re-bury Cassie, and untie him then.

Jeremy Gustaffsson wasn't the brightest kid in his class. This was the only plan he'd come up with, before burying Cassie and walking off to leave the unconscious Greg Tuttle tied up in old man Isham's cabin. He was counting on the fact that Greg Tuttle didn't know anything about what had happened to Cassie Chandler, since he'd been passed out.

Jeremy thought, *I'll get my car when I go back to untie Jenny's dad at midnight.* He had the additional thought, *At least the little pissants didn't notice that my car isn't parked outside. They'd probably find it pretty funny that I lost my pants, shoes and car in one day.*

Jimmy and Jeff were dumb, but they weren't that dumb.

CHAPTER 40

October 31, 2003, Friday
The Scrantons

Sally and Earl and Shannon Scranton had spent the time since Stevie disappeared plastering his sophomore high school picture around town on telephone poles and distributing them to various media outlets within a 150-mile radius.

The Scrantons had attracted some volunteers, mostly kids who knew Stevie and were, like him, a bit odd. Stevie's squished-shaped head looked off-kilter in the pictures the Scrantons stapled to every available surface. That was good. That was what Stevie looked like in real life.

The family had also divided the town of Cedar Falls and Waterloo into radiating circles. They planned to first search the circle closest to their home and the school and then move outward to the more remote areas. In brainstorming sessions, various friends of Stevie's would suggest possible places he might have visited and the logical places a kid on the lam would go were checked first, like the Greyhound bus station. Still nothing.

Then Shannon and Earl, who were frustrated by the long period of inactivity after the first flush of Stevie's disappearance, had the idea of going out to Burnham Woods and checking cabins. Tad McGreevy had already checked the one cabin he and Stevie used to use sometimes, to get away from it all and just be left alone, Old Man Isham's abandoned cabin, but Tad had not mentioned this to anyone else. Tad had done this early in the morning, before school. When...not if, but when...Stevie came back, Tad didn't want to compromise their secret club house location.

The Isham cabin was just off a gravel road where the oldest of the cabins built near the new penitentiary were located. After the feds decided to put the maximum security place up in that area, it made cabins located near there even more difficult to sell. Old Man Isham was in Fernwood Nursing Home. He'd been there for years now. His cabin sat alone and abandoned in Burnham Woods, mute testimony to the changing nature of recreation.

Kids didn't go camping any more. They sat inside playing video games or talking on cellphones or typing to one another on the Internet. For that matter, many of the adults who had frequented the woods to fish or hunt had given it up once the new prison began to rear its ugly head, turreted guard posts looming over the peaceful bucolic setting.

Shannon and Earl Scranton were alike in one respect. They were like caged animals if they were not allowed to do something physical for a long period of time. Shannon had been a star volleyball player in high school. She enjoyed anything physical. Her dad was much like her. Earl was probably the source of Shannon's athletic ability.

Shannon and Earl took off in Earl's beat-up Ford pick-up, the one he drove to his foreman's job at Rath's Packing Plant, and soon found themselves on the gravel road leading to Burnham Woods.

"Let's park the car. We'll walk down this gravel road. You knock on the cabins on the left. I'll knock on the ones on the right. Stick together." It was very early on Friday morning, the dawn of Homecoming Day. Tonight was Halloween.

Shannon walked up to the door of the deserted cabin where Ike Isham had once cleaned and cooked the fish he caught in nearby Cedar Creek. It was the same cabin where her little brother and Tad had played with their Mighty Morphin Power Rangers when they were far too old to get away with playing with them in front of others. It was the same cabin where Janice Kramer had lost her virginity to the star tackle of the Waterloo Warriors semi-pro football team, one night after a game. The cabin's existence was the best-kept secret at Sky High. Wild parties were not held here, for fear the location would be discovered by the authorities, if they overdid it, and then it would be shut down.

As Shannon climbed up the two stone steps that led to the cabin door, she was surprised to see the door was slightly ajar.

That's odd, she thought. Then a slight pulse of hope swept over her, as she thought of how it might mean that Stevie was here or had been here. Shannon called to her dad, lagging slightly behind her and knocking on doors of cabins on the right side of the gravel road.

"Dad! Come here a minute. I might have something." Earl Scranton came at a trot. He was fifty-eight years old. He had become a father at forty, but he was still in great shape for his age. Part of that had to do with the physical demands of his job at Rath's Packing Plant, but part of it was just genetics.

The two slowly pushed the door open and entered the abandoned cabin.

The first thing they noticed was an acrid odor. A blue tarp lay on the floor. Something limp and lumpy was bundled within it. On the kitchen table lay an array of kitchen utensils, mostly knives. The knives had been laid out symmetrically according to increasing size, culminating in a large butcher knife that looked worthy of one of the slasher flicks the kids were so fond of watching at the Cineplex. In those movies, there was always a camp near a location with a name like Crystal Lake. There was usually a killer on the loose who showed remarkable creativity with sharp pointed objects. The memory of such films made Shannon uneasy, as the room they were in looked very much like the cabin in the last slasher flick she had seen.

Suddenly, Shannon was afraid to open the blue tarp. She sensed that her father had the same reluctance.

Finally, her father took the lead. "Let's take a look around. You look in that old icebox, Shannon. See if it looks like anyone has put in any supplies or been living here. I'll open this blue tarp and see what's inside." Shannon smiled. Nobody but her father had called a refrigerator an "icebox" for twenty years or more.

Shannon was afraid to look as her father opened the lumpy blue tarp, but she was also afraid not to look. She finally made her peace with not looking, but, instead, doing as her father had asked and checking the ancient refrigerator.

She walked carefully and slowly towards the refrigerator, her footsteps making a creaking sound as she stepped on the weathered wooden planks of the floor. She opened the antique Norge refrigerator (a brand that hadn't been made since 1978). At almost precisely the same moment, her father unwrapped the blue tarp.

Ultimately, Shannon couldn't resist glancing at the large blue tarp. She turned just as Gregory Tuttle's bloody headless torso tumbled from the covering and fell onto her father's booted feet.

When Shannon actually looked inside the refrigerator door at its contents, what was left of Gregory Tuttle's head sat there, facing her, his mouth still taped shut with silver electrician's tape, his eyes wide with unspeakable terror. Earl Scranton instantly recognized the severed head as Gregory Tuttle, his broker.

Shannon promptly fainted.

CHAPTER 41

October 31, 2003, Friday
Michael Clay

The radio was playing the refrain "If you've got an impulse let it out" from some group that Michael Clay didn't know. *After my time*, he thought, of the group singing, but then he also thought, *NOW is my time*. He smiled. That's what he had told his old man after he had been arrested for the murders of those thirty-three men and boys buried beneath his house. He could have written this lyric.

He said, to his heartbroken father, "When I have an impulse, I have to let it out."

His father just stared at him, appalled.

He listened to the phrase ending the song, "I've got a hunger twisting my stomach into knots." Michael didn't have an intense hunger right this moment, because he had just had a nice interlude at the cabin in the woods. He had enjoyed letting his impulses loose on the bound and gagged Gregory Tuttle. It was almost as though his father—who had always known his son wasn't quite "right"—had left him an early Christmas present in the woods.

Michael had to hand it to his dad. His father stood by him right through the trial, testifying under oath that, aside from killing some squirrels or birds or rabbits when he was a young boy, Michael had never shown any murderous impulses. Dear old Dad just didn't know. He didn't know about the old woman Mike had murdered in the summer of his sophomore year of high school. During his eight years in the slammer, Dad had sent him letters and newspapers. He always came to visit.

If he had known about Gladys who had lived near Michael's grandmother's house in the country, would Michael Clay, Sr., still have come?

As a teen-ager, young Michael could see that Gladys was alone all of the time. Nobody really cared if Gladys lived or died. Whenever he saw her, before he killed her, he thought of the Beatles song "Eleanor Rigby." After he smothered her, he dissected her organs. They were studying biology that year.

Although it was messy, he put down her plastic shower curtain to keep the gore from tracking throughout her tidy frame house. At times, he would sit there, nude, actually sitting amidst the blood and entrails, comparing the actual insides of a living human being (well, not living at that exact moment, but previously living) with the aseptic illustrations in the textbooks. No wonder he got "A's" in science classes. The fields and friends near his Grandmother Clay's little cottage in the country provided an excellent laboratory for the curious boy.

He had graduated from amphibians, frogs and tadpoles, which they often dissected in biology class amongst the nervous laughter of classmates and the smell of formaldehyde, to birds, squirrels, rabbits, and, ultimately, Gladys. He sometimes thought that he had done Gladys a favor. She always said she never wanted to have to live in a nursing home. *Well, now you don't have to worry, Gladys*, he thought to himself as he removed the pillow from her face. Gladys didn't even struggle much.

But Belinda Chandler, now screaming in the back seat of Gregory Tuttle's stolen Pontiac LeMans, was going to be a harder kill. Although Michael needed to gradually head south towards Mexico and refuge, he knew that the rural fields of Iowa and the Midwest were absent of people after the harvest. If the field he selected also had a stream nearby, he could use the water to wash off the knives he had taken with him from the cabin. He could also cut Belinda up into smaller pieces. By putting her in the stream, she would decompose faster and be harder to identify. *Maybe even become fish food*, Michael thought. *Nothing like going green and helping the environment.*

Michael knew all the tricks of preventing identification of a dead body, but he did not have his full complement of tools and chemicals. One had to pay careful attention to the fingerprints, the teeth, tattoos, birthmarks. It would be best to utterly and completely destroy the identity of the struggling girl in the back seat. Doing so under these conditions was going to be a challenge. Besides, it was starting to rain. With each moment that passed, the thunder became louder and the downpour heavier.

Maybe I should wait. Maybe there's a better place?

Belinda's struggling in the back seat was making it hard for Michael to concentrate on doing things right. He needed some electrician's tape to shut her up. Maybe there was some in the trunk. He'd check. If there was, he could at least stifle her so he could think. After all, his early Christmas present back in the cabin had had silver electrician's tape over his pretty little mouth,

One area where Michael had gotten lucky was in the clothing department. He was no longer clad in an orange prison jumpsuit. The previous occupant of the cabin had been a rather portly man. Ike Isham's clothes, some of which were still hanging on hangers in the closet in the bedroom, had fit Michael perfectly. "Woodsman-fell-that-tree" flannel and overalls were not Pogo's normal style. *Still*, thought Michael with a smile, *at least it isn't a clown suit.*

Michael had had enough of dressing up as a clown. He only did it originally to satisfy his father-in-law, a guy whom he had never liked. His wife Marianne divorced him after the discovery of his sordid past. His father-in-law never came to the trial or visited Michael even once in prison.

And after all I did for him, too, he thought with bitterness. *It's not like I liked being a clown. I hate kids.*

After he gained notoriety as "the Clown Killer" he had capitalized on his infamy to paint a series of clown portraits while in prison. They had sold well. Everyone wanted a piece of Michael Clay or a painting by the most famous Killer Clown in history.

Yes, his clown paintings were exceedingly popular. He was only allowed to give the money to charitable causes. He was not allowed to personally profit. He had asked if he could donate the thousands of dollars to the Republican Party. In his clown heyday, he had once posed with George W. Bush's wife, Laura. She had personally autographed the picture of the two of them together. He liked the idea of donating money to the re-election campaign of George W. Bush. True, this was not an election year—yet— but Michael really wanted to see Laura's husband running the country for another term. He was a great president. Michael Clay could at least have as his legacy that he had helped George W. Bush retain power. The country would thank him for that.

As he drove, humming along to "The Sound of Settling" by "Death Cab for Cutie," Michael thought how apropos the song was.

He was driving a death car to a location where he hoped to kill a cutie, Belinda Chandler.

CHAPTER 42

October 31, 2003, Friday
The Cabin

After Earl Scranton placed the 911 call to the cops, he went to his unconscious daughter and tried to revive her. Shannon hit the floor as though she were a rag doll. Passed out like some floppy invertebrate toy.

Who could have done something so heinous to poor Gregory Tuttle? Earl knew that Greg had been screwing Cassie Chandler. It was inevitable in the life of a spouse of Andrea SanGiovanni—or so it seemed—that, at some point, Andrea's drive to become Slum Queen of Cedar Falls would impact negatively upon her personal life. Andrea's dedication to work had driven off Husband Number One, if rumor was correct. Was it any wonder that Husband Number Two had begun to feel neglected? Feeling neglected was something that Greg Tuttle would never feel again. He was deader than yesterday's road kill.

"Daddy! Daddy! Get me out of here!" Shannon Scranton was waking up. She wanted nothing more than to be gone from the smelly cabin in the woods, this house of horror, where she had just discovered a dismembered head in the refrigerator.

"Who would do something so horrible to Mr. Tuttle?" Shannon asked her father, who was gripping Shannon under the arms to help her to her feet.

"I don't know, Honey. We should go outside and wait for the police. Don't touch anything. Don't even glance at that blue tarp on your right as you leave." Saying this, of course, meant that Shannon was definitely going to look at that blue tarp on her right as she left.

All Shannon wanted to do was to help try to find her little brother Stevie. Now she was going to have to deal with the image of Gregory Tuttle's horrified expression on his severed head for the rest of her days. She could understand why poor Tad McGreevy had to take an entire year getting over everything he said he'd seen. But Tad had imagined it. Shannon was living it, up close and personal. Maybe some people would forget something so horrific, in time, but with Stevie Scranton still missing, it made Shannon, his sister, hysterical.

The revolving red cherry top of the first police car on the scene grew visible in the distance. It became bigger and brighter and louder as it bumped down the gravel road to the Isham cabin. The squad car screeched to a halt.

Charlie Chandler hopped out on the driver's side. His partner, Evelyn Hoeflinger, emerged slowly from the passenger side.

"What have we got here, Earl?"

Charles Chandler had been on the Cedar Falls police force for almost forty years. He had gone directly from high school graduation, to the altar with his pregnant girlfriend Cassie, to applying for a job with Cedar Falls' finest. Both his uncle and his father had been cops, so it was a logical choice for Charlie. It was a logical choice that was going to end soon. Charlie was being pressured to step down. Mandatory retirement loomed. He'd been giving that some thought. Charlie had no plan for his golden years.

When he'd joined the force, he needed a job fast. Cassie laid it on him that she was preggers when he was barely nineteen years old. The shotgun ceremony between the long-time high school sweethearts had taken place quickly. They lost that first child, a son. Cassie had seemed okay with that, but Charlie was heartbroken. This was his firstborn, a son that he had buried in a small white box in a ceremony attended only by immediate family. It broke Charlie's heart when the small box was lowered into the ground on a bitterly cold winter morning.

The couple tried again, but Cassie had trouble conceiving. It wasn't until 1984 that the Chandlers were successful in having Belinda. Belinda wasn't a boy, so Charlie wasn't nearly as enchanted with her as he had been at the prospect of having a son. By that time, he and Cassie had been married for almost twenty years. No children had come of the union— at least none that lived— until Belinda. Charlie realized that he'd have to make Belinda into the son he lost. There would be no new babies born into the Chandler household.

Belinda was nineteen now, no longer living at home. She was the exact same age that Charlie had been when he had married Belinda's mother in order to give their son his name. But Charlie was almost forty when Belinda was born to the aging couple. He was now fifty-eight—almost fifty-nine— years old. The department was insisting that he step aside soon. What did he have to show for the past twenty years?

The Chandlers had Belinda, of course. But Belinda was no longer the focal point of their lives. Charlie had his work with the police department, but he could tell that the Powers-That-Be were maneuvering to force the 58-year-old beat cop retire. Let the young lions have his job. In a bigger city, he'd already be gone, but Cedar Falls was still the middle of nowhere. They had let a few rules and regulations slide.

If I do retire, what will I do? thought Charlie.

Cassie filled her days with Lord-knows-what. She had adopted any number of screwy hobbies. She claimed she liked birdwatching, for instance, which Charlie Chandler thought was about as exciting as watching haircuts. When he saw Cassie pick up her binoculars from the kitchen table where they always were, he would get up and leave the room.

God forbid that she start warbling on about a crested sapsucker or some damned thing!

Charlie did not want to have to pretend to be interested in the same things that Cassie liked. It wasn't his nature. He just wanted her to amuse herself and leave him be.

Cassie came and went often on shopping trips. She couldn't be found for hours on end when she was in shopping mode. She worked a few hours on weekends at Hunter's Car Lot.

In the old days, when Belinda was little, Cassie had lavished attention on their only child. When Belinda turned eight, Cassie threw a huge party. All the little girls at the party came to Black's Tea Room in Waterloo. A manicurist did their nails. A magician performed his magic act. The parties went on until Belinda became old enough to protest that she just wanted her closest friends, girls like Shannon Scranton or Sharon McGreevy, to come spend the night or go skating or go to a movie.

The growing estrangement from his wife caused Charlie to focus more and more on his life in the police department. Without the police department, he felt he would have no identity at all. He felt like the Invisible Man in his own house. But at least he had his job, for the moment.

What am I supposed to do while Cassie is birdwatching and buying clothes and selling cars? Do I look like the kind of guy that likes to watch yellow-billed sapsuckers or sit and watch a 60-year-old woman try on lingerie?

That was how Charlie had explained to his partner, Evelyn Hoeflinger, why he kept on working, despite his arthritis, his dislike of the police bureaucracy, his bad heart, and his short temper. It was also why he began taking a little nip now and again: to stop constantly thinking about his impending retirement.

Charlie hadn't had a short fuse when he graduated from the Academy. Back then, life had looked a lot brighter. He had a new wife he loved and a son on the way. All that had come crashing down. "Life just walked away from me," Charlie once said to Evelyn, while they were on a particularly boring stakeout. "Sometimes you walk away from your life; sometimes, it walks away from you."

The most exciting crime that Charlie ever worked during his nearly 40-year career with the Cedar Falls police force was a riot in a park in The Heights. The Heights was an area quite close to the Waterloo/Cedar Falls border.

The Heights became the destination of choice for Mexican immigrants brought to town to staff Rath Packing Plant. It was the only area where they could afford housing. Once they got out of the Ramada Inn, their temporary hellhole of a home when they arrived en masse, the families found the most affordable housing options were in the rather elegant-sounding area dubbed The Heights

Charlie had once joked to Evelyn, "They ought to call that area either The Depths or Little Mexico."

The riot in Glendale Park resembled a bad casting of the Sharks and the Jets from West Side Story. Instead of Puerto Rican gangs, it was the townies versus the Mexican immigrants. From what Charlie could see, the immigrants were winning, hands down. They were ferocious fighters who would stop at nothing. It had taken twelve cops with billy clubs and mace—one of them a much younger Charlie Chandler— to break up that particular rumble in the park, back when the idea of immigrant workers brought to town to work the packing plant was new.

The white residents of the town didn't like the influx at all. They complained at City Council meetings, that the immigrants were ruining the town. "Sixty Minutes" did a special on how the town had gone downhill since the packing plant employees came. Yet, the children of the white residents of the town didn't want to work the jobs at the packing plant. Those jobs involved long hours and backbreaking labor with no insurance or benefits.

Alex and Roberto Jimenez, the boys caught half-heartedly fighting over the same girl (Heather Crompton) at school were from the Heights. That was where all the Mexican-American workers at the packing plant eventually ended up, once they graduated from the Ramada Inn. Alex and Roberto were cousins. Many of the Mexican workers were related. The Heights residents had large extended families. It was difficult to keep track of who was related to whom. Someone was always someone else's cousin or sister or half-brother or uncle or aunt.

Andrea SanGiovanni, a smart businesswoman (if not so smart as a wife) bought up as many of the small wood frame dwellings in The Heights as she could afford. Her divorce settlement money helped. Gregory Tuttle, her second husband, assisted her with leases and collecting rent. The ability to save money in the large Mexican families was non-existent. Any extra dollars were sent back to Mexico, to relatives who were struggling. Sometimes a personal visit had to be paid to tardy renters. It was Greg who made those visits.

As Charlie Chandler approached the huddled figures of Earl Scranton and his sobbing daughter, Shannon, standing together outside Old Man Isham's cabin, he greeted them with, "What's up, Earl?"

Earl and Charlie had been classmates at Sky High. They were the class of '63. They had played on the same varsity football team.

"Charlie, it's pretty unbelievable. Somebody cut up Greg Tuttle like he was a steer at the packing plant. Shannon here (a gesture towards his sniveling daughter) opened the refrigerator and found his head in the 'frig, severed from his body."

As Earl related this particular detail to his old classmate, Shannon began to whimper softly. He put his arms around her, patted her helplessly on the back, saying, "There, there, Honey."

Earl added, "You'd better go take a look for yourself, but put something over your face. It stinks like the rendering plant in there. I've seen a lot of animals slaughtered in my years at Rath, but I've never seen anything like this."

Charlie and Evelyn slowly approached the entrance to the cabin.

CHAPTER 43

October 31, 2003, Friday
Evelyn and Charlie

As Charlie Chandler and Evelyn Hoeflinger approached the cabin, Charlie said to his partner, "Maybe you should wait out here, Evelyn."

This was so like Charlie. He was so old school, so old-fashioned. In Charlie's world women did not become cops. They stayed home and baked cookies or watched birds or whatever it was that Cassie Chandler did in her spare time. And, quite frankly, from all the rumors that swirled about, Evelyn didn't really want to know too much about Cassie Chandler's extra-curricular activities.

What she did want to know was whether Charlie Chandler was going to "snap out" on her, as he sometimes did. Charlie had been getting loopier and loopier. Sometimes, his temper seemed out of control.

Although she didn't know this for a fact, Evelyn suspected that Charlie was drinking heavily. *Anything would be heavy for an arthritic nearly sixty-year-old cop with a pacemaker,* she thought.

Crime in Cedar Falls, before the massive influx of Mexican immigrants had damn near ruined Waterloo/Cedar Falls, had been minimal. Previously, when Charlie started on the job, the crime scene had been very minor. Robberies. Burglaries. The occasional rape. Muggings. Domestic violence incidents. They rarely had murder cases before the Mexican Mafia came to town. In Charlie's early days on the force, an exciting day might be rescuing a cat from a tree. Once the Hispanic macho men arrived, there was at least one knife fight every weekend and the local high school had put in a request for their own Officer Friendly, to help stem the violent tide, a spot filled by the insipid, one hundred and twenty pound weakling, Lenny McIntyre.

Everyone recognized that Charlie treated his partner Evelyn Hoeflinger as though she were a fragile china doll. He never respected her for her ability to defuse volatile situations. His protective father act was wearing very thin with Evelyn. Evelyn was right out of the Academy, only a few years older than Charlie had been when he had started on the force. She expected to be treated as an equal.

Evelyn sighed. None of the men on the Cedar Falls police force who were paired with women officers (of whom there were three) treated them as equals. There were jokes and comments and asides. You could certainly tell one generation of cops from another. At least Charlie was a kindly, paternal sort and wasn't hitting on her, as Rita Cernetisch said her partner Tom Tolliver sometimes did.

Evelyn liked having Charlie Chandler as her partner because he knew this town better than anybody on the force. He was a wealth of information about everyone. But she hated his patronizing "Little Woman" treatment of her. His suggestion that she remain outside what had to be a gory crime scene was just one example of that treatment.

"I'm going in, Charlie," Evelyn said. She drew her service revolver.

"What do you need that for?" Charlie looked genuinely puzzled.

"It's a crime scene, Charlie. What if the perp is still in there, hiding somewhere?"

Charlie Chandler actually snorted aloud. "Right," he responded, as he used his handkerchief to turn the doorknob to the cabin.

The pair entered a scene of appalling carnage. For Evelyn, it was a first. She had never seen a person who had been decapitated. She wondered what sort of force, what kind of weapon would be needed to completely cut through the bones and vertebrae to sever a person's head from the torso. Evelyn was holding her arm against her nose. The Scrantons had not been kidding about the odor. The two officers quickly exited the cabin, visibly shaken.

* * *

"Poor dumb bastard looks like he was tortured as well as beheaded." This remark came from Charlie. Evelyn looked at him, observing closely to see if he appeared to have heard the rumors about Cassie and Greg Tuttle. At least she knew where Charlie had been most of the night, if he needed an alibi. There was no way of telling how long Greg Tuttle had been dead until the forensics people arrived.

"We're going to need the FBI, Charlie," Evelyn said.

"Why? What possible good can calling in the FBI do?" Charlie retorted. He had been a rogue cop in his younger days. An independent cuss, he still didn't like turning his case over to the feds.

"Well, you know and I know that the FBI is better-prepared to do the fingerprint analysis and all the rest of it without having to wait weeks and weeks for it to come back from the crime lab in Des Moines." Cassie had a point. Although they did have more violent crimes than in the old days, the city was not likely to become the next location for a "C.S.I." television crime series.

"Let's just call it in to headquarters and see what they want us to do," Evelyn said.

"As you wish, M'Lady," said Charlie, parodying a grand bow. He returned to the squad car and Evelyn, who turned to interview the Scrantons, saw him reach for a flask in his back pocket and sip from it as he settled behind the wheel to call in the gruesome crime scene. She actually thought about asking him if she, too, could have a sip, after what they had just witnessed, but she didn't want to let on that she knew Charlie was a secret tippler.

CHAPTER 44

October 31, 2003, Friday
Andrea SanGiovanni

Word spread quickly that there had been a murder out at Old Man Isham's cabin. When the dead officer in the penitentiary van, Jim Kinkade, was discovered in Burnham Woods, not far from the cabin, the high school authorities, advised to do so by local law enforcement, canceled the Homecoming festivities.

"That stinks!" Jeremy Gustaffsson protested when he heard the news.

The game would still be played against Columbus High School, but there wasn't much the cops could do about canceling Halloween. The thought that an active serial killer was on the loose didn't make the local authorities want to encourage the teen-agers of the town to go out and park in desolate areas. When the identity of the escaped convict became public knowledge, the dance's fate was sealed. Michael Clay was from the area. He knew it well. He could be lurking anywhere. It was even possible that someone from his past might be harboring the fugitive. It was best if the Homecoming dance just didn't happen.

Principal Peter Puck felt a sense of relief that he wouldn't have to attend yet another of the boring rituals of youth. He put on a feigned show of disappointment when asked.

"Of course, it's too bad about the dance, but the game will still be played," he responded, when questioned by students and parents. "After all, better safe than sorry." Then he hustled off as though he had something important to do, which was never the case.

Jeremy wondered how he was going to be able to see Jenny SanGiovanni now. She couldn't use the excuse that she was going to Homecoming with a group of her girlfriends. Since it was her mother's new husband who had been found in the woods, trussed and butchered like a hog, Jenny's presence would be required at home, comforting her mother. He also had to call in and report his car as stolen, but he'd report it as having been taken from outside the gym.

"Shit! This really sucks. Here it is, my last year of high school, and they cancel the dance because wussy Gregory Tuttle went and got himself killed."

His companion, Stewie Truitt, said, "Well, you can still get together with Jenny, I'll bet." Jeremy said nothing.

Jeremy also failed to acknowledge the cause and effect of his kidnapping of Gregory Tuttle and abandoning him at the Isham cabin in the first place as a major contributing factor to Gregory Tuttle's murder. Ironic.

How was I supposed to know that that old queen Michael Clay would escape and kill him? AND steal my car! To be honest, Jeremy was far more upset to learn that his Pontiac LeMans had been stolen than to learn that Gregory Tuttle had been killed.

Jeremy cranked the volume on his father's truck stereo as AC/DC rocked and rolled. *Dad always plays oldies, but at least they're good oldies!*

Another reason Jeremy was upset was that Jeremy didn't like Andrea SanGiovanni, Jenny's mother. The feeling was mutual. Jeremy would usually follow mention of her name, when he was with his friends, by saying, "Andrea, the Dyke."

Word leaked to the community that Andrea was devastated by the news of her second husband's death. Her children gathered to watch over her, with Cynthia, Frank and Jenny arriving one by one. They were shocked to see their mother, who usually radiated strength and competence of an almost masculine sort, completely devastated.

"Serves her right," said Jeremy. "She should have taken care of her man. Tammy Wynette had it right, 'Stand By Your Man.' Jenny would stand by me, no matter what. That's what her mother should have been doing, instead of trying to corner the market in Slum City."

Jeremy's coterie of toadies, Stewie Truitt first and foremost, nodded their heads in agreement.

So far, there had not been anything to link Jeremy to any of the trouble. Jeremy was surprised to learn of Gregory Tuttle's death, but rather than feeling sad or upset, he simply viewed it as one less obstacle in his path to Jenny

SanGiovanni. Jeremy hadn't planned on killing Tuttle. In fact, he was glad he got the news early enough that he had not gone back to the cabin to release Tuttle at midnight. He had left Greg Tuttle tied up but otherwise unharmed. It was no concern of Jeremy's if Pogo went ahead and did the job for him.

This way, there's nobody to report that I harmed a hair on anyone's head. It's no skin off my ball sac. Maybe Tuttle will get blamed for Cassie Chandler's death—, if she turns up. People will probably think that Pogo killed her, too, thought Jeremy. He smiled the sly twisted smile of a psychopath.

He was amazed at his cleverness, although miffed that his maroon Pontiac was missing.

This was working out better than Jeremy had hoped. So far, nobody had reported Cassie Chandler missing. Jeremy was going to do everything in his power to get in touch with Jenny and see if she could at least sneak out and meet with him for a little while after the game. *If she isn't cheering at the game, maybe she can crawl out her bedroom window.*

Jenny had done that on two occasions over the summer, after her parents told her she couldn't see Jeremy. There was a tree conveniently near her window. Jenny had no difficulty getting in and out of the house unseen.

We could at least celebrate Halloween together this way.

Jeremy was pretty sure that Tad McGreevy never knew what hit him back in the SanGiovannis' garage. Tad was hit from behind. For all Tad knew, it might have been Gregory Tuttle who hit him in the head.

Yes, this is definitely working out well, so far.

I just hope my freakin' car is okay.

CHAPTER 45

Halloween: The Hospital
Jenny SanGiovanni

Jenny glanced at her mother's haggard face.

Why don't we just go home? she thought. It didn't make any sense to her. *Why are we just sitting here waiting for Tad to open his eyes? It's like a wake.*

She looked through her purse for her Kleenex pack. She gathered her scattered thoughts.

It might make some sense for me to wait. Tad's my friend. But Mom just wants to see if Tad can tell her what happened to Greg. What difference does that make, now?

The word had come to Andrea hours ago that Gregory Tuttle was dead. From her mother's stoic reaction, Jenny decided that she was in denial. There was no way that the family sitting up all night by Tad's bedside was going to bring Greg back from the dead. Jenny dabbed at her eye. She blew her nose for the hundredth time.

I shouldn't think this way. Tad is my best friend in the world. At least, my best male friend. I should want to be here when he wakes up, so I can make sure he's all right.

Jenny still remembered how nervous Tad had acted the very first time she met him at the movies.

Stevie was with him then. She dabbed at her eyes again and misted up. *Now, Stevie is missing. Tad is in the hospital. My stepfather is dead. What-the-hell happened? Who said that the only thing you can count on in life is change? Why do all my life changes have to be bad? It's like everything up until now was built on a foundation that collapsed. What can we count on, other than change? Why is the change almost never a good thing?* She glanced at the television set, set to "mute," where news of a horrible earthquake somewhere was playing. *It's like we're God's little playthings. He just wants to build us up to tear us down.*

Jenny wasn't a deep thinker, but she remembered hearing the police officer say, to Stevie Scranton's parents, "Sometimes, people just walk away from their lives." The policeman was suggesting that Stevie had run away from home. The entire police department was still operating on the theory that Stevie voluntarily left town. The Scrantons refused to accept that theory. The Scrantons were actively searching for Stevie.

At the time, Jenny had thought the policeman sounded like a moron.

Who walks away from their life? Especially when they're only sixteen years old?

Jenny thought that Tad's comment to her, afterwards, made more sense. He had looked at her with a sober express. Then he leaned over and whispered, "Sometimes, people's lives walk away from them."

Jenny hadn't asked what he meant at the time. She didn't want to appear dumb. Now, she hoped Tad would wake up. She hoped he'd be the same old Tad, her good friend, so she could ask him exactly what he meant that day, because she was beginning to get a glimpse of a future that changed with the wind. It wasn't very reassuring. Especially if you were only sixteen years old.

Although Jenny did little deep philosophical musing, Tad McGreevy often did. Jenny was usually cheerful and upbeat. She was also usually busy with school. Academic activities. Extra-curricular things. Cheerleading. Band. Chorus. Speech. Drama. Candystripers. If you kept busy enough, you could block out "the real world" outside the narrow school world. Jenny took part in nearly everything. You name it, and Jenny was involved with it. All that activity filled her life. It filled her mind, so that she didn't have too much time to think about her father in Boulder. She tried not to think about anything else that was painful. Sometimes, she felt like a hamster on a treadmill. Constantly doing and on the go. Often in perpetual motion to quiet the sad thoughts that tried to creep into her mind.

Stevie Scranton had once said, to Tad, "Why do you like Jenny SanGiovanni so much? She has all the emotional depth of a puddle. She's got to be dumber than dirt if she goes out with Jeremy Gustaffsson."

Stevie wasn't trying to pick a fight. He just wondered.

Tad had defended Jenny's intelligence. It was true that Jenny got good grades. Of course, it didn't hurt to be a dead ringer for Reese Witherspoon when seventy-five percent of your high school teachers were male. Jenny's upbeat attitude and winning smile always carried the day if it meant the difference between a higher or lower grade. Jenny studied hard enough. She had two older siblings who had done well in school. They had warned her about what teachers would give you a fair shake and which ones were to be avoided at all costs.

The only one she had tried to avoid,(but had been unable to keep off her schedule for next year was Mr. Kellogg), the chemistry teacher. Sky High didn't have anyone else qualified to teach chemistry. Jenny's mom said she should take chemistry, biology and physics if she was serious about a career in nursing.

I mentioned once, in fifth grade, that I wanted to be a nurse, after I had my tonsils out. Now, I'm stuck with that identity six years later, she thought ruefully.

Jenny usually did what she was supposed to do when she was supposed to do it. Andrea and Greg, as well as Frank and Cynthia had made it sound like chemistry was a "must-have" course for Jenny's medical career of the future.

The truth was, Jenny didn't know what she wanted to be when she grew up. She wondered when or if she would ever know what she wanted to be. She wondered when anyone was really grown up. She had seen some grown men who sure didn't act "grown up." Mr. Kellogg was one of them. He was always ogling all the young girls in his classes. He seemed particularly taken with Heather Crompton, Jenny's good friend. She dreaded next year when she'd be stuck in his class so he would be ogling her.

Some of the other girls she hung out with…Janice Kramer, for instance…talked about getting married as quickly as possible after high school.

That is definitely not for me, Jenny thought.

The truth was that Jeremy's constant pushing for sex had turned her off on sex ever since last summer when she had sneaked out of her room so she and Jeremy could hang out together.

He's like a walking hormone! Jenny thought.

Jeremy was good-looking, but he was always trying to give her a back-rub or cop a feel. He wasn't even subtle about it. Jenny felt like a piece of meat around him. Other times, when he would open up a little bit about his family, she felt sorry for him.

Once, at the movies, she had pulled her coat up around herself, like a blanket, in the frigid Cineplex. It wasn't more than thirty seconds after she draped her coat over herself to keep warm that Jeremy's hands were under the coat heading for her breasts. She didn't feel like being mauled in the theater with all their friends watching. Jeremy would have had her give him a B.J. right then and there if Jenny would go along with it, which, of course, she would not.

I really don't get what the Big Deal is about having sex. Kissing is nice, and being held and told you're pretty is nice, but Jeremy is never satisfied with just that. He's always pushing the envelope, always wanting more. More than I can give him, anyway. More than I WANT to give him. I don't want to have sex with anybody when I'm only fifteen years old. If I did, it wouldn't be with Jeremy.

Jenny liked the fact that Jeremy was the BMOC on campus, the starting quarterback, the leading scorer in basketball. She liked that the other kids considered him cool. And Jeremy was cute.

"Cute," Jenny had once joked, "If you like your men to look and act like a Hitler youth."

The other girls she was with had tried to compare Jeremy to the much hipper Daniel Craig, but Jeremy was much too tall to be compared to Daniel Craig, although he did have the muscled torso part down. The truth was that Jenny liked Jeremy Gustaffsson only when he behaved, when he opened up and talked to her, communicated with her. That was not very often. He was so aggressive, so needy, so "in pursuit" at all times. And, although Jenny was not Einstein, Jeremy definitely was not someone you could talk deeply with about the plot of a movie or a book. He was about as sensitive as a nail gun and twice as hard, most of the time.

"Come on, Baby," he would say after they'd been parked somewhere necking. "It isn't good for an athlete to have blue balls."

Jenny would pull away from the persistent Jeremy. She would laugh off his sexual advances and tell him she had to get home. Lately, the more she was alone with him the more aggressive he became.

The reputation Jeremy enjoyed as a hunk was in stark contrast to Tad's reputation at Sky High.

Everybody thought Tad was weird. It was a holdover from the year he had been out of school and tutored at home. His parents had said it was because he had mononucleosis. Other classmates had whispered about Tad's nervous breakdown when he was eight. Jenny had not met Tad until that night at the movies, eight years later. He seemed as normal as anyone else, to her, but a lot more sensitive, and considerably cuter than most of the boys in the class.

One of Jenny's girlfriends had commented on Tad's pale complexion. She said, "Tad always looks like he just saw a ghost. Or like he IS a ghost." Everyone had laughed, including Jenny, but, secretly, she felt guilty for laughing at her friend. He was pale, in a Conan O'Brien way, but he had dark hazel eyes and beautiful brown wavy hair. Tad McGreevy had definitely improved in the looks department since age eight.

Jenny had the feeling that Tad would be gentle. He would really care for her, if they were boyfriend and girlfriend. By contrast, she felt as though any warm body would suffice for what Jeremy had in mind.

Tad had given her such a soul-searching look when he made the comment about life walking away from you that she felt as though he could see right into her heart.

He probably sees how guilty I feel that I'm not as strung out over Stevie's disappearance as he and the Scrantons are.

Jenny didn't have anything against Stevie. She just didn't have anything *for* Stevie. He was kind of a weird nebbishy-little kid. It didn't help Tad to crawl out from under his "psycho" reputation to hang out with Stevie, the class clown.

On the other hand, Jenny thought, *It's really kind of touching that Tad has always been such a loyal friend of Stevie's, because Stevie looked weird when he was little and he has only gotten weirder-looking as he's gotten older.*

Needless to say, Stevie Scranton had never had a date with anyone. Perhaps the same was true of Tad, but Jenny had seen how a few of her more predatory female friends had been eyeing him lately. One had even whispered, "Nice buns!" when Tad walked away from them, down the hall to his locker.

Jenny wondered if Jeremy would ever be as loyal to his friends or girlfriends as Tad was.

I wonder if I even qualify as Jeremy's girlfriend any more. My folks said I couldn't keep going out with him. I really don't like the way he's been pressuring me. I'm a little bit scared of what he'll do when I really am sixteen.

She had a heavy heart just thinking about how the pressure from Jeremy would increase when she was no longer underage "jailbait" on her December 27th birthday.

Then, sitting there watching her mother and siblings sleep, she had a Eureka moment, an epiphany. *I don't have to go out with Jeremy any more. Homecoming isn't going to happen. It's been canceled. I can just quit seeing Jeremy. No obligations. He can't MAKE me go out with him, after all. I really just don't want to deal with him—.with IT… any more.*

With this thought, Jenny felt better than she had felt in weeks. It was as though a huge weight had been lifted from her slender shoulders. Then she thought, *Who should I date for the rest of the year, if I don't go out with Jeremy? After all, Prom will be coming up in the spring.*

With the same light-dawning-in-the-forest clarity, it occurred to her that Tad would take her to any social event she wanted to attend—not that a good many other boys in the junior or senior class wouldn't line up to take her out, if they heard that she were available. Some might shy away for fear of Jeremy Gustaffsson's famous temper, but Tad wouldn't.

Tad would like me for me, she thought. *He wouldn't always be pressuring me for sex. He would listen to what I say.* She had noticed that Jeremy hardly ever listened to anything she said…really listened. To be honest, they didn't do much talking about anything when they were alone together. All Jeremy wanted to do was get her alone. After that came the groping.

At first, Jenny had been flattered that Jeremy Gustaffsson, the school's leading scorer in several sports, was that "in" to her. Then she realized that he would never be satisfied until he "scored" with her, as well. Jenny was no different than the opposing players on Waterloo Columbus' football team. They were a force to be overcome by the persistent Jeremy Gustaffsson and Jenny SanGiovanni was, likewise, simply an obstacle to be overcome. Jeremy was so used to wearing down his opponents, whether they were team members or his parents, that he would never quit. That was when the conflict and the pressure had started to build between them.

The moment she realized that Jeremy's hardscrabble childhood made him an insatiable suitor, she knew that she had to break it off with him completely. This time, it wouldn't be because her parents were on her case. It would be of her own free will.

She was sympathetic to the hard-luck life Jeremy had lived with his alcoholic father, his hyperactive little brothers, and the Gustaffsson family's constant moves around the countryside following the horses to various harness racing tracks.

But enough is enough, she thought. *I'm not going out with Jeremy Gustaffsson any more.*

With that thought, she also realized that she was very glad they were all waiting for Tad to awaken from the coma. She hoped she would be there when he did awaken. No sooner had Jenny formed that thought, contradictory to how she had been feeling before her realization of her options, than her mother walked over to her and said, "Officer Peterson says we should all go home and try to get some sleep. I'm beginning to think he's right. Even if Tad does come out of it in the next couple hours, his family will want to be with him first. Gather your things. Wake Frank and Cynthia. We're going home. I've got funeral arrangements to make tomorrow. First, I'll have to stop by the office to make sure that it can run smoothly without me for a few days."

CHAPTER 46

Halloween Day
Andrea SanGiovanni

Jenny had been getting very tired of sitting at the hospital waiting for Tad McGreevy to awaken. Her mother had really been getting on her nerves. The presence of so many cops who kept asking the same questions over and over hadn't made the night go any faster. The announcement that they were going to leave was welcome news.

Jenny had wandered down the hall to the candy machine during the evening, then thought better of it and returned to the family waiting area where Andrea, Frank and Cynthia sat silently. The SanGiovannis sat on one side of the room. Jeanne, Jim and Sharon McGreevy sat on the other. Tad might hold the key to the question of how, exactly, Greg Tuttle ended up a corpse in Old Man Isham's abandoned cabin, his head inside an old Norge refrigerator.

When Andrea announced that they were leaving, as she just had, Jenny felt a tremendous rush of relief. *Twice in one night,* she thought. *Before, when I realized I could just break it off with Jeremy, and now that we're leaving.*

The McGreevys, of course, were just praying that Tad would wake up at all. If and when he did wake up, they prayed that he would be normal. Jim McGreevy didn't have as much hope in that particular area as Sharon and Jeanne did. He wasn't sure if his only son would ever emerge from his unconscious state. If he did, what would he be like? Memories of how Tad had behaved after his eighth birthday party kept flooding back.

For her part, Andrea SanGiovanni, getting her keys out to drive the kids home, knew that the only way she was going to be able to survive the pain of Greg's loss was to throw herself back into work. All the things that Greg had previously assisted her with were now going to have to be handled by Andrea alone. She knew that she would be criticized for this plan, her survival plan. The townsfolk already called her the Slum Queen behind her back. They thought she didn't know it, but she did.

Let them grow up like me, with a drunk for a dad and no money in the house for food half the time, and then let them come and criticize me for being ambitious, she thought. Sullen. Defiant.

Andrea remembered when Joan Rivers' husband, Edgar, committed suicide. Joan had thrown herself back into her nightclub act and other projects immediately. Joan Rivers, too, received harsh criticism for going back to work so soon and so energetically, but grief was a killer. Liam Neeson, after Natasha Richardson's death, said, "I think I survived by running away...running away to work." That was Andrea's plan. It was the only plan she had.

I can't just sit home and think about Greg. I can't do it. I'm better off working until I can't feel anything any more. We, as a family, are better off going home. The SanGiovannis headed for the hospital emergency room exit. It was interesting that Jenny threw herself into everything related to school to keep from feeling things, and her mother planned to throw herself into everything connected to work to keep from feeling.

Andrea felt as though everything she had worked to achieve was built on a bed of shifting sand. Everything could be taken away from you by chance or circumstance. Just when you thought you had worked hard to provide a secure future for your family, the rug could be yanked out from under you. The life she had built was walking away from her, dropping through her fingers, disappearing like a cloud formation as it changed shape in the heavens.

She had tried so hard to put behind her the rejection she felt when Jenny's father left her for another woman. Andrea would always know that she had been the one who had been left, not the other way around. She thought that she and Jeff had a happy home: three great kids, all the creature comforts. Then he came to her and told her he was profoundly unhappy.

Although he had denied that another woman was involved, soon after this statement, he remarried Tammy Tolliver and they moved to Boulder. This, too, seemed like a betrayal of the American dream Andrea had worked so hard to achieve. It wasn't supposed to be like this. She and Jeff were supposed to be happy in their half million-dollar home with their three beautiful children.

Why wasn't Jeff happy with me? Why is no man happy with me?

Andrea knew that both of her husbands had come to the conclusion that she was neglecting them, neglecting the family unit because she wasn't at home making dinner or cleaning or playing June Cleaver. The fact was that she had a compulsive need to achieve and to succeed. She needed to prove to her parents that she had worth. She needed to ensure the financial stability she had not known as a child.

She also knew that, like Scarlett O'Hara in the classic *Gone with the Wind* a relevant line, for her personally, was, "As God is my witness, I will never go hungry again." Andrea wasn't absolutely sure that was the exact line, but the meaning resonated.

She was going to make damn sure that her own family never wanted for anything. Her kids were going to have the opportunity to go to the best colleges and live in the finest houses in town. These were all things she had not had as a child. If it meant she had to work long days while other women shopped or gossiped over lunch, that was just the way it would have to be.

Her mother had taught her, years ago, that no woman could depend on a man for her self-worth or her income or her status. She had learned that rule well and had self-cast herself as the primary breadwinner in the family, even though Jeff SanGiovanni made a good living as the local Budweiser distributor. Andrea would not have had to work at all, or, at least, not as hard as she did work. That became grounds for many arguments in the months leading up to Jeff's announcement that he wanted out of the marriage.

How could he just walk away from his life...from our life? That wasn't supposed to happen.

Andrea, on the other hand, was perhaps in denial, pretending that when they got home, Greg would be there to greet them and rub her feet, as he always did when she had put in a particularly long day. He would hug her and tell her that he loved her. Andrea was hurting, right now. She didn't think she could hurt more, but she was going to find out that she was wrong.

The only blessing, so far, in all of the night's developments, was that they had not yet asked Andrea SanGiovanni to come to the coroner's office and identify Gregory Tuttle's mutilated corpse.

Be thankful for small favors, she thought.

And then the door of the ICU opened with a pneumatic "swish" and she and her children walked into the cool, crisp, ozone-charged night air.

CHAPTER 47

Halloween Night
Pogo

The rain was coming down harder. Lightning strikes were illuminating the autumn leaves. Michael Clay was not going to wade into some Iowa field in this sort of weather just to take care of Belinda Chandler. He'd have to deal with his captive at some other location.

Belatedly, Michael had rigged a gag for Belinda. He had removed one of her socks. Using a shoestring from Belinda's tennis shoe, Pogo had stuffed the sock in Belinda's mouth and tied it around her head with the shoestring. Since her arms were bound behind her back, she couldn't remove the gag. At last, Pogo had the silence he needed to think.

The worst part of town is going to be nearest the packing plant, he thought.

There always used to be plenty of empty properties ringing that godforsaken area of town, bordered on one side by the railroad tracks, with the smell from the packing plant drifting down to Deer Run and The Heights. Michael was not as up on the current status of real estate in his old hometown, but he was pretty sure that some eternal truths prevailed. One of them was that the worst part of town always had a railroad track running through it. The other was that it usually had a noisy or smelly business nearby. Sometimes, a toxic one.

Michael turned the dented maroon hood of the Pontiac towards the shady side of town. When he had crossed the tracks and was heading towards the north...always considered the poorest part of the city...he began paying attention to the houses that were boarded up. The authorities always did that, to prevent vandals from breaking out the glass in the windows to gain entry. With the tools Michael had taken from the trunk of the Pontiac, those Jeremy took from the McGreevys' garage, he was pretty well prepared for any household task.

He could remove a door at the hinges or remove a head at the neck or dispatch anyone who got in his way with a few quick thrusts of the deadly-looking kitchen knife he had removed from the Isham cabin. He had also taken Gregory Tuttle's bank card. Using information he extracted while conducting some creative questioning, Pogo sailed through an ATM outlet and removed the maximum amount in cash. He pulled the flannel collar of the shirt from Old Man Isham's cabin up around his neck and face, to obscure his features from the security cameras.

Now Michael had money, weapons, a car and cash, but he could see that he would need to act to take care of the obnoxious girl in the backseat. His other option was to keep her with him and use her as a hostage. In the event he was located, she could be a worthwhile bargaining chip. He'd have to think about that. She had been so loud and annoying that he couldn't wait to slice her up. Now that she was gagged, he was able to ignore the muffled noises she was making. It wouldn't be long before the cops began to look for Jeremy Gustaffsson's vehicle. He had to think of stealing a different car from the neighborhood he was now entering, but it couldn't be helped.

Or could it?

The last street on the right after he crossed the tracks and near the Protestant cemetery (the Catholics were buried on the south side of town, where the rich people lived) had several houses with boarded-up windows. Pogo selected one that sat further back from the others and had an attached garage. Neighbors on either side were similarly boarded-up abandoned houses. Nobody would be looking out his or her window to see Pogo breaking and entering.

If I can put the car inside a garage for a while, maybe I won't have to find another car, he thought.

For a guy fresh out of prison, Pogo was developing real-life coping skills.

The rain was pouring down now. Lightning provided much-needed illumination as it lit up the sky in jagged electric arcs. Pogo's efforts with the crowbar to pry the plywood off the back door of the older two-story house were successful. He was able to pry the plywood covering off and smash the glass of the back door window in less than five minutes. He reached inside, grabbed the doorknob, and opened the back door.

Next, he had to half-drag, half-carry the uncooperative teen-ager from the backseat of the Pontiac into the dark kitchen of the old house. Belinda was dead weight.

But not as dead as she will be, thought Pogo.

Although he was anxious to take care of business and get on his way to Mexico, overwhelming fatigue now gripped him. After all, it had been eight years since Michael Clay was convicted of murder and sent to Fort Madison Penitentiary. Eight years of hard labor had followed, working in the furniture shop and the machine shop. Some inmates were even hired out to local farmers, although Michael never had been. He had been judged too high a security risk. Michael Clay had been fifty-eight years old at the time of his arrest and conviction. The eight years since then had been harsh ones. He was sixty-six years old. Right now, he felt every single day of it.

He regarded his prey, Belinda Chandler.

She's not going anywhere, he thought. *And neither am I, tonight. The car is safely inside the garage. Nobody will be looking for me here. I've got no connection with this house or this neighborhood.*

As much as he wanted to put an end to the ceaseless annoyance that Belinda Chandler represented, he was exhausted. He needed to rest for just a few hours.

With that final thought, he dropped Belinda to the cold linoleum of the kitchen floor, where she landed with a dull thud. Moving on into the poorly carpeted living room, Michael threw the blanket from the trunk of Jeremy Gustaffsson's car on the floor of the deserted house and instantly fell asleep.

CHAPTER 48

Halloween Night
Pogo and Belinda

When Michael Clay threw Belinda to the linoleum floor of the slum kitchen and staggered off into the carpeted living room to collapse in exhaustion, Belinda did not sleep. She looked around the room, assessing her options.

There was a very old stove with a broiler drawer at the bottom. The black handle to the broiler portion of the stove was broken in half. The broken handle had a sharp edge. It became Belinda's goal to cut through the ropes that bound her hands behind her back by rubbing the ropes against the sharp edge of the broiler oven door handle.

First, she moved her face back and forth across the handles of the broiler oven handle, dislodging the shoelaces that were holding her gag in place. She spat out the sock that Pogo had stuffed in her mouth, working quietly, with desperation. The white sock tasted like sweat. Even though it was her own sweat, it was disgusting.

Not yet, she thought. *Don't start screaming yet. Get your hands free. Maybe you can even sneak out of here while that sadist is still sleeping*

Belinda worked to cut through or dislodge the ropes that bound her hands behind her back, ropes that cut deeply and painfully into her wrists. There had been rope in the trunk of Jeremy's car. There was a shovel in there, too. Belinda had no idea why there would be a shovel in the trunk of Jeremy Gustaffsson's car. It was just as well that she didn't know the truth: Jeremy Gustaffsson had used the shovel to bury her mother in a shallow grave near Ike Isham's cabin three hours ago.

Belinda knew nothing regarding Gregory Tuttle's torture and death, which was also just as well.

When Belinda saw Jeremy Gustaffsson's familiar maroon Pontiac LeMans slowing to a stop for her, she didn't immediately realize that it was not Jeremy Gustaffsson behind the wheel. Still upset over her spat with Kenny Kellogg, by the time she realized that it wasn't someone she knew driving the car, Michael Clay had locked all the doors. He warned her not to scream. She had screamed anyway, reflexively. In fact, she kept screaming right up until that bastard had stuffed her own dirty socks in her mouth and tied them around her head with shoestrings from her own tennies.

Rope. He had to stop and remove rope from the trunk, warning her before he fetched the roughly braided hemp that her passenger side door was locked. It would do no good to try to escape. She had tried to open the door to run, anyway. Pogo was right. It was locked from the driver's side control panel. Pogo also had a knife in his lap. It looked like some prop from a pirate movie. *No, not a pirate movie, more like that Halloween movie*, Belinda thought. It was one big ass knife.

She was no longer a girl walking home alone, angry, after a rendezvous with Kenny Kellogg at her girlfriend Billy's place in the woods, but a damsel in distress held captive in one of the worst parts of town by a crazy-ass nut job with a big hunting knife. Belinda had not recognized Pogo. Michael Clay had been in prison for eight years. Belinda was only eleven years old when news of Pogo the Killer Clown's arrest and trial filled the local airwaves.

Working with determination, she was able to slip one hand free from the thick itchy rope. Slowly, she was able to wriggle the second hand free from its prison. Both hands were numb from being pinioned behind her back. She began untying her feet, which were bound together at the ankles.

Belinda had been working on freeing herself for so long that she could see, through the kitchen window that the sun was coming up over the neighbor's garage. The kitchen looked out over a narrow alley with detached garages set along the narrow lane, the garages standing there like sentinels saluting the sunrise.

Her circulation had been impaired by the tight ropes. Belinda felt woozy as she cautiously began to get to her feet. She finally managed to stand, barefoot, and tiptoed towards the back door of the kitchen. To do this, she had to pass the open door to the room where Pogo lay.

Just as she was reaching for the doorknob, she felt the big man grab her from behind. Belinda began screaming, yelling as loudly as she could.

This startled the woman whose key had just opened the locked back door, Andrea SanGiovanni, the realtor selling the house. Andrea was as shocked to see Belinda as Belinda was to see her. In fact, Andrea dropped her keys and reflexively put her hands up in a defensive posture in front of her face. Both of the women were terrified by the large man in the flannel shirt who was now holding the large knife to Belinda's neck.

"Come in. Sit down on the floor. Don't make a sound or I'll slit her throat, and then I'll slit yours." Pogo sounded like he meant it. He scooped up Andrea's keys, picking them up from the floor where she had dropped them in surprise. The key ring featured a picture of Andrea, Jenny, Frank, Cynthia and Jeff SanGiovanni. The key ring was the kind you make as a Christmas gift for family. Andrea did as she was told, her head spinning.

This is like a bad dream. This can't be happening. Andrea was still in shock over everything that had happened. Now this.

After leaving the hospital, going home, cleaning up and getting a few hours of sleep, Andrea had decided to check on the work the plumbers were supposed to have completed on this property. If it was done, she could rent the small house immediately. She had a Mexican-American family that wanted to take possession. Andrea knew the Jimenez children, cousins Alex and Roberto Jimenez, because both boys were crazy about Heather Crompton. Jenny had told Andrea about the knife fight between the two boys over Heather's affections. Heather actually loved the attention, Jenny told her mom.

"Two boys are fighting over me!" Heather had squealed on the phone. Jenny had tried to explain that it wasn't cool that one boy attacked another one with a knife, all because they both liked the same girl, but Heather was drunk with the romantic nature of it.

"I've never had two boys fight over me before," she burbled, seemingly not even hearing Jenny's admonitions.

"What if one of them had been seriously hurt, Heather? Would you think it was so cool then?"

Jenny's reasoning with Heather did no good. Heather was, quite simply, drunk with power.

In the old days, Andrea could have sent Greg to check on the work in this neighborhood, but, after she checked out this property and told her secretary to let the Jimenez family fill out the proper papers to become her new tenants, she was on her way to the local funeral home. She had to take care of funeral arrangements for Gregory Tuttle. This stop had been the last work-related stop she planned to make this week, a week of mourning that she was organizing in her usual efficient, businesslike fashion, trying to keep from thinking about what it all meant.

This house in the Heights might be the last stop Andrea SanGiovanni ever made.

All Andrea could think of to do was to try to calm the hulking figure who was holding a knife to the frightened young girl's neck. She thought she recognized the girl. In her terror, she couldn't think of her name.

"What are you doing? Don't hurt her. Put the knife down." Andrea spoke evenly, with authority, addressing the hulking brute.

These were fairly stupid things to say, but Andrea was heavily dosed with Xanax and still in shock from the death of her husband. Unlike Belinda Chandler, she did recognize Michael Clay, aka Pogo the Clown. Her mind was slowly beginning to deal with the fact that Michael Clay had killed her husband. Now he might kill her, too.

If it had been just her own life at stake, Andrea would have made a run for it. With Belinda involved, she dare not. She was trying to stay on an even keel, trying to assess the situation, trying to think her way through to find a way to keep them both alive.

Belinda Chandler, meanwhile, was screaming as loudly as she had ever screamed in her life. Most of it was just noise. But amongst the noise was the phrase, "Don't kill me," repeated over and over. It was really beginning to annoy Michael Clay. He hauled off and slugged Belinda right in the face. The terrified teenager slumped to the linoleum floor, unbound, unconscious.

Michael Clay approached Andrea SanGiovanni.

"Lie face-down on the floor," he said. His voice, like gravel, sounded like pain.

Andrea, seeing little opportunity for effective resistance, did as Pogo asked.

"Put your hands behind your back."

Again, Andrea complied. She felt rough rope being wrapped around her wrists, knotted, and pulled tight.

Then, she saw Pogo approach the now-unconscious figure of Belinda Chandler and re-tie her hands behind her back. Pogo replaced the makeshift gag that Belinda had removed.

"There," said Pogo. "That ought to shut her up for a while."

It would, indeed, shut Belinda up. Belinda was now in no condition for conversation. She was unconscious. She had a broken jaw, a fractured skull and a concussion from the force of Pogo's blow. He might be old, but he was still a 300 pound powerfully-built man who had overpowered much bigger prey.

Outside the small house, the two Jimenez cousins, Alex and Roberto, were just pulling up in the alley when they heard high-pitched screaming. They noticed, through the window of the garage, a car that had not been there during their visit yesterday. A female voice was heard screaming, "Don't kill me!"

The Jimenez family was planning on taking possession of the house by week's end. They had been sent over by their family to check on the plumbing repairs that the landlady had said would be done by today. In fact, the landlady, herself, Mrs. SanGiovanni, had said she would be there to show them around the house and point out the improvements. She was supposed to bring the paperwork.

Now, with screaming coming from the house, the boys rushed into the house and into the fray. There was nothing they liked more than a good fight. Seeing the pudgy man and the two bound women on the floor, the boys rushed at Michael Clay.

Unfortunately, Michael Clay had more than one large knife in his possession. He shoved the large butcher knife into Alex's stomach and grabbed a second one from the small of his back where he had concealed it. Alex dropped in his tracks, grimacing in pain. Roberto was still bandaged from the fight the two boys had with each other at school over Heather Crompton. His arm was in a cast and a sling. He used the cast to protect himself as Michael slashed at him with the second knife. The first knife was currently embedded deep in his cousin Alex's stomach.

Pogo, true to his nickname, hopped over the prone women bound on the floor and ran for the garage. He was able to open the garage door and start the engine of the Pontiac. Roberto checked on Alex very quickly and dialed 911 on his cell phone. Then, Roberto, more brave than smart (he always said, "I'm the brave one, not the smart one.") threw the phone at Andrea SanGiovanni, saying, "Tell them where we are. I'm going after that son-of-a-bitch."

Pogo led. Roberto, cast and all, gave chase in his own vehicle. It was a car chase between a souped-up, heavily-decorated Monte Carlo lowrider and Jeremy Gustaffsson's maroon Pontiac LeMans.

The race was on.

CHAPTER 49

Morning after Halloween
Race to the River

Pogo had a headstart on Roberto Jimenez. For one thing, Roberto's lowrider Monte Carlo had starter issues. The boys had been too busy working on putting in solid lifters and the hydraulic system to make the car dance, like the cars of the other members of their gang, the Latin Kings. Ordinary things like issues with the starter had been ignored. The car always started...eventually. It just didn't always catch on the first try.

Whenever someone criticized this, the two would just say, "It's no different than that piece of crap lawnmower Poppy has. You just have to keep trying. Turn it over a few times is all."

And that, in fact, was what Roberto now had to do before he could begin his pursuit of the fleeing Pontiac.

Back in the house, Andrea SanGiovanni rushed to Alex Jimenez' side. She grabbed the hilt of the bloody knife and pulled it from his stomach, despite the excruciating pain she knew it was causing. She used the bloody knife to free Belinda Chandler's rope-bound hands and feet. The police were already on their way, thanks to Roberto's 911 call before handing his cell phone off to Andrea. (Maybe Roberto was more than just "the brave one." Maybe he was also "the smart one.")

As soon as Belinda was free from the ropes that bound her, Andrea instructed Belinda in a desperate attempt to try to save Alex's life. Alex was groaning and moaning in extreme pain. He was doubled up on the floor, clutching his stomach, bleeding profusely. Blood everywhere. Andrea hoped that the Cedar Falls EMT's rescue times were quick.

Otherwise, this kid doesn't stand a chance, she thought.

Because of Jenny's interest in a nursing career, all of the SanGiovannis had taken a number of first-aid courses at the local hospital where Jenny was a candystriper. Some of the things they had learned did not apply now (no heart attack here), but some of them did.

"Quick! Take off your blouse. Place it over the wound. Use it to staunch the flow. Press down hard!" Belinda did as she was told. Beliinda had no sense of false modesty over removing her blouse. After all, she had on a perfectly acceptable Victoria's Secret bra and she had been totally nude in bed with her chemistry teacher approximately four hours ago. Now was not the time to quibble.

Andrea spoke with the 911 operator.

"What is your emergency?"

"We have a young male who has been stabbed in the stomach. He's bleeding out."

"You need to find something and put pressure on the wound," said the dispatcher.

"Yes, we're already doing that," Andrea answered.

"What is your address?" the dispatcher asked next.

" We are at 511 Fremont Street in the Heights. Look for a white house with green shutters. You'll see a silver Prius parked in the alley." Andrea was describing her own car. She had seen the taillights of Jeremy's car disappearing with Pogo behind the wheel and noted Roberto's attempts to give chase. It had taken three attempts to start the souped-up Monte Carlo. Andrea doubted that a Monte Carlo that old could compare to the Pontiac Lemans Jeremy was always tinkering with. But she was rooting for Roberto.

Andrea didn't realize that Alex and Roberto were major gearheads.... boys who loved to tinker with cars. One of the social things of the Latin Kings were competitions where the souped-up lowriders were made to "dance." There were also chicken races involving the cars where the fastest car won. The 1980 Monte Carlo was plenty fast, but was it as fast as Jeremy Gustaffsson's Pontiac?

Meanwhile, in the Monte Carlo giving chase, Roberto had cranked the stereo of the car. It was blaring Hispanic music. The only song Andrea would have recognized, had she been able to hear it, was "La Bamba," an old Richie Vallens song recently covered by a local band, "Los Amigos."

Michael Clay was driving as though he were the devil himself. He was heading for the bridge over the Cedar River. If he could cross that bridge and make it onto the new Interstate that led to the east, he could exit onto gravel roads that led to nowhere. In the dark, no one would be able to find this car in the tall foliage of autumn's husked cornfields. Michael had money, clothing and weapons. All he had to do was find a remote farm, steal a different car, abandon this one, and be on his way south.

But, for the moment, he had to outrun one of the Latin Kings, Roberto Jimenez, who, if he weren't the devil himself, was a good imitation of His Satanic Majesty.

Roberto and Alex, in addition to installing the superior hydraulic system for the lowrider (the ride suffered, but the car danced like a ballerina), rather than the cheaper bladder system that other gang members used, had installed an after-burner device. During drag races, this would give the car an edge at the starting line. Alex called the vehicle "the Batmobile."

When Roberto saw the Pontiac approaching the bridge, he threw the switch on the after-burner device. The Monte Carlo accelerated as though its fuel tank had exploded. The Monte Carlo came so close to Pogo's bumper that, as Michael Clay almost reached the bridge that crossed the river and led away from town into the remote rural area where Pogo hoped to ditch this car and steal another, there was impact.

The impact was sudden and strong. The Pontiac, out-of-control, rammed from behind, headed through the bridge railings, flipped over twice, and dropped into the dark turbulence of the Cedar River below.

CHAPTER 50

The Hospital
Tad Awakens

When you awaken from a dream, it seems real. It doesn't seem as though it didn't happen. Consciousness grabs you. Your heart is pounding. Your palms are sweaty. Your heart rate is accelerated.

At least, all these things are true if you are Tad McGreevy awakening from a dream that is not a dream. Tad had been comatose for nearly 48 hours.

During those 48 hours, he had seen Michael Clay kidnap Belinda Chandler. He had seen Andrea Chandler wander unsuspectingly into danger. He had seen Roberto Jimenez give chase in his Monte Carlo. He saw the resulting accident that plunged the Pontiac with Pogo at the wheel into the Cedar River. He knew what happened after that.

When he awakened in the hospital's intensive care unit, Tad McGreevy was breathing heavily, perspiring, muttering, and eventually, practically screaming, "I've got to save Jenny. Got to save her!"

At Tad's bedside were his mother, Jeannie, and a representative of the Cedar Falls Police Department. There could be no more than two visitors at a time in the ICU. Mr. and Mrs. McGreevy were taking turns, along with Tad's sister Sharon. Waiting. Hoping. In the case of the McGreevys, praying that Tad would come out of his comatose state and be able to tell the police some of the details of what had happened in the SanGiovannis' garage.

Unfortunately, Tad was not able to shed any light at all on what had happened in the darkness of the garage that day.

"I saw something on the floor. I went towards it. I couldn't make out who or what it was. It looked like it was a woman, facedown. She was lying on top of a man, but I couldn't tell who the man was. I never saw her face. Then I was hit from behind."

This was not what the police wanted to hear.

"A woman? You say there was a woman?"

The questioner was Officer Nels Peterson. He felt kind of sorry for the kid. He felt even sorrier for the family. He remembered the Michael Clay case, eight years earlier. Nels remembered that this was the kid who said he'd seen the murders, seen colors that told him Michael Clay was evil. The kid who said he saw violent crimes in his dreams.

Tad McGreevy had had some kind of psychotic break with reality after that. He hadn't been right for over a year. Then, he had gotten better, thanks partially to Dr. Eisenstadt, the psychiatrist. He spent a year at home being tutored. After a year of home schooling, he was well enough to return to school and he'd been fine. Until now.

"Are you sure you don't know who this woman was?" Nels was hoping for more.

There had been no reports of any missing woman. Nels Peterson thought it was probably just the poor kid's scrambled brain. After all, he had sustained a pretty serious head injury, according to the doctors. It was just lucky that Tad hadn't remained comatose for weeks or months.

But now the kid was screaming about Jenny SanGiovanni, who had just left for home with her mother and brother and sister a little over two hours ago.

What is he talking about? wondered Peterson.

Peterson turned to Jeannie McGreevy and asked, "Can I speak with you in the hall a moment, Mrs. McGreevy?"

Jeannie was only too happy to talk to Nels in the area outside the ICU.

Jeannie said, "Just let me get my husband. He'll want to talk to Tad, now that he's awake. Then we can talk."

She rushed off to the waiting room to inform her husband and daughter that they could take the two chairs in the ICU. They could be there to welcome Tad back to the land of the living.

Peterson looked Jeannie McGreevy in the eyes. Haggard. Hair mussed. Make-up gone. She had aged ten years in the past two days. The unmistakable pallor of someone who has not seen the light of day for a while. Her complexion was a sickly gray-white.

"Mrs. McGreevy, I don't mean to upset you any more than you already are upset, but Tad claims that he can see things in his dreams. I know that he claimed this back in 1995 when Pogo was on the loose. Do you think there's anything to it?"

Nels Peterson, a kindly police veteran, held Jeannie's gaze as he asked his question.

Jeannie McGreevy had always believed that Tad did, in fact, see the world a different way. He was more sensitive. He was more intuitive. She had never doubted that he was telling the truth. Now, for the first time, she was determined to tell the truth herself.

"I think that Tad does have some sort of precognitive ability, Detective Peterson, but my husband doesn't believe in it. He refused to let me mention it, back in 1995. He just wanted Tad to be a normal kid. Lord knows, we went through hell with him back then. But I have to say that Tad's predictions about Pogo's victims were too accurate to be mere coincidence. Jim wouldn't believe it. Still won't. He wouldn't let me speak of it, except to Dr. Eisenstadt. Both Tad's sister and I think there is something to Tad's story. I don't know what kind of power it is, or what your police force would call it. But I know psychics are brought in to help the police find victims' bodies sometimes. Tad has said that he can tell if a person is good or evil because he sees auras around them. Auras are colors. He sees these colors around everybody, including you. We told him not to speak of it after what happened in 1995."

She looked almost apologetically at Nels Peterson, "I think you can appreciate why. The Pogo murders almost destroyed our family. In fact, we had Tad committed for a brief period of time. That just seemed to make him worse. Dr. Eisenstadt agreed with us, finally, that Tad should be released and tutored at home. After about a year, he regained his strength enough to go back to school. He quit having the horrible dreams once Pogo was caught and sent to prison. Now, he seems to be having them again. As you know, Michael Clay is apparently on the loose." The strain on Jeannie. McGreevy showed in her eyes.

Nels Peterson chewed reflectively on his bottom lip before speaking again. "What I'd like to do, with your permission, Mrs. McGreevy, is bring Dr. Eisenstadt back into this situation, back on the case."

Jeannie McGreevy looked doubtful. "I—I don't know. My husband probably wouldn't like it. I know he wouldn't like it if it means thousands and thousands of dollars of medical bills again."

Nels Peterson interrupted the haggard woman. "No. This would be on the police department's dime. I just think that we need a professional in the field of psychiatry. Since Dr. Eisenstadt is already familiar with the case, I'd like your permission to bring him in…at the department's expense, of course."

Upon hearing this, Jeannie seemed more receptive. Nels asked another question, "Does Eisenstadt believe that Tad has special powers?"

Jeannie cocked her head in an almost birdlike fashion. "I don't know what he thinks about Tad," she finally answered. "At first, we had high hopes that he could make Tad better. I think we were naïve about how much a good psychotherapist can do. But it was because of Dr. Eisenstadt's recommendation that we committed Tad to Shady Oaks. I think that sanitarium did Tad more harm than good."

Jeannie reached into her pocket for a Kleenex. She dabbed at her eyes with the tissue. "I do know this, once Pogo was locked up, the bad dreams stopped. Tad hasn't had them since 1995. But when Pogo escaped and began killing again…." Her voice trailed off.

Peterson continued, "But Eisenstadt saw, for himself, that Tad's predictions were very nearly eye-witness accounts of the killings, right?"

Nels Peterson had been on the Michael Clay case eight years ago. He remembered the young boy's vivid rantings, all of which were dismissed as psychotic breaks with reality…until they turned out to be nearly perfect, detailed accounts of the horrors police investigators found in the crawlspace of Michael Clay's house.

"Yes, I think he finally did realize that Tad had some sort of insight into Pogo's crimes, that he really did see something in his dreams, but, after Pogo was caught and prosecuted, things returned to normal…slowly but surely. It took a long time."

"Why do you think that Tad woke up screaming that he had to save Jenny SanGiovanni?"

"I don't know," Jeannie said, shrugging. "He left our house to go over there saying the same thing. I tried to stop him, but he just bolted from the dinner table and left. That's when he was attacked and why he ended up here."

"Well, let's get Eisenstadt over here to take a look at Tad—with your permission, of course."

Jeannie McGreevy, looking wan and frail, nodded her consent.

CHAPTER 51

November 2, 2003
Belinda

Once the 911 call for emergency medical help came in from Andrea SanGiovanni in the Heights, Charlie Chandler became aware that his daughter, his little girl, had been held hostage along with the SanGiovanni woman.

And not in a very good part of town, either, he thought, as his police intercom crackled with the news. He instructed Evelyn to drive. Charlie Chandler picked up his cell phone to call Belinda's mother. The only problem was, Cassie seldom had her cell phone turned on. When she did, she often didn't hear it ring.

I'll just call the house and leave a message. She should get it there.

Since all hell had broken loose, Charlie had not been home. He hadn't given so much as a moment's thought to his wife or her whereabouts. He grabbed a couple hours of shut-eye at the station. He and Evelyn Hoeflinger began the paperwork that all cops hate, paperwork made necessary following their trip to Ike Isham's abandoned cabin and their gruesome discovery there. To be honest, Charlie hadn't given Cassie Chandler much thought in the last twenty years. He was just glad that he was here and she was.... wherever she was.

But now, as they sped towards the location where his little girl had been held captive and traumatized, *but, luckily, not killed by that son-of-a-bitch,* Charlie thought he should try to contact Cassie and break the news to her.

Kids want their mothers when something like this happens. I've got to get word to Cassie and break it to her gently, so that she doesn't lose it.

* * *

It was still dark at the crime scene at Ike Isham's cabin. No one had yet realized that a second murder victim was buried in a shallow grave near the ramshackle structure. There were police technicians on the scene and forensic crime scene investigators working the interior of the cabin and some of the exterior. Crack CSI investigators they were not.

As Larry Mason, chief local CSI investigator on the Isham crime scene, stopped briefly outside to catch a breath of fresh air, he dimly heard a cell phone ringing. At first, he thought the phone belonged to one of his staff.

"Jake…is that your cell phone going off in the car or something?"

"No, Boss," Jake Gordon responded. "I thought it was yours."

There were only 3 technicians working the case. One, Jake Gordon, was dusting for fingerprints. Bob McHenry was photographing the crime scene. Larry Mason was doing everything else. Conducting a crime scene investigation in Cedar Falls, Iowa, wasn't Las Vegas. They didn't have unlimited numbers of crime scene technicians to dispatch to a crime scene, no matter how bloody, gruesome, or interesting. None of the CSI folks were beautiful buxom blondes, like in the movies and on television.

Larry cocked his head like a bird taking the measure of a tree branch. He perked up his ears, a cat about ready to pounce. Larry had always had good hearing. No loud rock music had caused his hearing to deteriorate. His musical tastes ran more to Beethoven than the Beatles.

Larry walked three paces closer to the source of the sound. It was very muffled, but here in the woods there was no traffic noise to drown out the insistent ringing of what could only be a cell phone. It would ring, then stop. Ring, then stop. Larry advanced on the sound with each successive spate of its chiming.

Soon, the constant phoning that Charlie Chandler was making to his MIA wife would lead the crime scene investigators to yet another body in the woods, this one buried in a shallow ditch and hastily covered with dirt by Jeremy Gustaffsson.

In her coat pocket, Cassie Chandler's cell phone and Prius keys.

* * *

Meanwhile, Evelyn Hoeflinger drove towards 511 Fremont Street in the Heights while Charlie tried first Cassie's cell phone and next their house number, over and over again. He left messages both places. He really wanted to talk to Cassie in person, to break the news of their daughter's rescue gently. Charlie kept calling one number, then another, feeling that, at some point, Cassie would pick up one or the other. But Cassie Chandler, whose cell phone was on, this time, and in her right-hand jacket pocket, would not be taking calls ever again.

Soon, the squad car with Charlie and Evelyn inside was pulling up in the alley behind the small house in the Heights and the two officers saw that the ambulance attendants were rolling a young man out on a gurney.

A second gurney carried Belinda Chandler. Charlie Chandler forgot his duties as a police office. He became just a worried father, racing to her side.

"Are you all right, Honey? Did he hurt you?"

"I'm fine, Daddy. They just want to take me in to theck me over. He didn't hurt me thoo bad. Nothing that won't heal up fast." Cassie's speech was sloppy. She didn't mention how much her jaw hurt or that she was still seeing stars from the blow to her head.

Although Belinda had a sheet covering most of her body from the waist down, she had raised her upper torso up on one elbow to talk to her father. Her father blurted out, almost without thinking, "What happened to your top?"

Charlie meant her blouse, of course…the one she and Andrea had used as a makeshift bandage for the gaping wound in Alex Jimenez' stomach wound.

"It's nothing, Daddy. I'll tell you all about it at the hospital. Can you get Mom to come? I'd like to thee her." Belinda pulled the sheet up around her now-dirty and blood-soaked bra in a show of modesty that she only half felt. Her words came out muffled, "I'd like to thee Mm." No vowels. No sibilants, but Charlie got the message.

Charlie Chandler smiled inwardly at the accuracy of his prediction that his little girl would want her mommy. All little girls—and little boys—do, when they're hurting. And Belinda was hurting. He also smiled because Belinda had a lisp for a few years before the speech therapists at school worked with her. Her damaged jaw took him back to when she was only 5 years old. After hearing Belinda's story of her rescue at the hospital, he realized he owed Andrea SanGiovanni a huge debt of gratitude.

I'm going to have to swing by and thank that woman and try to help her, if I can, Charlie thought. *If it weren't for her, my little girl might not have made it. And what Andrea's gone through in the past twenty-four hours can't have been easy.*

This private thought was interrupted by Belinda asking Charlie, for at least the tenth time, "Where'th Mom? When will thee get here?" Belinda's face was swelling like a chipmunk's and the bruising was turning purple fast.

"I'm working on it, Sweetheart. Just hang in there. When I get your mom on the phone, she'll be here."

But, of course, the only room in the hospital that Cassie Chandler would be visiting tonight was the morgue.

CHAPTER 52

November 2, 2003
Nightfall

Michael Clay lay there quietly. He didn't move. He barely breathed. He simply was. Pogo was hiding out until the last rays of sun sank below the horizon.

When he swam through the window of the sinking Pontiac as it dropped deeper into the roiling Cedar River, he had one goal. *Let them think I'm dead. Let them think I went down with the car.*

Michael had ripped off all of Gregory Tuttle's earthly goods thoroughly before gutting him like a fish. He had taken Tuttle's money, his wallet, his credit cards, his driver's license, and his keys. Only the keys remained in Pogo's possession after the Pontiac crashed into the river. The keys were attached to a spring-like mechanism attachable to a belt loop. Michael had taken advantage of that feature. He also had taken a good hard look at Gregory Tuttle's address and photo ID. And, of course, there was the Christmas key-chain with pictures of the happy, smiling blended SanGiovanni family. Pogo was appreciative of the display; it made his next step easier.

It had occurred to Pogo that Gregory Tuttle's empty house might make a nice hideout, but Tuttle, between bursts of tears and screaming, had mentioned his wife and stepdaughter would be there. The unoccupied house on Fremont Street seemed lower risk, after Pogo realized that Tuttle's house might have other occupants.

It's funny how my life has turned out. I was an up-and-comer. Everybody said so. Michael Clay had been rising in the ranks of the GOP rank-and-file. Precinct committeeman. Campaign worker. Everyone said he was a natural. Even Laura Bush personally thanked him for his fund-raising efforts.

Instead, I end up locked away for eight long years. My life just walked away from me. I really got screwed.

Pogo had no sense of guilt or responsibility for his torture and murder of 33 young boys and men. He just felt upset that his bright future hadn't turned out the way it was supposed to.

* * *

Pogo knew it was all the fault of that last young boy he had approached. Pogo's last would-be victim was a nervous redheaded, freckle-faced slim kid who looked like he had stepped right out of a Norman Rockwell painting. He was reedy and weak. Michael liked them that way. Then the kid had begun screaming.

The screaming brought Mrs. Michael Clay (Marianna) to the top of the basement stairs. She wasn't usually at home at that time of day. That wasn't supposed to happen, either. Marianna was appalled at what was going on at the bottom of the stairs. Marianna Clay called the cops. It had been all downhill for Michael Clay ever since that phone call.

But now I can start over, in Mexico, he thought. To do that, Michael Clay was going to have to go to the Tuttle well again. It was true that Gregory Tuttle's ID and credit cards and cash had been lost, along with his wallet, in the rushing waters of the Cedar River during Pogo's escape from the sinking car. But the keys to the Tuttle house in the Harvest Homes subdivision, complete with Christmas picture key ring, still dangled from Pogo's belt loop.

Pogo even had a good idea of exactly where Harvest Homes was located. It was a new subdivision that had sprung up since he had been sent up. In his chats with Gregory Tuttle, he had extracted many tid-bits of information. Knowledge of the location of the Tuttle home was just one of many such useful bits of knowledge that Michael Clay had filed away for future reference, in case he needed an ace in the hole. Pogo was now ready to play the Ace of Spades: the Death card.

I'll lie low until sunset. I can stay hidden in the fields that surround the subdivision, until I find the house. With any luck, there'll be money or jewelry in the house. Maybe a weapon. I can clean up and get some food. I can use the key and maybe there's a car key on here, too. Pogo fingered the keys still dangling from his belt loop.

Pogo realized with growing distress that he hadn't eaten anything for almost two days. His stomach was sending out signals. It was time to feed it some real food, not just the Tic-Tacs in Belinda Chandler's purse.

Michael Clay began trudging along through the woods that bordered the road along the river heading towards Harvest Homes subdivision, where, just now, Jenny SanGiovanni was home alone. Frank had left to play video games with his best friend. Cynthia had gone back to her small one-bedroom apartment. Andrea, as usual, was working and also planning her second husband's funeral.

* * *

As Michael Clay walked slowly and cautiously through the forested roadside area, Captain Charles Chandler was learning a disturbing bit of news.

Cassie Chandler, his wife of 39 years, was dead.

At first, Charlie went numb. Her loss hit him as though he had come into the house and found the couch was missing. He had liked the couch, but he could get another one. Cassie's loss was a little like losing an old family pet, like their tabby cat George. George threw up every day. When they finally had to put George down (feline leukemia) Charlie had missed George, even though the reasons why he missed him were not completely pleasant.

At one time, he had loved Cassie, but that time had been close to 40 years ago when they were teen-agers in high school. Married at nineteen, passion had fled. His life began drifting away from him. He could find another Cassie, but he wondered what he should tell Belinda. Belinda could not find another Mom. Charlie approached Belinda's bedside quietly, like an animal that isn't quite sure how it will be received.

Belinda stirred. "Daddy? Is Mom here yet?" Belinda's articulation was improving. The doctors didn't think she'd need to have her jaw wired shut, after all. The blow from Pogo had caused a fracture, but it would heal.

"No, Honey. We need to talk. There's been some sort of horrible accident."

Actually, neither Charlie nor anyone else knew, at this point in time, how or why Cassie Chandler's body was buried in a shallow grave near Ike Isham's cabin. The first guess was that she was another of Pogo's victims, joining Gregory Tuttle and prison transfer Officer Jim Kinkade. There was no reason to suspect the involvement of a second killer, and the forensic evidence would be a long time coming.

"What do you mean...'horrible accident'?" Belinda sat up in bed, looking fragile and frightened, wide awake.

"It's your mother, Honey. Something has happened to her. We don't know exactly what yet."

"But she's....she's all right, isn't she?" Belinda's eyes revealed that she suspected and feared the worst. She hugged her knees tightly.

"No, Honey. I'm afraid that she's not all right. It looks as though she may be one of Pogo's victims. They found her body out near Ike Isham's shack in the woods. Greg Tuttle's body was inside the cabin. Your mother was buried in a shallow grave nearby."

Charlie didn't think it was necessary to add that it was Cassie's ringing phone, as he repeatedly dialed her cell phone, that had led crime scene investigators to her dead body.

Belinda Chandler collapsed and fell back onto her hospital bed, sobbing. Charlie eventually pushed the call button for the nurse, hoping that they could give his only child something to help make her pain go away.

As he did so, he was surprised that he felt no pain, only a sense of release and relief. If it weren't for Belinda's reaction, he would not have felt much of anything.

Regardless of how he felt about his wife's death after thirty-nine years of wedded bliss, he loved his daughter with all his heart. Right now, all he wanted was to help her any way he could.

I must be a bad person not to feel more, Charlie thought. He lowered his head and studied his work-calloused hands, rubbing his rough fingertips together—a habit of old. The other thing that Charlie habitually did when nervous was to remove his wedding ring and play with it. Cassie used to berate him for this.

"Charlie, if you didn't take your wedding ring off in the first place, it wouldn't have rolled all the way up the aisle of the plane! How embarrassing!" or "Charlie, if you'd just quit playing with your wedding ring and leave it on your finger, it wouldn't have fallen under the bleachers at the volleyball game. How do you think it looks when you're always taking your wedding ring off in public like that?"

Charlie felt ashamed of his shortcomings as a human being and as a husband. He would have to try much harder as a father than he had as a husband, even if Belinda was no longer a child.

He had failed his wife. He mustn't fail his daughter. He must work to become a better person, any way he could. And he could think of several ways he could improve, right off the top of his head.

CHAPTER 53

November 2, 2003
Near Midnight: Harvest Home Subdivision

There it was again: a rustling sound. Jenny walked to the window and pulled the drapes aside to see what was out there.

She had begged Cynthia to stay overnight with her, but Cynthia and her mom hadn't seen eye-to-eye on very many things over the past ten years. Cynthia just wanted to go back to her own apartment and sleep in her own bed. Frank was over at Buddy's, as usual. Andrea had said she was dropping off some papers in the Heights for one of her rentals.

That had been a good three hours ago. It didn't surprise Jenny that her mother wasn't back, because she had said that after she dropped off the paperwork for the Jimenez family and made sure the plumbing issues had been addressed, she was going to Green's Funeral Home to "make some arrangements."

She didn't ask Jenny to go with her. Jenny was thankful for that, at least. She didn't want to go with her mother to pick out a casket or an urn or anything even remotely connected to a corpse—especially one that had been decapitated and was now in pieces.

If there was one place on the planet that gave her the creeps, it was a funeral home. She couldn't imagine herself married to a mortician. Or actually *being* a mortician. She had read once that the comedian Whoopie Goldberg, before she was Whoopie and had a normal name like Karen Johnson, used to do the make-up and hair for dead people in a funeral home. She couldn't imagine touching the corpse, the cold dead body of a stranger, on a routine basis. *The Corpses of Strangers.* It sounded like a book title. She shivered as she curled up in the Lazy Boy recliner. She knew it was a childish, squeamish thing. It was just something she knew about herself. Another of her shortcomings in life. According to her mother, she had plenty. That was why she wasn't sure she wanted any part of nursing, either. Ick.

With my luck, my patients will all die and become corpses immediately, she thought. *The two things I hate most: patients and corpses in the two places I want to avoid most: hospitals and mortuaries. It's true that I like to help people who are hurting, but what if they die? Patient to corpse. Two horrible conditions in life—or death.*

Jenny shook her head to clear it of images of dead bodies on metal tables having God-knows-what done to them to prepare them for their funeral home visitations. She thought of the old TV series "Six Feet Under." She shuddered. It was so barbaric. She definitely needed to get up the courage to tell her mother that the nursing thing had been a passing phase. Right now, she couldn't think of anything she'd rather do less than work in a hospital. Unless it were to work in a mortuary.

Her mother was probably touring Green's Funeral Home right now with Mr. Green, selecting a casket or urn for Greg, deciding what sort of service to hold. It was creepy as hell. Jenny wanted no part of it. She was not afraid to stay home alone, normally, but the recent violence in the woods near the prison had spooked everyone. There were people locking their doors at night who had never locked a door in their lives in Harvest Homes Subdivision. She wondered if the Chandlers' doors were all locked up tight as a drum. She thought that Charlie Chandler was probably pretty busy with bodies turning up in the woods. That would mean that Cassie and Belinda might be home alone, too. If she needed anything, she could always call the Chandler house or walk over to their house. After that thought, she pulled herself together and repeated, *I'm fine. I just need to calm down.*

Jenny had not heard the news about Cassie's corpse being discovered in a ditch or Belinda's near-escape from almost certain death. The SanGiovannis had left the hospital before that particular bit of gruesome news broke. The news about Greg had been bad enough. Jenny had been watching recorded episodes of her favorite shows on their TiVO in the family room ever since.

When Jenny pulled the curtains aside to look out, she could see that the wind had picked up in the nearby fields and the slight rustling noise she was hearing were the dry, sere harvested corn stalks, standing forlornly together like a crowd awaiting a speech. They reminded her of an IMAX documentary she had seen entitled "Journey to Mecca."

The documentary showed thousands of pilgrims to Mecca making their journey to the holy place and then circling the stone altar in a sort of arena. Some kissed a black stone that was supposedly the cornerstone laid by Mohammad, himself. The cornstalks in the darkness looked like weary pilgrims. Their fruit had been harvested over a month ago. Now all that was left were dry husks, rotting forlornly in the field. The rustling sound was the wind amongst the dead or dying leaves.

Jenny thought she heard a louder, sharper sound. It was a noise like glass shattering. It was probably her imagination playing tricks on her. Or it might be one of their cats.

They had 5 indoor-outdoor cats: Merrill, Pierce, Fenner, Smith and Beane. Smith, in particular, was as clumsy as any cat she had ever owned. He loved to come in the house and leap to the ledge above the refrigerator-freezer and then into the cupboards that housed cushions for their patio furniture. Half the time, Smith made the leap and failed to reach the ledge because of his immense girth. He had been an adorable tiny black-and-white kitten when they first got him, but he was either eating too many groundhogs in the fields behind their house or eating too much cat food in their basement, where they kept the cats' bowls. Andrea suspected that he ate all his cat food and many of the other four cats' food, as well.

The cats' bowls. I'll bet that's it. One of the cats has knocked over its heavy glass bowl. Maybe Smith even managed to break it, as clumsy as he is.

Jenny settled back into her chair in the family room and flipped the TiVO device to "list" to see what she could watch while she was waiting for her mom to return. There was an unwatched episode of Jon Stewart's "Daily Show" that looked interesting. She queued it up.

* * *

Meanwhile, Michael Clay was cautiously letting himself into the house through the window and trying to avoid the broken glass of the basement window that he had just smashed. He listened warily to see if there were sounds of people moving about upstairs. He could barely see in the darkness. Only the full moon gave wan light. He didn't want to unintentionally signal his presence. It wouldn't do to tip off the upstairs residents and have them lock the door to the basement, trapping him down there. He was banking on the fact that 99% of house owners don't lock the door to the basement. Why would they?

As he stood there, trying to acclimate his eyes to the darkness, he saw two pair of eyes staring at him. It was unnerving. He also saw a door, opened it. He looked down what appeared to be a long corridor or tunnel. *I wonder if that tunnel leads to a bomb shelter?* he thought. *Rich people always have too much of everything...too much time...too much money. Or maybe it's a wine cellar. They always have those, too. Damn moneyed sons-of-bitches. It looks like it goes a long way. Interesting.*

Then Pogo heard the soft meowing of two cats. Michael Clay hated cats. He was allergic to them and they seemed to enjoy making him miserable because of that characteristic. *Give me a good dog like a Labrador Retriever any day of the week*, he thought.

Now that he was fully inside the SanGiovannis' basement, he could smell the odor of cat piss and cat litter boxes. One of the automatic cat boxes went off at just that minute, in fact, startling him. *Just how many cats do these people have? I'm hearing about five motors going off at once!*

Michael slowly crept towards the bottom step of the basement stairs, when Merrill, who didn't like men in general...hadn't ever since Frank and his friends had teased him when he was just a kitten...came towards Pogo, hissing and making a low, growling noise like a dog.

Jesus H. Christ! thought Pogo. *That damned cat sounds just like a dog!*

Merrill made an even lower growling noise deep in her throat, a sound which went up and down in tone and frequency.

Following Merrill's lead, Pierce and Fenner also began making low aggressive growling noises. The noise sounded like three giant refrigerator-freezers humming in the darkness—guttural threatening sounds.

Nice kitties, Michael said, as he slowly moved through the crush of cats that was beginning to gather around his ankles. He just needed to get free of all this cat dander and cat hostility before his allergies kicked in and he began sneezing. Not a good idea to start sneezing and let the residents upstairs in on his presence in their basement.

Just be nice kitties and go do your thing somewhere else, Michael muttered under his breath.

I hate cats. Why won't you suckers leave me alone? He shook Beane free of his pant leg. He began to make his way up the basement stairs.

CHAPTER 54

November 3, 2003
12:01 A.M.

Stealthy step by stealthy step, Michael Clay climbed steadily towards the top of the SanGiovannis' basement stairs. When he reached the top step, he stretched out his hand towards the doorknob. At first, the doorknob, although it turned, didn't open the door. Michael applied more pressure, pushing with slightly more force. The door was stuck. He would have to apply greater force to gain entry. He hoped it wasn't locked, as that would mean breaking the door down. If anyone was on the other side, they'd have time to dial 911 while he was breaking down the door.

So much for my theory about people not locking their basement doors, Pogo thought, just before the door gave, and he was able to slide, like a phantom, into the house.

* * *

In the family room, Jenny SanGiovanni heard a noise. She knew it was probably just her imagination. She had been through this before with her parents. They always cautioned her about panicking unnecessarily. The SanGiovanni house had a hot water heating system. The hot water was pumped around the perimeter of the rooms in metal ducts. It often made loud cracking noises. It was usually the case that the heating system had caused Jenny to become frightened, when nothing at all was wrong. She had become the butt of jokes. But, this time, if she were to cry "Wolf!" would her cries be answered?

* * *

Back in the hospital, young Tad suddenly sat bolt upright in his hospital bed and glanced with wide, frightened eyes at his parents, who had been taking shifts waiting by his bedside until he regained consciousness.

* * *

Tad's eyes opened. He gasped, "Dr. Eistenstadt!"

Dr. Eisenstadt was in the room. He had been contacted by the McGreevys to come, at Officer Nels Peterson's suggestion. The Cedar Falls Police Department had not brought him in as a special consultant. Dr. Abraham Eisenstadt already had made a habit of stopping by the young man's room if he were in the hospital seeing other patients.

Dr. Eisenstadt had always felt guilty over Tad's commitment to Shady Oaks, which seemed to be the final straw in the boy's break with reality eight years before. After that stay in Shady Oaks, Tad had had a complete mental and physical breakdown. Dr. Eisenstadt was well aware that he had contributed to the breakdown by not listening to the boy or believing his stories. What Tad was trying to tell him about Pogo, the clown, turned out to be true, but Abraham Eisenstadt had completely dismissed Tad's visions as poppycock. Dr. Eisenstadt had felt guilty about it ever since.

If he ever tries to tell me some outlandish story again, you can be damn sure I'll be all ears. That kid has some kind of power, thought Eisenstadt.

Eisenstadt had come by on each of the evenings Tad had been hospitalized, stopped to chat with Mr. and Mrs. McGreevy. He had observed the unconscious form of the teen-aged Tad, noting how much larger he had become since their first encounter eight years earlier.

"Yes?" Dr. Eisenstadt answered as though a comatose boy's suddenly sitting bolt upright and saying his name was the most normal thing ever in his world. The doctor's eyes, like a raven's, shone darkly in his sharp-nosed skull. The young boy commanded his entire attention. Dr. Eisenstadt had an intense way of looking at you, even if you were not his patient. He was all eyes now. His ears wouldn't miss Tad's warnings this time, either.

"Jenny! Jenny is in danger! Help Jenny! Get Charlie Chandler! Send Captain Chandler to help Jenny!"

Tad was gasping as he finished. Tad's first words in days got the attention of Abraham Eisenstadt and everyone else in the room. Abe had silently sworn that if this kid ever told him anything again, he was going to listen and listen hard. The fact that it was the most Tad McGreevy had said in days was another reason to pay close attention.

Dr. Abraham Eisenstadt immediately pulled his cell phone from his pocket and dialed 911.

"What is your emergency?" asked the robotic female voice on the other end of the call.

"Please…patch me through to Charlie Chandler. He's got to get over to the San Giovannis' house immediately," said the doctor.

"Who is this?"

"My name is Abraham Eisenstadt…Dr. Abraham Eisenstadt. There is an emergency at the SanGiovanni house."

"What is the nature of the emergency?" the female voice of the 911 service asked.

"Just get someone over there stat!" shouted the doctor into the phone.

In his distress, the doctor had dropped into med-speak from his long-ago medical intern days.

"Can I be patched through to Charlie Chandler?" asked the psychiatrist.

"We will dispatch an officer to the house, Sir," said the emotionless female voice.

"He said to send Charlie Chandler. Send Charlie Chandler."

"Who said to send Charlie Chandler?" asked the anonymous female voice.

"Nevermind," answered Dr. Eisenstadt, "I'm telling you that there is a real emergency at the SanGiovannis' home in Harvest Home subdivision. Captain Charles Chandler needs to get over there right away! He's the one who must deal with it." Dr. Eisenstadt didn't know if Tad's vision required this particular cop, but he was going to honor the kid's request. It was the least he could do.

"All right, Dr. I'll take care of it."

The line went dead.

* * *

At this point, Tad was sitting bolt upright in bed, his red Opie-like hair plastered to his sweaty face, his eyes wide with fright, a sort of blank stare on his face, as though he telepathically were seeing mayhem. His eyes had fluttered back into his head so that just the whites showed. The expression on

Tad's face struck everyone in the room. No one was speaking, other than Dr. Eisenstadt making the 911 call. All were thunderstruck by the sudden vehemence of Tad's return to consciousness. The fact that he returned and spoke with such urgency only added to the intensity of the drama.

* * *

The call went out to Captain Charles Chandler of the Cedar Falls Police Department and Evelyn Hoeflinger, his female rookie partner. Despite the news that his own wife had been a victim of a crazed serial killer this night, Charlie rose from the bedside of his now-sedated daughter and strode into the corridor, where Evelyn waited.

"Let's roll," he said. "Something's wrong at the SanGiovannis' house. We've got to get over there!"

They sprinted for their squad car, which, in Charlie's case, meant that he John Wayne walked to the vehicle where Evelyn was already behind the wheel, ready to roll.

CHAPTER 55

November 3, 2003, 12:15 A.M.
To the Rescue

As they accelerated in the older-model Crown Victoria Ford squad car, heading towards the Harvest Home subdivision, Captain Charles Chandler tried to imagine what the emergency might be at the SanGiovannis. He was happy to help. He owed a debt of gratitude to Andrea SanGiovanni for saving his daughter from Pogo. But he was curious about the call.

All he had been told by the dispatcher was that there was an emergency, that he had been requested by name, and that time was of the essence. Hysterical citizens dialing 911 didn't usually ask for a certain cop by name. They were glad if anyone at all showed up. They wanted any officer, the sooner the better.

"Why do you think the SanGiovannis asked for me by name?" Charlie asked Evelyn.

"No idea," Evelyn said. She was thinking about her weekend and how it had gone down the tubes.

At this point, with Charlie gunning the old Ford as fast as it could go on such primitive country roads, Evelyn was trying to decide whether she'd survive the crash if Charlie hit a tree. She didn't know why Charlie wouldn't let her drive. He'd made her move to the passenger side, pulling rank, when she was perfectly capable of driving and had reached the car a good twenty seconds before the much-older and slower Charlie had sauntered over to it. Evelyn was sulking now. She knew that it was a gender thing and an age thing. Charlie wanted to be "large and in charge."

She also knew that her partner occasionally ducked into the men's rest room to down vodka from a flask he carried, so she wasn't particularly reassured by his archaic attitude towards letting a woman take the wheel. For a moment, smiling, she thought of Carrie Underwood's song *"Jesus Take the Wheel."* She wished she could suggest that option to Charlie. She'd prefer Jesus driving right now, rather than allowing her only half-sober partner to drive them into a ditch or a cow or worse.

*Jesus is probably busy with more pressing matters tonigh*t, thought Evelyn. *But Jesus certainly wasn't looking out for Charlie's wife.*

Evelyn had seen this male chauvinistic attitude time and time again in her own parents' marriage. It didn't matter how snockered her dad got at the party. He still insisted that he would drive home. It was stupid, really, when you thought about it. Even after her father got that DUI for driving so slowly that he resembled a little old lady from Dubuque, he didn't let Loretta Hoeflinger drive…despite the fact that she had been drinking only Diet Coke for hours, while Harry Hoeflinger had thrown back double vodka chasers and too many beers to count.

Evelyn sighed as the struts of the squad car took a beating.

My butt is taking a beating, too, thought Evelyn. *This had better be good .It better not be a cat stuck in a tree or another damn false alarm from that airhead blonde daughter of Andrea SanGiovanni's, Jenny.*

There had been a few 911 calls from the SanGiovanni house when young Jenny SanGiovanni was left home alone. She had become spooked by strange noises. The noises turned out to be the hot water heated furnace ducts of the house making their usual clatter. Evelyn did have some sympathy for a young kid who had just found out her stepfather had been brutally murdered. But she was in a foul mood, knowing that Halloween weekend was going to be a total waste. She'd had a date for a costume party, and now that Playboy Bunny costume would go to waste.

Maybe if Andrea SanGiovanni would work less and stay home more, her kids wouldn't be calling in 911 calls about the furnace, Evelyn thought.

But Evelyn didn't say anything aloud, because she knew that Andrea SanGiovanni had been instrumental in helping save Charlie's daughter's life during the past twenty-four hours. Charlie Chandler wouldn't take kindly to criticism of Andrea. He would want to help her, just as Andrea had helped Belinda, if he could. That's the way Captain Charles Chandler was: Old School.

The squad car screeched to a halt in front of the San Giovannis' house in Harvest Home subdivision, siren blaring, lights flashing.

* * *

Inside the house, Michael Clay had just used his 300+ pounds to force the door to the basement open. The stairs to the basement were off the kitchen. Luckily, that was too far away from the family room to be seen by someone sitting in the family room. This was a big house. The kitchen might as well have been ten rooms away. There was no way that Jenny SanGiovanni could see Pogo or hear him from where she sat watching her program, if she stayed put watching her Jon Stewart episode. The only way she would detect the big man's presence was if she decided to go to the kitchen to get a soft drink or a snack.

Michael slipped from the basement, glad to be pushing the door shut on the swarm of cats that had accompanied him up the stairs, curious kitties all and, depending on the cat, hostile or friendly to the intruder—most of them meowed in chorus all the way to the top. They didn't like being shut in the basement, but Jenny, too, had some minor allergies to cat dander. She just didn't want to deal with the cats tonight. She was too stressed out.

* * *

Jenny again thought she heard a noise. This wasn't the familiar water-gurgling sound she had so often confused with something more serious. This was a louder noise, like a door being forced open or a book being dropped. She could swear that she also heard the cats meowing, but that sound quickly stopped. She paused. She put the television temporarily on mute. Nothing. She almost got up, went to investigate. Part of her was too tired to investigate, part of her was too scared, and yet another part of her felt that she'd rather be the victim of a catastrophe than face her mother if she made another bogus 911 call. Or any kind of 911 call. She was still taking heat for contacting the authorities to come help Tad.

I wonder if I'm just jumpy because I know my mother's in a funeral home picking out a casket today? Or maybe it's the death of two people, one of them my stepfather, the other Cassie Chandler. I guess I have every reason to be skittish, but if I panic and start calling up Frank or Cynthia or—worst of all—

Mom, they'll just make fun of me. I need to learn to be braver and not imagine things where there is nothing at all to be frightened of. Or, she thought, *if I really think there is an intruder in our house, I could always go to the attic to get a gun.*

At the thought of rushing to the attic, where her father's gun collection was stored, to get a piece, Jenny smiled involuntarily. She knew absolutely nothing about guns or firing them and she didn't have the key to the gun cabinet, anyway.

Her father, Jeff, on the other hand, had been quite an expert shot and an avid collector. He had a large collection of firearms, was a card-carrying member of the NRA (National Rifle Association), and went target shooting nearly every weekend, when her parents had been together. It was but one of many bones of contention in her parents' marriage. Jeff intended to take the guns with him to Colorado, but he and Tammy had so many things to coordinate that, in the heat of marrying and moving, the firearms had been temporarily left behind in Andrea's attic. Not to worry. Jeff would retrieve them, sooner or later. Later, it appeared, since the guns were still in the attic one year after her parents' divorce.

"Next trip," he'd always tell Andrea, when he spoke to her on the phone. "I'll get them on our next trip out, when we pick up the kids."

Andrea SanGiovanni hated guns. She did not want guns in the house.

Jeff SanGiovanni, the Budweiser distributor, loved guns. He felt they were part of his Constitutional right to bear arms. Andrea suspected that he also liked the macho image that being a gun guy gave him. When she really wanted to mock him, Andrea would call him Charlton. He did not find it nearly as amusing as she did. Andrea would just roll her eyes when he announced that he was "going shooting." Once, he went to take target practice on her Saturday birthday, totally forgetting that it *was* her birthday.

They argued about his fondness for guns good-naturedly before their marriage. It was only after the children were born that Andrea insisted that all guns be taken to the farthest reaches of the house and locked up. They were to be kept under lock and key at all times.

"You know what happened to Wanda's son, Sandy," she said to Jeff during one of their arguments about his gun collection. Andrea was trembling as she shouted those words, uncharacteristic of the strong woman she normally was.

Their housekeeper, Wanda James and her husband, Harold, had adopted a son, Sandy. Wanda and Harold James had a biological daughter, Janet, who was in Frank's class at school. The James' had tried repeatedly to have a second child. After two miscarriages and an ectopic pregnancy, the James' decided to adopt the son they wanted so badly. Andrea and Jeff SanGiovanni had even been asked to vouch for the older couple, as to their suitability as parents. They wrote a statement and submitted to an in-house visit to help their housekeeper realize her dream of completing her family by taking Sandy in as her own son. After all, Wanda had baby-sat for their own three kids many times. She was the best housekeeper they had ever had, a loving mother, and a good person.

It seemed like the happiest of endings when the child was allowed to become Sandy James in a private adoption. It quit being the happiest of stories the day that little Sandy and a friend, Johnny Martoriano, were left home alone for twenty minutes at the James' house.

At the time, the two boys were in eighth grade, old enough to be left home while Wanda made a quick grocery store trip. The boys were in junior high school. It was a Friday after school. They should have known better than to get into Harold's unlocked gun cabinet and take out several of his guns to play with.

Wanda had just run to the store to get ice cream for the 12-year-old boys. Johnny was going to sleep over at Sandy's house. The two had been best friends since kindergarten. They had been looking forward to this night all week.

When Wanda walked into the James duplex, a split-level, returning from the grocery store, she descended the stairs and entered hell. Both boys were dead, shot with the firearms that Harold kept in an unlocked gun cabinet. Both had sustained grievous wounds to the head.

After much investigation, the police determined that the two 8th graders had been playing with the guns while Wanda was gone, as young boys who thought they were invulnerable have been known to do. Little Sandy had accidentally shot his best friend Johnny in the head, killing him instantly. Overcome with grief and unable to bear the realization that, in a careless moment, he had shot and killed his life-long best buddy, the distraught Sandy turned the gun on himself and committed suicide, putting the 38 caliber revolver in his mouth and pulling the trigger.

The scene, when Wanda entered, was bloody chaos, a room of ruined dreams and heartbreak.

Wanda never recovered, never quit blaming herself. In fact, the James' marriage broke up within a year of the deaths of the two boys. The funeral was a closed-casket affair. There wasn't a dry eye in the house. Just to make matters worse, the parents of Johnny Martoriano sued Wanda for negligence in supervising the boys and won a huge judgment in court. The James' were ruined financially.

This tragedy made a deep and lasting impression on Andrea SanGiovanni. She knew that what had happened to Wanda could have happened to any loving attentive parent. It wasn't true that Wanda had been negligent. She had merely been human. Life had walked away from those two young boys. There had been guns in the house in an accessible unlocked gun cabinet. The result was the senseless loss of two young lives.

In late-night conversations, Andrea and Jeff, now the parents of three young children themselves, talked about the death of their dear friend's child.

"How could this have happened?" said Jeff to Andrea. "You know Wanda was a good mother. She was a great babysitter for us."

Andrea and Jeff had relied on Wanda to supervise their own three young children many times. Wanda was mature and responsible. They trusted her implicitly.

Andrea became obsessed with one fact of the unfortunate deaths. She brought it up to Jeff almost immediately after the tragedy. She would not let the issue rest.

"It was the guns, Jeff. Wanda and Harold had guns in the house. All kinds of guns. The guns were easily accessible. I know that neither Wanda nor Harold ever dreamed that something so horrible could happen, but it did. I don't want guns in my house. We have three kids. Who's to say that young Frank might not do exactly as little Sandy did? If your guns are in the house, they have to be far, far away from everyday traffic, locked up, and inaccessible.

Wanda left the house for less than twenty minutes. In that twenty minutes, the boys got the guns out, loaded them, and were killed. Twenty minutes. Two young lives snuffed out. Two families that will never be the same. Two young men who will never grow up, never grow old, never have kids of their own. And this happened to Wanda…one of the most loving and responsible people you and I know. If you keep those guns, they have to be put far, far away…somewhere like the attic. They have to be kept under lock and key at all times. You have so many weird guns, too. Why do you have semi-automatic weapons, anyway? No hunter needs to have those in his collection."

Jeff actually never hunted anything. He just liked to shoot things, in a senseless show of machismo. The faster the gun fired, the better he liked it.

At first, Jeff protested that having to go to the attic to get his guns out to go target shooting was an inconvenience. He checked with the target range to see if he could keep his very favorite guns under lock and key there, for a fee, and found out that he could. He didn't protest much after that. The funeral service for Wanda's son had just been held. It had been one of the saddest funerals he'd ever attended. Pictures adorned the closed casket of the 12-year-old boy. Wanda was a sobbing, broken woman.

Andrea just fixed Jeff with a baleful stare. She said, "I'm sure it was an inconvenience when Wanda had to bury little Sandy, too."

After that, Jeff dutifully purchased a gun cabinet with a lock and dragged it to their spacious attic, which had a full floor and a dormer window, left his favorite guns at his favorite target range in a locked locker, and the couple never argued over Jeff's gun collection again. But Jeff secretly resented the need to go to such lengths to access his precious gun collection. One of his many resentments. One which, like buried resentments in general, festered like a boil over the years. Like most parents, Jeff thought, "That could never happen to me or my kids."

Jeff and Andrea had argued over other things—like Andrea's seeming preference for work over home—but there was never another argument about keeping Jeff's gun collection in the attic. It was locked inside a glass case. The key to the case was always on Jeff's key ring. The attic, itself, could only be reached by means of a pull-down ladder. Jeff kept his growing resentment close, too, deep in his mind, where the festering blister grew more infected every day it wasn't lanced.

CHAPTER 56

November 3, 2003
12:30 A.M.

Pogo considered several approaches to taking Jenny hostage. With the arrival of a squad car outside just as he emerged into the kitchen, he decided that the stealthy approach he had intended to use, sneaking up on the distracted teenager, would have to be jettisoned. Instead, he intended to draw her attention to the kitchen immediately and grab her from behind when she came to investigate.

There was a bowl of fruit on the granite countertop. He dumped the fruit out and dropped the heavy glass bowl to the hard tile surface of the floor, where it promptly smashed with a loud noise. He waited, poised to grab the young girl as she entered the kitchen. He did not have to wait long.

When Jenny rounded the kitchen corner, coming out to find out what that loud noise had been, he grabbed her from behind, stuffed a dish towel he had found hanging on the oven door in her mouth, and cautioned her.

"Be cool. Don't scream. Just be cool. I'm going to ask you a question, and then I'm going to take my hand away from your mouth so that you can answer. If you answer my question calmly, I'll let you live. If you don't, I'll snap your neck right now as easy as I'd snap a twig. Don't lie to me, or I'll kill you."

Jenny was paralyzed with fear. The dishtowel that Michael Clay had stuffed in her mouth was successful in silencing her.

Pogo said, "Are there any guns in the house?" He removed his hand from her mouth and pulled the dishtowel from her mouth, so she could respond.

"Y—y—yes," Jenny answered, in a shaky voice.

"Where are they?"

"In the attic," Jenny responded.

"Take me to them."

Just then, the doorbell rang. As the two officers approached the house, they could hear the television set in the family room through the door, but no one answered.

No one answered because Pogo was half-dragging, half-walking the terror-struck girl up the stairs to the highest point in the two-story house.

When they reached the second floor, a pull-down ladder must be activated. This was done quickly. Pogo motioned to the girl to begin climbing to the attic.

Jenny, however, who was complying with Pogo's every command, was so terror-struck that she literally couldn't move. Her vision clouded. She felt herself becoming light-headed and dizzy. In less than five seconds, she fell to the floor, her head making a loud "thumping" noise as it hit the hardwood surface. She lay there, unconscious.

Pogo realized that carrying her up the ladder to the attic was going to be quite difficult. He was not a small man or a young man. Simply climbing up there himself was going to require some finesse. He hoped that the officers were there on routine business and would just leave if no one answered the door, but he also had an idea. If it worked, Pogo might have to kill again, but he would live to fight another day.

Sunny Mexico was not yet out of Pogo's reach.

Quickly climbing the approximately fifteen stairs to the attic, Pogo gripped the wooden sides of the ladder and prayed that he would be able to find the lightswitch for the attic space. He also hoped it wasn't a crawlspace situation with just a few boards to stand on. In that hope, his prayers were answered. The attic room was spacious. If a real staircase had been built, the room might almost have been used as a bedroom. A large glass gun case stood on the wall to his right as he entered. It was filled with various weapons in a variety of calibers. There was even a semi-automatic machine gun. Pogo could see the ammunition boxes for each weapon neatly laid out near the gun within the cabinet. He murmured appreciatively, "The Mother Lode."

He had found the bare light bulb pull string immediately. Now all he needed was something to break the glass in the gun case, since he had tried the cabinet doors and they were locked. Looking around the attic, he saw a small table lamp on a child's old-fashioned school desk. Pogo reached for it. He used the lamp base to smash the glass in the gun cabinet. Glass shards sprayed and splintered and created a loud noise.

Outside on the porch, Charlie and Evelyn had just about decided that Jenny must have decided to take a shower or was indisposed in some other way when they heard the sound of breaking glass. They backed up onto the lawn, since the sound seemed to come from the second floor, trying to see what rooms on the second floor were illuminated.

As they backed further from the front door, off the front porch and into the yard, they heard more glass breaking. The barrel of a shotgun could be seen protruding from the attic window. Both officers were wearing bulletproof vests, which was standard practice in the department, but a bulletproof vest does not protect you from a head shot fired from above.

The first shot whistled past Evelyn's left ear. Charlie yelled, "Get down! Get down! Get back on the porch!"

Evelyn didn't need to be told three times. She lunged forward onto the porch, flattening herself against the surface of the porch's weathered wood. Charlie, meanwhile, decided to make a break for the squad car, in order to call for back up. He knew it was risky, but without the radio in the squad car and with a shooter above them, they were trapped, not able to escape and not able to enter the house for fear of a direct assault. The duo didn't know if it was one person or several shooters inside the house.

Just as he reached the curb where the squad car was parked, Charles Chandler felt a white-hot pain sear his left side. He knew he'd been hit. Despite the pain, he also knew he had to get to the radio in the squad car and call this in, or else Evelyn and he would be as dead as poor headless Greg Tuttle.

I'm the only parent Belinda has now. I've got to get some help. I've got to get back to Belinda.

Pushing forward by dint of sheer determination, Charlie managed to yank open the squad car's passenger side door. As he did so, he was hit again, this time in the leg. He half-crawled, half-pulled his body into the squad car, the pain somewhat offset by the adrenaline pumping through his system.

He managed to grab the radio walkie talkie and bellow, "Officer down! Officer down! 523 Harvest Home Boulevard. Send back-up!" before he passed out.

All the while he was thinking, "Is it Pogo inside the house shooting at us? If it is, is Jenny SanGiovanni still alive?"

CHAPTER 57

November 3, 2003
The Hospital

Back at Cedar Falls Memorial Hospital Dr. Abraham Eisenstadt sat by his young charge's bedside.

* * *

After Tad's outburst and his insistence on the need to rescue Jenny SanGiovanni, Tad McGreevy had become disoriented. He was no longer in a coma, but he wasn't making sense, either. Dr. Eisenstadt followed Tad's fevered instructions and used his influence to send a squad car to the SanGiovannis' Harvest Home two-story frame house, but he'd been unable to communicate further with Tad to ask him what he saw in his half-waking vision.

* * *

What danger did Tad know about that the others in the room were unaware of?

* * *

"Tad? Tad? Can you hear me?" Dr. Eisenstadt stood up from the chair he had been sitting in by Tad's bedside and, using a small penlight flashlight he always carried with him, tried, by shining the light in Tad's eyes, to see whether Tad was conscious, talking in his sleep, verging on slipping back into a coma, or simply exhausted.

He could tell little or nothing about the reasons behind the young man's frantic commands.

If Tad has a telepathic ability, he could be a great asset in so many ways, thought Abraham Eisenstadt.

Dr. Eisenstadt had written several books on fugue states, precognitive ability, and other similar little-documented phenomena. He felt rather foolish that he had completely failed to recognize a savant eight years ago, when Tad's powers first manifested themselves. Here he was, a so-called expert and yet he had ignored Tad and dismissed his stories, even after they were shown to be accurate. Now, Dr. Eisenstadt was very interested in finding out how much of the future Tad could "see." How did Tad's special power work?

* * *

The doctor was also very curious about what was happening at the SanGiovannis' house. After Tad remained unresponsive to his questions, Dr. Eisenstadt rose to follow his own impulses.

"If you folks will excuse me," said the psychiatrist, "I'm going to go follow up on what is happening at the SanGiovannis...if anything. After all, I was the one who made the 911 call." No one objected, so, without much fuss, Dr. Eisenstadt gathered his coat, said his good byes, and left Tad's room.

As he walked to his BMW parked in the doctor's area of the parking lot (Dr. Eisenstadt had privileges at the hospital), he mused on the behavior of the young boy and wondered what he would find when he drove to Andrea SanGiovanni's and Greg Tuttle's home.

It's not far, he thought. *In fact, it's on my way home, anyway.*

The good doctor lived in an equally nice subdivision called CherryWood that was slightly older than Harvest Homes subdivision. The SanGiovannis' house was approximately ten minutes from the hospital and another ten minutes beyond that Dr. Eisenstadt would arrive at his own home, where he lived with his wife, Sarah, and their two daughters, Rachel and Zoe, 13 and 16.

As the luxury sedan approached, Dr. Eisenstadt could hear what sounded like firecrackers. Loud percussive noises. He was now within walking distance of the two-story, four-bedroom home but caution told him he should leave his vehicle here, three houses away, and walk the rest of the way to the SanGiovannis' house.

As the good doctor was approaching the large frame residence, two police cars, sirens wailing, screeched by him and stopped, blocking the street in front of the large two-story frame dwelling. Those two cars joined one squad car already parked at the curb. Four officers piled out, two from each car. Instantly, there was that percussive sound again. Each officer ducked behind his squad car.

One of the officers on the scene was Lenny McIntrye, the Officer Friendly of Sky High. He wasn't really the officer on duty…in fact, he had been on his way home from having a few beers with his dart-playing buddies when the call had come for back up. He knew he could swing by the SanGiovannis' house and help out, and Lenny was nothing if not helpful. Because Lenny had been off-duty, he was in his street clothes, all 120 pounds of him. Don Knotts on holiday.

The first squad car contained partners Jake Gordon and Larry Mason, the second Tom Tolliver (ex-husband of Tammy Tolliver, now Mrs. Jeff SanGiovanni) and Tom's female partner, Rita Cernetisch. Tom Tolliver had been very curious about what might be going down at the SanGiovannis' residence. His partner, Rita, was the best shot on the force. From the cries of "Officer Down" and the repeated call for back up from a veteran cop like Charlie Chandler, Tom and Rita had gotten the idea that something big was up. An ambulance, siren screaming, immediately followed the two squad cars.

And here, on foot, almost walking into the midst of a killing field, was the unarmed psychiatrist whose curiosity had led him to follow up on his initial 911 call, a call he made at the behest of Tad McGreevy.

As soon as the EMT's jumped from the ambulance, rapid fire from above drove them back into their vehicle. In fact, although they realized that the injured officer was very likely trapped inside his car, which was parked outside the house and sustaining a steady rain of bullets from on high, they moved down the block, closer to where Dr. Eisenstadt's BMW was parked.

"Christ Almighty!" said Rita Cernetisch. "Who is shooting at us, and why?"

Her partner, Tom, said, "We have to assume that the shooter is the escapee Michael Clay, but there's no way of knowing whether that is the case until we get a visual I.D. or make contact with him. Do we have a bullhorn?"

Rita shouted to Jake and Larry, the first officers on the scene, who were now hunkered down behind their vehicles, "Do we have any way to talk to the shooter?"

Just as Rita shouted this to the men in blue crouched behind the other squad car, she spotted the unarmed civilian who had come to a halt on the sidewalk about fifty yards from the house. She also noticed that a Channel 5 news truck was one of the vehicles now beginning to clog the street. She instantly realized that they were going to have to cordon off the street and get any nearby residents out of their houses. Fortunately, since there was such a great distance between houses in this new subdivision, that task would not be difficult. There were only the Chandlers, whose house sat empty now, and the Yundts, whose turreted mansion gave testimony to elderly Able Yundts' good fortune in business and in the stock market. Able owned the now-closed theater downtown. The multiplex at the mall had supplanted his old converted opera house theater.

The Channel 5 news truck's presence was pure happenstance.

Bob Black, father of Rodney—or tattoo boy, as Stevie Scranton liked to call him—was a sports photographer for Channel 5, the NBC affiliate. He had been on his way home from working on a highlight reel of football action for the league-leading Eagles when he passed the intersection and heard the shots. He pulled the station truck he was driving down the street and soon realized, from the presence of two squad cars, at least five officers, and one gawking civilian on the scene, that something out-of-the-ordinary was happening. He grabbed his heavy video camera and began shooting film of the house, the officers and the ambulance. Just as he panned the street —a bullet whizzed past his ear. Later, on the morning news, it would be Bob Black's film that all stations would play, with the talking heads asking those listening at home to pay close attention to the many shots.

It was apparent from the footage that the person shooting from the attic window of the SanGiovanni home had access to automatic weapons, but there were also some old-fashioned shotgun blasts that pierced the night air. Unfortunately, some of those shots had pierced the body armor of the first back-up responders on the scene.

Both Jake Gordon and Larry Mason were wearing protective bulletproof vests, but the shooter was shooting down on them from above. They had been hit almost immediately. They were now down, in the street, bleeding from gunshot wounds to the head and upper torso. It did not look promising for either man.

Jake was 48, married, no kids, a by-the-book kind of guy with salt-and-pepper gray hair and a mustache. Larry was 39, father of three, a man who looked like he could hold his own with any combatant in a fair fight, but this was not a fair fight. Larry's bald head—he shaved it—was bloody. Neither man was moving or responding to the cries of Rita and Tom.

Rita yelled at Tom, "Lay down some fire and cover me. I'm going back to the ambulance and get those EMTs to help our men. They also need to find Charlie Chandler. He must still be in his squad car." The squad car, of course, was taking a beating. It was so bullet-riddled by this point that it looked like a prop in a movie, perhaps a remake of "Bonnie and Clyde."

Rita made a break for the ambulance, which was down the block now and, therefore, slightly out of range and off to the side of the view afforded from Pogo's perch. She reached the ambulance only to find the two attendants crouched inside, terrified, and unsure what to do. Both male EMTs looked like they were stunned by the ferocity of the firefight.

"Guys. I need you to try to get our officers out of the line of fire. We can distract the shooter by gunfire, ourselves, to help you out. Do you think you can get our men into the ambulance? We think that Charlie Chandler is still inside his vehicle. He was hit when he called this in. He needs help, too."

The EMTs looked grim, but they were not cowards. Rita explained that she would be shooting at Pogo's perch and would give the men a sign when they should make their run to rescue the three policemen trapped in the hail of bullets.

"I'll wave you on right before Tom and I begin rapid fire on the shooter. Make your move then."

Just as Rita finished these remarks in detailing the plan that would hopefully lead to the rescue of the downed policemen, Dr. Eisenstadt made his way to the back of the ambulance.

"I'm a doctor," he said, "a psychiatrist. Can I help?"

"Sure, Doc. We've got at least three wounded officers and someone needs to try to talk the shooter down or at least talk to him to distract him so these two (Rita cocked her head at the stunned EMTs) can do their job."

"Fine. I called this in. I'll be glad to try to talk to the shooter. If you need me to assist, I can help with the wounded."

Ordinarily, on a routine ambulance call, you did not get a trained doctor. Those who responded to emergency calls were instructed in transporting victims to the nearest medical facility. The emphasis was more on heart attacks than on gunshot wounds to the head. With a trained physician on the scene, and a psychiatrist at that, maybe these policemen had a chance."

"I'm Dr. Abraham Eisenstadt. I'll help any way I can." Abraham Eisenstadt meant that with all his heart. He immediately set to work following Rita's lead.

"OK, Doc. Come with me," said Rita. She zigzagged her way back to her own squad car and her own partner. Their vehicle was not taking direct fire at the moment. They had pulled up slightly later and slightly behind the first two vehicles, one of which was Charlie's, still parked at the curb. Those two cop cars were directly in the line of fire. The pinging of bullets on their metal surfaces continued, uninterruptedly, throughout Rita Cernetisch's shouted conversation with the doctor on the scene.

Charlie's car, in particular, was beginning to resemble a metalicized piece of Swiss cheese.

CHAPTER 58

November 3, 2003
Sunrise over Slaughter

The standoff began around one o'clock in the morning. It was now nearly seven hours later.

Dr. Eisenstadt used a bullhorn provided by the police to try to talk to Michael Clay. That provided a few moments of silence in the onslaught. In those precious moments, the three wounded officers were extracted from the scene. Both Jake Gordon and Larry Mason were pronounced DOA at Cedar Falls Community Hospital.

Captain Charlie Chandler had lost a lot of blood. He was in critical condition, but he was hanging in there. He had a broken leg and internal bleeding. It looked like he might lose a kidney, if not his life.

Meanwhile, the crime scene had escalated into a full-blown media extravaganza. Only Bob Black from Channel 5, the sports reporter who had wandered onto the scene by accident, had footage of the wounding of the first two back-up responding officers on the scene. It played continuously, all morning long. All other programming was set aside as the drama unfolded. It was almost like an instant replay of the O.J. Simpson Ford Bronco chase, as the cameras kept coming until the street outside the SanGiovannis' house resembled a circus or a craft fair. Yellow crime scene tape and sawhorses kept spectators at bay. Even Andrea SanGiovanni was refused access to the grounds of her own house and quickly shepherded to a safe waiting area the responders had set up down the block.

For now, the only civilians allowed anywhere near the site were Dr. Eisenstadt, who had been helping the police since the beginning of the siege, and Bob Black. Other cameramen from other stations showed up, of course, but they were kept at bay by the sawhorse blockades, the crime scene tape, and what must have been at least thirty officers from a variety of police departments that had rushed to the scene.

Andrea SanGiovanni sat inside a police van parked far enough away to be safe and was frantic.

Should I tell them about the tunnel? she thought. Andrea was torn. *What if Jenny isn't even alive any more? If she is still alive, will it help Jenny or hurt her chances of survival?* Andrea was torn. She wanted to do the right thing for her daughter, but the right thing is not always immediately apparent.

The big problem initially was how to get to the wounded men. That problem was solved once Rita Cernetisch was provided with a rifle with a scope. It was not any secret that Rita was the best shot on the force. Rita had even qualified for the Olympics once, although she didn't medal.

* * *

Rita's pinpoint shooting kept Pogo out of the catbird seat just long enough to get the three wounded men into the ambulance. The van carrying the three heroes sped away around two in the morning. After that, it became a waiting game.

"What about the girl...Jenny SanGiovanni?" asked Dr. Eisenstadt.

Nobody knew what had happened to Jenny. Fears that Jenny was being held hostage in the house kept the team from rushing the door with a battering ram.

Around three in the morning, with Evelyn Hoeflinger still pinned down on the porch, but safe from the firing, and with the three wounded officers transported to the nearest medical facility, the officers saw, through binoculars, the slim, dazed figure of a blonde girl appear in the doorway of the house.

Jenny SanGiovanni had remained unconscious for nearly three hours after slumping to the floor of the upstairs hallway where the pull-down stairs to the attic were located. She eventually regained consciousness. Her only thought was of escape. She slowly and unsteadily got to her feet and, clutching the banister, because she had sustained a concussion in the fall and her world was reeling, she descended the staircase to the front door, unlocked it, and appeared, framed in the doorway. Evelyn Hoeflinger shouted the young girls' name: "Jenny. Jenny. Come to me." Meanwhile, she shouted to the officers in the street, "Hold your fire!"

Jenny's mother, Andrea, down the block and anxiously waiting, now had the decision about whether to reveal the secret of the house answered for her by Jenny's appearance in the doorway. Andrea felt faint, but she also felt a wave of relief sweep over her.

Jenny stumbled a few steps to Evelyn Hoeflinger, who was still crouched on the SanGiovannis' large porch. This had turned out to be a relatively safe place throughout the shoot-out, but getting off the porch was going to be a different matter.

After discussion with the officers in the street via walkie-talkie, the best course of action for rescuing Jenny was selected. Evelyn would escort Jenny around the perimeter of the porch which greeted visitors and wrapped around the house, providing a friendly, old-fashioned front entrance. Once the porch ended, the pair must hop over the porch railing to the ground below and run for the back of the house.

The street in front of the house had turned into a killing ground. The officers who responded had their hands full trying to keep bystanders, townsfolk, newsmen—all potential victims— away from the front of the SanGiovannis' house.

Michael Clay was holding shooting practice. Sometimes he'd rake all vehicles within sight with automatic fire. Sometimes he'd target just one cop car or one particular spot below him, as when he made the Channel 5 camera a target. During the time that Rita Cernetisch had used her sharpshooting talent to pierce the window with shot after shot that came perilously close to the ex-con, Pogo had lain flat on the floor of the attic room and waited patiently. She would stop, sooner or later. Then he would kill all of them, if he could.

I'll kill all those pigs in the street, thought Pogo. *It'll serve 'em right, after what they did to me in the pen for the last eight years.*

At one point, assuming that it was Michael Clay in the upstairs attic, Dr. Eisenstadt had played the part of hostage negotiator. The problem was, Pogo had no hostage. He would have had the little blonde chippy who showed him how to get to the attic, had she not passed out right when they were about to climb the stairs. Pogo thought about going back down the stairs to get her. The fact was, he had been kind of busy since all the shooting started. He did have a thought about something else he might do if he went back downstairs. If this constant barrage of gunfire didn't let up, he'd have to put Plan B into action.

I don't know if that wine cellar or bomb shelter in the basement is very big, but if whoever the hell is shooting at me keeps getting this close, maybe I should try to take cover there. I'm not going down. I'm not gonna' be taken alive, if I can help it. I won't spend another eight years inside.

More and more cop cars and officers and spectators and ambulances and yellow crime scene tape appeared in the street below until the place looked like an auction was being held. Pogo saw a news camera from Channel 5...a new one. He took a couple of pot shots at it. Further down the block he could see the TV news van with "Channel 8" written on the side.

How did the television station get wind of this so fast? Pogo wondered, but then he remembered that those types usually had police scanners. The media were like parasites or vultures, coming late to the kill. He remembered how many news people had ringed his house after the news got out about the bodies buried beneath it.

As the hours wore on, Pogo had three main thoughts. He had to take a piss. He was hungry, and he was not going to be taken alive.

I ain't going back to prison for no man. That's for sure. I'll go to hell first.

Soon, the FBI arrived. Conversations were held about trying to use tear gas to smoke him out. The officers could not get near enough to the house to launch a tear gas canister that would get to the attic. They could fire through the windows of the house, but would the fumes reach the attic? Unlikely.

"This is beginning to remind me of the Symbionese Liberation Army shoot-out in Oakland in the sixties," Dr. Eisenstadt commented. He looked around at the officers on the scene. He wondered if he was the only one old enough to remember that shoot-out, when a house in Oakland had been placed under police attack while black militants defended from within, also with automatic weapons.

Rita Cernetisch, who was only thirty-two, definitely did not remember that shoot-out. She did have the presence of mind to ask the psychiatrist, "How did they get them out of the house?"

"If I remember correctly, after the tear gas didn't work, they set fire to the place," said Dr. Eisenstadt.

Rita shook her head "no" vigorously. She was athletic and muscular for a woman. Her short cropped brown hair gave her a masculine air of command.

"We can't risk fire," she said. "The fields around here are very dry. The wind would carry the flames to the houses nearby. You'd burn down the whole subdivision. It's too great a risk to try burning them out."

Tom Tolliver, Rita's partner, said, "What about getting a bulldozer and knocking the place down?"

Everyone, at first, looked at Tom like he had just said the stupidest thing ever. Then they began to think about it.

It just might work.

CHAPTER 59

November 3, 2003, Dawn
Bobby Hurley

Dawn was at six in the morning. Pogo had been inside for six hours.

The officers outside had relayed Tom Tolliver's idea for removing Pogo from the SanGiovanni house to headquarters. Tom Tolliver rather liked the idea of knocking down the house that belonged to his ex-wife's new husband. The place was easily worth half a million dollars, even in a rural community such as this one. He sure wouldn't shed any big crocodile tears if his ex's new squeeze or his ex-wife Andrea lost a few bucks while he, Tom Tolliver, was doing his job.

Headquarters sprang into action. They checked the available crane and demolition services in the yellow pages. Their search led them to Bobby Hurley.

Bobby was a short, rusty-haired graduate of Columbus High School in Waterloo. A good Catholic boy, Bobby had been an altar boy with Charlie Chandler's immediate superior, an old school cop by the name of Paul Nicholson. The teacher, Miss Nicholson, was Paul's aunt.

When the two boys were younger, they resembled one another. Both were short and Swedish, with blonde hair and blue eyes. Sometimes, they were asked if they were brothers when they were serving mass with Father Brugg. They weren't. They were just good friends, classmates, and altar boys doing what their parents thought they should to insure their entrance to the Promised Land.

Now, when the plan was laid out for the head honcho of the local police force, he immediately thought of his old friend Bobby, who had made a small fortune amassing large cranes and wrecking balls and various pieces of heavy equipment that were used to demolish buildings.

Bobby had never struck Paul as being particularly bright, but, then, the feeling was mutual. The fact that Paul Nicholson, nephew of Miss Nicholson, the old maid schoolteacher each of them had had in sixth grade, had risen to be the top cop in the community was astounding to Bobby, when he heard it. Paul had always seemed very meek and mild—especially around his wife.

Bobby had done his best to corner the market on heavy equipment in the town. With John Deere being such a big player in the area, it hadn't been easy. He had to keep one step ahead of that giant corporation and go them one better. John Deere and International Harvester might have a shitload of heavy-duty trucks, bulldozers, and the like, but only Bobby Hurley had a genuine wrecking ball. Bobby didn't have just one. Bobby had three cranes with wrecking balls, each one capable of knocking down the wall of any structure in this town.

Maybe if this had been Vegas and they were talking about demolishing the Desert Inn, Bobby would have been out of his league, but for Cedar Falls, Iowa, Bobby Hurley was the best game—almost the only game— in town. Bobby Hurley's televised business slogan was, "You build it; we tear it down."

His wife had suggested, "If you build it, we'll tear it down," a take-off on "Field of Dreams" but Barney didn't think his wife Nicollette, a petite blonde with a killer figure, was all that smart, either, so he had stuck with his own slogan.

"Waddaya' mean, '*IF* you build it?' If we're tearing it down, it's already been built, Nicollette. There's no 'if' about it. That's just a stupid idea for a slogan." Nicollette didn't agree, but it wasn't her business.

She went back to re-painting her acrylic nails, rolling her eyes at Bobby's inability to grasp anything clever.

As Paul had often thought, Bobby wasn't the sharpest knife in the drawer, but he sure had one good idea and it had made him a shitload of money. His wrecking equipment was now going to do a good deed for the community while also making Tom Tolliver's day infinitely brighter.

And if Tom Tolliver never had another good idea, at least he'd had one today.

CHAPTER 60

November 3, 2003, 6 AM
Bringing Down the House

In addition to the wrecking ball and bulldozer, the SWAT team brought in a heavy-duty armored car, something impervious to the implacable rat-a-tat-tat of Michael Clay's intermittent machine gun fire strafing the street.

"How many clips do you think he has with him in that attic?" Rita Cernetisch asked Tom Tolliver, her partner.

Tom had a very bad nicotine habit. He was definitely in need of a cigarette right about now. The two of them were the last of the first responders to still be on the scene. They had arrived shortly after one in the morning. It was now approaching seven A.M. Tom also had a bit of a "thing" for Rita, but she didn't seem to be feeling it. This made Tom cranky, as Rita was the second woman to reject him recently. Tom just shrugged by way of response to Rita's question. She was on his shit list this week. Maybe next week, if she learned to play nicely with others, he'd feel differently.

Sometimes, during the gunfire volleys, there would be a lull and the Cedar Falls police would grow hopeful. During one such lull, a phone call came in from someone claiming to be Michael Clay.

"I'm hit," the man's voice said. "Send in some medical help and I'll stop shooting."

"Who is this?" asked the policewoman taking the call.

At that point, the phone went dead. Was it really Pogo, calling from his attic lair? If so, where did he get a cell phone? The number was traced. The phone belonged to Belinda Chandler. That strengthened the probability that the call was legitimate. This monster had already shot and killed two of their own in cold blood and wounded a third. Nobody on the Cedar Falls police force was too worried about whether Michael Clay had an "owie."

"We're going to knock the walls of that house down right around your ears, you son-of-a-bitch," Tom Tolliver yelled in the background. The use of the wrecking ball and bulldozers had been his idea, and he was pretty damned proud of it.

Tolliver continued, bellering, "If you want to live, come out now with your hands up."

When there was no response and the call went dead, plans went forward for razing the house. The cab of the crane that held the wrecking ball had been rigged with a protective bulletproof windshield and metal shield near the grill that housed the motor. The operator of the crane merely had to swing the ball towards the house. Destruction would ensue. Nobody was sure just exactly how this would affect Michael Clay, but the general level of concern for his well-being could best be described as low to non-existent.

It had been seven long hours, with newsmen, neighbors, volunteer psychiatrists, and police personnel from counties as far away as Buchanan and Cedar and all the way over to Dubuque called in. Even the FBI was on the case. They all just wanted this siege to be over.

Jenny SanGiovanni was safely in their custody and either Pogo soon would be taken alive, if wounded, or he'd be dead. Either way, it would be a welcome relief to all the men in blue working the case. It would mean that Tom Tolliver, a three-pack-a-day man, could finally light up. His fingers twitched at the welcome prospect.

* * *

The first contact between the metal ball and the north side of the house produced a gaping hole and a sound like a car accident. Gunfire continued to be directed at the men in the street and at the crane operator. It produced a pinging sound, like a bee bee hitting a metal garbage can. If it was going by the cameraman's sound equipment, it made a "whooshing" noise, picked up on tape and replayed in a continuous loop on all the late-night newscasts.

After the third mighty swing of the wrecking ball, the entire right side of the upper story of the house—the level of the attic and the four bedrooms immediately below—were exposed and the sounds of gunfire ceased. The noises made by the bullets fired into the street actually stopped before the final blow of the wrecking crew. A good ten minutes of silence had been a welcome non-sound for all those in the street watching the drama play out.

Rita Cernetisch had once seen a house look like this after a tornado sheared off the side of the Chi Omega Sorority House in Iowa City. The individual bedrooms inside the Chi Omega house looked like they were contained within a giant dollhouse, with the bunk beds still in place and everyday items untouched. There was no side on the SanGiovanni dollhouse, or on the Chi Omega one, which she had seen five years ago. At any moment, the floors could give way or the bunk beds tumble to the street below. Rita remembered that the sheared-off half-house after the tornado roared through had been an unusual almost surreal sight.

So was this.

* * *

Swing number four of the wrecking ball. The entire top floors were now one with the bottom floor of the house. Debris rained down on Andrea SanGiovanni's Steinway grand piano. Various pieces of attic foam insulation drifted down to the ground like dirty snow.

Officer Friendly, Lenny McIntyre, who had been here nearly all night long, nervously biting his fingernails and watching, fascinated by the standoff at Harvest Homes subdivision, became aware that his school day job was about to begin. Back to the real world. He scurried off to find a McDonald's that would serve him an Egg McMuffin so that he could report to Sky High and tell one and all of his adventures.

Lenny hadn't really done much. After he realized how dangerous it was out in the street, he had ducked inside one of the last-to-arrive squad cars and watched the entire drama unfold from a discreet distance. When the top floor collapsed onto the bottom floor below Lenny was heard to mutter under his breath, "Dog-gees! That's what I'm talkin' about!" It was a good thing that Lenny had arrived in his street clothes, because he could go directly to Sky High from the crime scene. He might be tired and wearing the clothes he'd had on since yesterday, but he'd have some good stories to tell in the halls of Sky High.

* * *

Reports from the hospital regarding the condition of Captain Charles Chandler indicated that the old man had fluid around his heart, had taken a bullet that was lodged near one kidney, a kidney which might have to be removed, and that he had a broken femur. Charlie wasn't a kid. If he lived, it was going to take him some time to heal up.

Lenny took off for school, trying to remember every detail of the most exciting thing he could remember happening in this town in all of his twenty-seven years of life.

CHAPTER 61

November 5, 2003
The Hospital

Charlie Chandler was out of danger. The grand old man of the Cedar Falls Police Department would survive. He was pretty banged up. He had lost one kidney. His left leg was in a cast where the femur was broken. His heart problems were under control. He would miss his dead wife's funeral, but Charlie would live to fight again.

* * *

Tad McGreevy was being discharged from the hospital. He would have been eligible to go home at least two days prior, but for the news of the SanGiovannis' house being razed and the search for Pogo's remains. Dr. Eisenstadt knew that Tad would have vivid dreams about Pogo's continued rampage if Pogo escaped and were out there killing innocent victims.

Investigators were still sifting through the rubble, trying to find anything that appeared to be the corpse of the escaped convicted serial killer, remains which were mysteriously missing in the rubble. Dr. Eistenstadt had urged authorities to keep the boy under observation.

When Pogo's remains were not located, but a tunnel from the basement into the nearby fields was discovered, Dr. Eisenstadt, without wanting to seem like a nut case himself, urged that the precognitive boy in Room 1013 not be sent home just yet.

"If Pogo managed to live through all that and escape, he's going to kill again, and Tad McGreevy is going to see him killing again, in his dreams."

This was Dr. Eisenstadt speaking at a staff meeting at Cedar Falls Memorial Hospital. Abraham Eisenstadt had more reason that the others on staff to believe in Tad's powers.

There was an uncomfortable silence after the doctor spoke. He knew it made him look odd. He realized that some of the younger members of the staff said his name and then made little jokes with strange looks, sometimes humming themes from "The Twilight Zone" or "The X-Files." But those members of the staff had not been responsible for sending eight-year-old Tad McGreevy to Shady Oaks. Dr. Abraham Eisenstadt had been skeptical of Tad's claims then.

He was a believer now.

The other doctors on staff had looked at Eisenstadt like he was balmy.

"What are you talking about?" a young intern asked, clipboard in hand.

"Tad has special powers. He sees auras around people...colors that tell him whether someone is good or bad." Dr. Eisenstadt tried to keep his voice calm and steady. He tried not to sound like he was taking offense at the condescending attitude of young doctors half his age with half his experience, and none of his past history with Tad McGreevy.

The young intern snickered. "It's pretty clear that Michael Clay was bad. He was doing life for murder before he holed up in the SanGiovannis' attic. How does seeing some color or other around another person mean that Tad has any special powers?"

The intern could not have been more than twenty-five. His specialty was pediatrics. He had very little credibility with the 65-year-old psychiatrist. That feeling was mutual.

He's missing the point, thought Abraham Eisenstadt.

Abe continued, "The police haven't found Michael Clay's body in the wreckage of the house yet. He was a big guy...over 300 pounds. We do know he was wounded. Doesn't that make you suspicious? Doesn't it make you the least bit worried that he might still be out there? That he might kill again?"

"Wounded? How do we know he was wounded? He probably committed suicide when it was obvious that the police were closing in on him."

Young Mr. White Coat speaking again.

"He phoned us," Abraham Eisenstadt responded, shrugging, hands out, as he argued for keeping Tad just a few more days. "That's how we know he was hurt. He told us. He was using Belinda Chandler's cell phone. Don't you see? He could still be alive! He could still be out there!"

Dr. Eisenstadt had lost the fight to keep Tad hospitalized so that he would be available for help in recapturing Pogo, should Michael Clay still be alive. Two days was all the attending physician would sign off on for keeping Tad in his charge. That was only because Tad took a temporary turn for the worse.

* * *

Tad seemed to lapse into a deeply depressive state when he heard that Andrea SanGiovanni was sending her daughter Jenny to Boulder, Colorado to live with her father and attend school there the second semester of her junior year. It was November now. Jenny would not miss that much school with Thanksgiving and Christmas chewing up what was left of the semester.

She could make up her first semester credits with a home tutor while attending a high school near her father's home. Tad didn't know it, but Jenny was looking forward to getting away from Jeremy Gustaffsson and her mother's sadness after Gregory Tuttle's death. She was walking away from the entire idea that one day she had a house and a room in it and a normal life, and the next day her house was rubble, her stepfather was dead, and her mother was just one catastrophe away from a complete breakdown. Her mother needed a break from life. So did Jenny. She was ready to walk away from her life in Cedar Falls, for the present.

"It's just for the semester, Tad," Jenny had reassured her old friend during a visit to his bedside. "Mom isn't herself. She says she isn't strong enough, right now, to be the glue holding this family together. She just buried Greg. She's a mess. She knew I wanted to go live with my dad some day. That day is now." Seeing how sad Tad looked, Jenny quickly added, "But it's just temporary. Naturally, Mom contacted Dad about all this.... Greg's murder. Our house being destroyed. Dad and Tammy agreed to let me live with them. I can finish this year at their local high school. I'm coming back, Tad. I don't want to graduate with a bunch of kids I don't know that well. I want to graduate with you and Stevie...."

Realizing her miscue, Jenny came to an abrupt halt.

Tad looked down at his knuckles, folded together in his lap as he sat upright in bed, white from stress.

"I mean, I want to graduate with all of my friends. That means you and everybody in our class."

Jenny thought this might be the most diplomatic way out of her faux pas. She didn't want to mention Jeremy and how Jeremy was not among the "everybody" she wanted to graduate with. It might have made Tad feel slightly better about her temporarily leaving, but it would lead nowhere good to discuss Jeremy with Tad.

For one thing, Jeremy had already begun contacting her, pressuring Jenny to sneak out and secretly meet him. It was just one small step to imagine him pressuring her for sex again, underage or not. Jeremy was one big reason that Jenny wanted to leave and go to Boulder to finish out her junior year, even though she'd be "the new girl" in class.

The way Jenny had it figured, Jeremy would graduate...finally...and when she came back to finish school with Tad and all her girlfriends, Jeremy would be yesterday's news. He was a year ahead in school. As a fifth-year senior, he'd have graduated and gone on with his life. She wouldn't have him pressuring her to attend this or that school function as his date. She wouldn't be placed in the awkward positions she had been placed in this year.

"After this semester, I'll be back. You'll see." Jenny reached out and took Tad's hand in a friendly gesture of concern and affection. "We'll talk every day on AOL."

"What about Frank? What about Cynthia? What about your mom?"

Tad asked logical questions, which the doctors also noticed. For a kid who had been comatose and incoherent just days prior, Tad McGreevy seemed to be tracking the conversation and current events pretty well.

Jenny replied, "Well, Frank wants to live in the dorm with Buddy Attenza while he's going to Cedar Falls Junior College. He's been wanting to do that for a while, anyway, but Mom insisted that he stay home to save money. Now that we don't *have* a home..." Jenny trailed off again. "But Mom says the city is going to reimburse us for destroying our house. She says that Frank can use the money to pay for his dorm room at the University of Northern Iowa when he finishes junior college this semester. There might even be enough to pay for my college, after I graduate next year. I kind of want to go away to school for college."

Tad's heart sank even further on hearing that. "Your mom? What about her? Where's she going to stay? How do you feel about her plans?"

"Mom is going to move in with Cynthia until she decides where she wants us to live. It might just be me and Mom, but my family will survive in Cedar Falls somewhere. Because we *are* going to be back together, Tad. I'm not leaving forever. Neither is Mom and neither is Cynthia. Cynthia has a small apartment near Layne's Insurance where she works. It has a pullout bed. But Cynthia's only got one bedroom. It'll probably cramp her style for a while, but my mom is going to stay there until she gets back on her feet. Mom's going to look for a new house for us. She needs the time off from taking care of Frank and me. She has her business, but she doesn't have Greg any more. Frank is practically gone from the house, anyway, and will be after this. I think Mom feels kind of lost."

"As long as you're coming back, Jenny. Promise me you're coming back." Tad looked at her with large liquid eyes.

"Don't be silly. Of course, I'm coming back," Jenny said, with a smile. "You don't think I'd leave you to fend for yourself in your senior year of high school, do you? I'll be back, Tad. It's just for a little while."

Secretly, Jenny thought about the saying Tad used to repeat: *Sometimes you walk away from your life; sometimes it walks away from you.* Jenny wanted—at least for a little while—to walk away from her old life. She wanted a shiny new one without Killer Clowns and dead stepfathers and threatening boyfriends.

She now understood why even a young person might feel like walking away. She understood why her mother might have the same impulse, although Mom was adamant about not leaving Frank and Cynthia alone in town. Right now, Jenny felt just the opposite. She wanted to get away from everyone and everything for a little while. She didn't mind that she'd be odd girl out in a new school to do it. She'd cope somehow. There'd be no Jeremy Gustaffsson pressuring her to have sex or sneak out and meet him, when she knew her folks would disapprove. There'd be no Tad McGreevy, with his sad spaniel eyes, looking at her as though she had just broken his heart.

Jenny added, "To be honest, I'm glad we're getting a new house somewhere else." She said, "Still here in town, of course. That house in Harvest Home always gave me the creeps. There were weird noises in it all the time. You remember me complaining about it. And we really didn't have any neighbors near enough to feel like we had neighbors. Only the Chandlers. I don't think Mr. Chandler and Belinda will stay in that big house, either. Not after what happened to Mrs. Chandler. Belinda had already moved out, but she'll have to help her dad for a while. He's another one who'll be lost, without his job on the police force."

Tad did, indeed, remember Jenny complaining about the strange noises at all hours of the day and night in her house. It was always explained away to Jenny as the sound the hot water heat in the baseboards made while circulating. Tad wasn't so sure. He wasn't sure of anything any more. But something about her comment about how lost Charlie Chandler would be gave him an idea.

And then she left. Jenny walked away from her life in Cedar Falls. For a little while, Tad's own desire to get better and go home from the hospital left with her.

Doctors didn't initially connect the news of Jenny's leaving town for Colorado with Tad McGreevy's relapse, but two more days were required before Tad regained the color in his face.

Two days after Jenny's visit, Tad began to act more like his old self. He was responding normally to questions asked of him by the nursing staff. He was watching episodes of Jon Stewart's "The Daily Show." While he seemed quite glum, he was no longer silent or incoherent.

In fact, Tad asked when he could speak to Charlie Chandler, who was recuperating on the fifth floor. Those were normal things. With the return of a semblance of normalcy to Tad's life, the attending doctor and the nursing staff agreed that he could continue his recuperation at home.

* * *

So it was that, two days after the attack on the SanGiovanni house, Tad walked into Charlie Chandler's room on the fifth floor of Cedar Falls Memorial Hospital wearing his street clothes, ready to leave for home. Soon, his parents would drive him back to his old room, filled with bittersweet memories. There were the model airplanes that he and Stevie had spent hours assembling and the posters that each had on their bedroom walls. ("Thursday" was one musical group they both liked. And "Modest Mouse.")

Tad entered Room 501 and looked at the man in the bed, who was an imposing physical presence even when flat on his back with tubes running to and from his body and his leg in a cast.

"Mr. Chandler," Tad began, "I've got something I want to talk to you about."

CHAPTER 62

November 5, 2003
The Search

Rita Cernetisch, Tom Tolliver and Evelyn Hoeflinger were at the crime scene, the SanGiovannis' house in Harvest Home subdivision.

For two days, continuously, during daylight hours, crime scene technicians sifted through the rubble of the home, which was little more than a concrete foundation now. The failure to discover Michael Clay's body was eclipsed by just one bit of news from the scene of the fatal shoot-out: there was a secret tunnel that ran from the basement of the SanGiovanni house approximately two hundred yards into the nearby fields, corn fields that were now dry and dead-looking in shades of tan, awaiting the first snow of winter. The tunnel stopped just short of the meth lab the cops had discovered three years ago.

Everyone in town knew that Andrea SanGiovanni bought up properties in the Heights, the Mexican part of town, cheaply and resold them for a profit. Few were aware that Andrea, in the course of her work as a real estate businesswoman, had discovered that the brand-new, expensive home in Harvest Home subdivision she quickly moved to purchase after her second marriage had previously been owned by a meth maker and distributor, a single man who went by the name Clint McClintock.

The tunnel from the basement of the house led to no building now. Authorities had discovered the meth lab in the woods and torn down the ramshackle structure, hidden amongst corn fields and forested land that seemed to have been the main manufacturing site for what must have been a profitable crystal meth production operation.

The police had not arrested anyone in connection with the apparently abandoned lab when they found it, and they hadn't discovered the tunnel to the house that stood at least two football fields away. The stairs down to the tunnel, ingeniously hidden inside a dead hollow tree, would require someone one whole hell of a lot smarter than Jake Gordon and Larry Mason to ever notice this Disney-esque touch. Jake and Larry needn't worry about their incompetence reflecting poorly on their work. Both were dead, Pogo's second and third police victims after Jim Kinkade.

The authorities had seized and sold the land, which included the SanGiovanni house on three quarters of an acre, at auction. It was Andrea, during an inspection of the house that had appeared on the market quickly, up for sale, cheap, who had discovered the hidden door and the tunnel from the basement of the house.

Andrea SanGiovanni never said a word.

"It's perfect, Greg," she told her new husband-to-be. "The house has everything we've ever wanted, and we can get it for a song."

Gregory Tuttle was, at that time, in perfect harmony with his new wife's ways. They both enjoyed the finer things in life. Greg, at least, enjoyed getting them for little or no effort. His financial advising business meant that he was going to be spending a lot of time in any new house he and Andrea purchased. He liked the amenities of this one: hot tub, in-ground pool, large in-home theater— anything you could desire. They'd just tell the kids that the tunnel was designed as a wine cellar and bomb shelter. Kids don't go around talking about their houses. In fact, if you lived in a mansion, you downplayed that, in order to fit in.

Greg had quickly agreed to the plan to purchase the house in Harvest Home and keep their respective mouths shut about the tunnel. Of course, by the time that it might have done the police some good in entering the house undetected during the recent siege, in an attempt to rescue Jenny, Gregory Tuttle's head had been removed from his body. Greg wasn't going to be doing any talking to anyone ever again.

If either Andrea or Greg had mentioned the tunnel development, the police would undoubtedly have wanted to more strenuously look for the previous owner, Clint McClintock, for questioning. The department could be expected to poke around in the house, looking for clues to the abandoned operation. They might even hold the house as evidence for a potential court case.

No, it was definitely the smarter move to keep their mouths shut about the existence of a tunnel—most probably a drug tunnel—that led from the ritzy SanGiovanni house to a dilapidated shack in the woods where someone had been cooking crystal meth. After all, crystal meth was all over the Midwest. In fact, Oelwein—which wasn't that far away in Fayette County— had been the subject of a recent best-selling book, *"Methland."*

Greg Tuttle had thought, at the time, *I've got to hand it to McClintock. Buying a fancy house like this in a remote subdivision was the perfect cover. With the tunnel, if the authorities ever did come poking around while they were cooking, they could pop down the rabbit hole and disappear.*

Andrea did not want the secret of the SanGiovanni happy home known by anyone other than her new husband. Greg Tuttle contributed roughly 25% of the cost of the place. That was probably less than 5% of its true value on the open market. The auction price was $100,000. The house and land were easily worth half a million dollars—maybe more, as the subdivision continued to be developed.

Right now, Harvest Home subdivision had paved roads and electricity and they had finally gotten off sump pumps in this area and were hooked up to the sewer lines. But there were very few side roads that led to the property and there were very few residents of Cedar Falls who could afford the normal going rate for such a fine house.

Cassie Chandler's parents had money—old money—and she had inherited it. Otherwise, Cassie and Charlie, who existed on an honest policeman's salary—would never have been able to afford their house, which was nearby. But it was also true that, as one of the first houses in the subdivision, and one they contracted for and built themselves, Cassie and Charlie had been able to make a nice home for their only child, Belinda, for far less money than today's going rate in the area.

For one thing, the Chandlers' house was basic, only three bedrooms. It had no pool, hot tub or other amenities, and was at least five years older than the McClintock/SanGiovanni place. Plus, when they built, the place barely had roads. You had to take a bumpy gravel road that damn near broke your car in half, as Charlie often complained. Things had changed in Harvest Homes subdivision.

No one ever called the house Andrea bought "the McClintock place."

Andrea's motto was, "This house is our house now, mine and Greg's. Nobody else needs to know its history." But, of course, it would have been helpful to the cops to know that they could send a SWAT team into the house through a secret underground tunnel to rescue Andrea's young daughter Jenny. But Andrea never breathed a word. She said, later, that word of Jenny's rescue reached her just as she was going to tell the authorities, but that was a lie.

Even as the shoot-out with Pogo that had taken place all during the day, played out live on local television and two brave police officers died, Andrea had kept quiet about the secret tunnel. She almost had told the police when they were discussing whether or not Pogo might have Jenny with him as a hostage and the police were trying to decide whether or not to rush the house to rescue her, but a few moments later, Jenny had wandered out onto the porch of the house. She was dazed and confused, but safe. Jenny had been spirited away from the mayhem by Officer Evelyn Hoeflinger.

Once Jenny was safely out of the house, Andrea definitely saw no percentage in informing the police. At that point, they were talking about knocking her house to the ground. Sad and upset as she was about Greg's death and Jenny's rescue, Andrea was secretly cheering the police on in their mission.

Tear down the Meth Mansion, she thought. *It has nothing but bad memories for me now.*

Sometimes, you walk away from your life. Sometimes, it walks away from you. Both were happening in Andrea SanGiovanni's life as she watched the assault against her home with a wrecking ball on live television and felt the guilt of her silence.

CHAPTER 63

November 5, 2003
Tad Talks to Charlie

Charlie Chandler knew his days on the force were numbered. He'd had visits from the brass. It was clear they'd prefer he hang it up. He was, after all, getting up there in age. Charlie wasn't opposed to the idea of "retirement," per se. His problem was that he wondered what-the-hell he was supposed to do in retirement. Cassie was dead. Belinda was no kid any more. She wouldn't want to live at home with her old man indefinitely. Charlie wasn't even sure that he wanted to return to the house in Harvest Home. It would be too spooky to be there alone.

As he was pondering all this and thinking about the events of the past few days, a young boy hesitantly entered his room. Tad knocked lightly before entering. He had made sure, by asking at the nurses' station, that it wasn't a bad time.

"Mr. Chandler?" Tad began.

"Yes...that's me," replied Charlie, reaching for his glass of water with the bendable straw. As Tad saw the injured man straining to reach the glass, he quickly retrieved it for him.

"I'm Tad McGreevy...the kid who had Dr. Eisenstadt make the 911 call?"

"Good call, Kid," said Charlie. His voice was gruff. "How did you know that the escaped con was at the SanGiovannis?"

"I'll tell you the whole story about that when you're feeling better, Mr. Chandler..."

"Call me Charlie," the cop interrupted.

"The reason I wanted to talk to you tonight really doesn't have anything to do with the 911 call, though," Tad said. "I'm here about my best friend, Stevie...Stevie Scranton."

"Isn't he the boy who disappeared a month or so ago?" asked Charlie.

"Yes, Sir, and that's what I wanted to talk to you about. I don't know if you ever do any private detective type work, trying to find missing people, but my best friend is missing, and I'd do anything to find him."

Charlie sat up a bit straighter. A plan was forming in his mind. A purpose for Chapter Three of his life.

"There's nobody looking for him now?" asked the veteran policeman.

"Well, you know how it works, Sir. They look for a while..." Tad's voice trailed off. He didn't want to say that the Cedar Falls Police Force couldn't find their collective butts with a flashlight. That would serve no useful purpose. He knew that, just like a school, within even a bad school you could have "good" teachers who upheld standards. The same was true of a police force, and Tad had always heard that Captain Charlie Chandler was a good cop.

"I don't have much money, but I would pay you what I could. I work summers mowing lawns and sometimes I make a fair amount. I've been saving it for my college fund, but Stevie was my best friend ever since we were little kids in kindergarten. I can't just sit back and do nothing. There has to be someone who saw him or who knows where he is and why he disappeared." Tad looked at the man in the hospital bed with hope in his eyes. Charlie had to smile at the sincerity of the boy. *Ah, the innocence of youth*, he thought.

"Well, I'll tell you, young man," said Charlie, adjusting his hospital blankets slightly. "It's a real fine thing you're doing...trying to help locate your friend. I wish every young boy had a friend as good as you."

Charlie looked out the window, squinting toward the Cedar Rapids Memorial hospital sign in the distance to hide the moisture that was threatening to leak from his eyes. Charlie was a very soft-hearted guy, deep down. The thought of this young man offering him his college money, money he would earn mowing lawns, to try to find his missing friend was touching.

" I think I'm going to be cashing in my chips at the police department after I get out of this hospital bed. I'm pretty sure that the Powers-that-Be would just as soon an old relic like me stepped aside and let some younger blood into the department. Since my wife recently passed away and my only child is grown, I think I will have some extra time on my hands, and I would enjoy helping you find your friend."

Charlie smiled an encouraging smile at Tad.

Tad's beaming smile told Charlie all he needed to know.

"That's great, Sir," said the young boy. "I know you have to heal up first, but I thought I'd come and ask and see if there's anything you might want me to do before you get out...before you're well again." Tad looked at Charles Chandler's weathered face with a mixture of hope and eagerness.

"Well, Tad. I do have some ideas we might be able to put into action before I can actively pound the pavement. Why don't you and I plan to get together at my house the day after I'm released? I'm not sure when that is going to be, but the sooner the better."

Charlie had already made arrangements for Belinda to help care for him while he was recuperating. Belinda and he had had the conversation about Charlie possibly selling the big house in Harvest Home and moving to an apartment closer to where Belinda lived. Maybe even an apartment in her complex.

Charlie had said, to Belinda, when she suggested that Charlie might like to join her at the Regency Suites, "Won't that cramp your style?"

Charlie was smiling as he asked, and Belinda was smiling when she answered, "I don't know. Do you plan to barge in without knocking? Because I'd like to think that I brought you up right and there'd be nothing going on that my old man couldn't walk in on."

Even Charlie smiled when she said this. Belinda was a good kid and very funny.

Belinda just laughed after her joke and said, "Oh, Daddy." She had always idolized her father. Now that her mother was dead, she wanted to spend more time with her father.

"I'll stop by the apartment office and see if they have any units for rent, Dad. I'd love to have you nearby. I don't blame you for not wanting to go back to Harvest Home. That was always Mom's thing. She enjoyed the birds and the close-to-nature thing, but I think you'd go stark raving crazy out there by yourself."

Charlie just nodded assent. He had had much the same realization about his life after retirement. He needed a project, and he thought that one might just have been handed to him on a silver platter.

What Charlie didn't know, when he and Tad spoke, was that he might need to be searching not just for Stevie Scranton, but for Michael Clay, aka Pogo the Clown, as well. The police department had not yet informed Charlie that the body of the man who shot him was not found in the wreckage of Andrea SanGiovanni's house.

CHAPTER 64

One month later
Loose Ends

Christmas was bearing down on Cedar Falls like a runaway freight train. In just a little over three weeks' time, everyone would gather to sing carols, exchange presents and give thanks. This year, Stevie Scranton would be missing, so his mother didn't need to worry about him opening his presents early.

* * *

Jenny SanGiovanni had settled into a new routine with her father and his second wife and her new classmates. Andrea and Cynthia SanGiovanni were both counting the days until Andrea moved into her own small house in a new part of town, in CherryWood, next door to the Eisenstadts, in fact. Frank was happy in school, rooming with Buddy Attenza. Jenny kept in touch with Tad by computer and excelled in her schoolwork, although she had not made many close friends in Colorado. Her mother was getting a new place. They'd be together for Jenny's senior year at Cedar Falls Sky High, just as Jenny had promised Tad.

* * *

Over at the Gustaffsson's house, Jeremy was still glorying in the fact that he had, literally, gotten away with murder. He missed Jenny SanGiovanni, but Jeremy was a believer in the old cliché, "If you can't be near the one you love, love the one you're near." Jeremy was doing okay in the "love-the-one-you're-near" department. He had a few prospects. Janice Kramer was way more accessible to him than Jenny had ever been. When Jeremy's little brothers gave him any lip, he'd wrestle them to the floor and dominate the little creeps, which he could still do. He had a new car now, an old Corvette, and it was a chick magnet.

* * *

Principal Peter Puck was preparing for a Christmas trip to Chicago. He would stay with his old friend David Simpson. They would do some Christmas shopping and visit the Manhole, a Chicago institution. David was his old college roommate. He knew where all the skeletons were buried. He knew about Peter Puck's fondness for young boys and men. But David was discreet. He had enough skeletons in his own closet to fill a graveyard.

* * *

Over at Cynthia SanGiovanni's apartment, Andrea SanGiovanni was making the hide-a-bed into her "room" in the living room of Cynthia's one-bedroom apartment as she had done for over a month now. She was counting the days until she took possession of a small frame house in CherryWood, an older subdivision of Cedar Falls, but one that was equally nice. Her next door neighbors would be Dr. and Mrs. Abraham Eisenstadt. Rachel and Zoe were such nice girls. They weren't quite as old as Jenny, but she was sure that the two girls and Jenny would become friends, when Jenny returned. She smiled thinking of the day when Jenny would come home to her.

* * *

Frank SanGiovanni was playing video games with his roommate Buddy Attenza in their college dormitory room. He was losing, but he was still having a good time. Frank had been giving serious thought to going to school to become a video game designer, but he was afraid to tell his mother or father that that was his ambition. He'd keep it to himself for a while.

* * *

Kenny Kellogg was boning one of his students and hoping that Belinda Chandler kept her big mouth shut about his fondness for young stuff. He had no particular girl in mind, but he was always on the lookout.

* * *

Lenny McIntyre, Officer Friendly at Sky High, was telling his fellow teachers, for the umpteenth time, about the exciting day when he nearly single-handedly captured a serial killer. Except for the fact that Pogo was still on the loose, it was a great story and infinitely preferable to talking about his days patrolling the corridors of Sky High. When he got to the exciting parts, he couldn't resist biting his fingernails.

* * *

Stevie Scranton's parents were gathered around a kitchen table with ex-Cedar Falls policeman Charlie Chandler and Stevie's good friend Tad McGreevy. They were discussing plans to try to find Stevie Scranton.

* * *

Stevie Scranton was crying in a dank, dark basement prison, comforted only by the presence of another young man, another captive, Scott Flugle. Daniel Malone would be home soon. He wouldn't like it if he found his boys crying.

* * *

Driving a stolen car, Michael Clay was arrested just short of the Mexican border in Brownsville, Texas, on a hot, muggy windy day. The border guards at the bridge that crosses into Matamoros, Mexico were on the lookout for the stone cold killer. For once, they got their man. Michael Clay—also known as Pogo the Killer Clown— was taken to the Brownsville Jail. He awaits transfer to a maximum security facility. But Pogo has no intention of walking away from his life of crime. Michael always was a hard worker and a creative one as Republican precinct committee chairman. Michael Clay's last gruff comment to authorities bundling him into the van to transport him from the Texas border to a cell was, "Don't put me in with no fruit-picker. I ain't no fruit-picker."

What Michael Clay was and always has been is an extremely crafty and dangerous psychopathic personality, and one with a true genius for escape.

THE END

RED IS FOR RAGE

BOOK TWO of the Trilogy, *RED IS FOR RAGE* continues the story of Tad McGreevy and Jenny SanGiovanni.

It is Tad and Jenny's Senior Year at Sky-High.

Find out what happened to Stevie Scranton.

Read more about Pogo the Killer Clown and Jeremy Gustaffsson.

Check out:

www.CONNIECWILSON.COM

www.WEEKLYWILSON.com

www.THECOLOROFEVIL.COM

for updates on publication dates. Check AMAZON.com and BARNES & NOBLE.com for the E-book.

The Saga continues soon in Red Is for Rage, Book Two of the series.

Opening Line of Book Two:

"She stood there, white dress covered in blood, clutching the 38 caliber revolver, body shaking uncontrollably."

About the Author

CONNIE (CORCORAN) WILSON taught composition at 6 IA/IL colleges and wrote for 5 newspapers. She currently writes for 6 blogs, was named 2008 Content Producer of the Year by Associated Content (2009), Midwestern Writing Center *Writer of the Year* (March 30, 2010) and reviews television, movies, and politics for Yahoo.

A graduate of the University of Iowa, Berkeley, Western Illinois University, Northern Illinois University and the University of Chicago, she was film and book critic for the *Quad City Times* during the 70's and 80's. Her (Jan., 2011) nonfiction release *It Came from the '70s: From The Godfather to Apocalypse Now* consists of 50 reviews written during the seventies, with 76 photos, major cast and interactivetrivia.

Connie's short story collection, *Hellfire & Damnation*, placed 7th (of 45) on Preliminary Stoker balloting [3 places ahead of Stephen King's *Full Dark, No* Stars, a distinction she cherishes.] Both books were awarded Silver Feather awards by the IWPA (Illinois Women's

Press Association), and E-Lit awards. Her screenplay based on her novel *Out of Time* was a winner in the 2007 "Writer's Digest" competition.

Up next:*The Color of Evil* (first in a trilogy, a novelization of "Living in Hell" from "H&D") and *Hellfire & Damnation II* plus the E-book version of *Ghostly Tales of Route 66*, a humor collection *Laughing through Life*, and a children's illustrated book, *The Christmas Cats in Silly Hats.*

In addition to interviewing Kurt Vonnegut, William F. Nolan, David Morrell, Joe Hill, Frederik Pohl, John Irving and Anne Perry for print and online publications, Connie taught for 33 years, founded and was CEO of 2 businesses (Sylvan Learning Center #3301 and Prometric Testing Center #3301), has a son (Scott) and a daughter (Stacey) born 20 years apart, is married 43 years to husband, Craig, and has 2-year-old twin granddaughters, Elise and Ava.

She lives in Chicago and in the IA/IL Quad Cities.

[*She also plays the oboe, the accordion and the piano, but don't let that get around.]

www.CONNIECWILSON.COM

www.WEEKLYWILSON.com

www.THECOLOROFEVIL.COM

12933097R00134

Made in the USA
Charleston, SC
07 June 2012